MW00943317

Road to Redemption

THE RETRIBUTION SERIES BOOK 2

Jorge G. Reyes S.

ROAD TO REDEMPTION

COPYRIGHT © 2015 JORGE G. REYES

Mystery, Thriller, Suspense,
International Thriller

All rights reserved. No part of this e-book may be reproduced
in any manner whatsoever, or stored in any information
storage system, without the prior written consent of the
publisher or the author, except in the case of brief quotations
with proper reference, embodied in critical articles and
reviews and certain other noncommercial uses permitted by
copyright law. For permission requests, write to the publisher
or author of this work.

Cover design by SmartApps
Images, designs, and artwork: Copyright © SmartApps
Formatting by Added Touches

All quotations and trademarks are respective of their
originators.
All use of quotations is done under the fair use copyright
principal. All of the characters in this book are fictitious. Any
resemblance to actual persons, living or dead is purely
coincidental. They are the product of the author's imagination
and used fictitiously.

ISBN-13: 978-1517328894
ISBN-10:1517328896

Printed in the United States of America

DEDICATION PAGE

This book is dedicated to:
My nephew and his lovely wife who spent endless hours
helping me with proofreading and editing.

I would be remiss if I didn't thank
Barbara and David for their technical expertise
and support at a crucial time.

I also want to thank my wife for her unyielding support
and encouragement to keep on writing.

TABLE OF CONTENTS

TABLE OF CONTENTS Cont'd

ONE

She went on rummaging through the desk drawers. Folders and papers came out to be discarded everywhere. She kept grumbling and complaining to herself. The large office with a massive antique desk and walls covered with books was in total disarray. The shock of her husband's death had dissipated after a few minutes.

A paid informant in the police department had called her. Her husband, Victor, had been killed less than an hour earlier at the airport. Since then she had been rifling through various file cabinets. "Aah, here it is." Sighing with glee and relief she allowed herself to relax on the wide leather chair.

Her thoughts brought her to Victor's partners. They would try to take over and move her aside but she had other plans. Another thought entered her mind; whoever had killed her husband had done her a big favor. She spit on the floor when she remembered having to go to bed with him.

The cartel leader, Fabian, she thought was the dangerous one. She figured that Eric would be in her pocket in no time. "I'm the new boss. I'm going to be the coca queen." She muttered to herself. "I have to let the men know I'm running things now. And I will find the bitch he kept in the guesthouse. And that good for nothing maid, instead of coming to untie me, turns around and runs away."

She stared at the hundreds of books lined up in their bookshelves of the large wood paneled office. "Did you ever read any of these books Victor? I doubt it. Where did that *malparido*, good-looking Tarzan, what's his name? Oh, yes Andres. He went with them." *Assholes. I'm going to kill them all.* "Where is the dammed phone?" She found it hidden under a pile of discarded files and called the guardhouse. "Mario, come here now."

A maid eavesdropping behind one of the doors scurried away.

Minutes later, a corpulent man with the demeanor of an ex-soldier knocked on the door. "Señora Claudia?"

"Open the door." She yelled.

He did and faced her from the doorway. He didn't betray his surprise at the messy room.

"Get closer, I'm not going to bite you. I guess you already heard that Victor has been killed."

Mario simply nodded.

"I'm making you my head of security. I heard that Rolando and Hugo were in charge of a large group that attacked a ranch. How much do you know about it?" *I didn't like that fat fuck Hugo, always leering at me. Rolando, on the other hand, hmm, I liked him, had a nice butt. A shame, I could have used him for other things.* Her tongue came out and she licked her lips.

"I heard about it, yes." He said.

"Do you know where the place they attacked was?"

"I think it's called *Los Cielos.* Somewhere between Santa Fe and Turbo."

"Tell me more." Claudia contemplated the now disorganized desktop.

Mario made a scratching noise with his throat.

She looked up at him. "Well?"

"Don't know much more Señora Claudia. They say the army killed them both and the rest of the gang is in jail."

"Find out everything you can and get back to me, and don't fuck up." Claudia gave him a hard look.

"Si, *Señora.* I'll do that but I need more men. I want to replace the ones that led those *maricas* escape."

"Get rid of those coward *malparidos*. You know what? Kill them in front of the others."

"I...cannot do it here."

"Why not? Get a fucking knife and quarter them like pigs. That's what they are. Make them an example of what happens when you fuck up. Use the guesthouse; I'm going to blow it up anyway."

"Count on me *Señora*." *Bitch. But I wouldn't mind taking her to the sack.* He turned around to leave.

"The Miami guy and Fabian...do you know them?"

Mario swiveled in his boots and faced her. "Eric and the Mexican? Yes."

"Good, go away, I have to take care of other business." Claudia dived into the paper mess and extracted the desk phone. She pressed the numbers written on a card while admiring the dazzling diamond ring in her wedding finger.

"*Quien llama?*" A gruff voice with a Slavic accent said.

"Claudia, Victor's wife, no, widow. Victor was killed this morning. I'm taking over."

"*Ty che, blyad?*"

"What was that you said? She asked in a somewhat angry tone.

"Sorry, it's a Russian curse for what the-"

"What the fuck? You can say it." She said.

"When? How...did his plane crash?"

"No, some motherfucker did him in and his bodyguards are dead too. You're now working for me."

"Señora, I don't want to live in the jungle much longer."

"We can talk about it when you get here. Did Victor say anything about a place called *Los Cielos?*"

"Let me...he said something about a large ranch near the Caribbean."

"Did he give you a name?"

"No...Don Victor told me he wanted more workers...something about expanding the crops." *Victor, dead? He is untouchable. Who would dare go after him?*

Somebody has big and I mean big cojones. Should I mention the cocaine? No, not on the phone.

"What else?"

"All he told me was that the place was big. He asked me if *El Químico* could handle two locations and if we had enough chemicals to produce the stuff…you know what I mean?"

"Of course I know. You think I'm stupid?"

"Victor never told me you knew about the business."

"Anything else?"

"We have a problem; the chemist, but I do not want to talk about it over the phone."

"How soon can you be here?"

"A shipment is ready to go. I can leave with it."

"Call me when you're sure." Claudia-Lucia hung up. *Let's see how soon he gets his ass here. Maybe he's good in bed. I better call Fabian and Eric. Let them know who their new partner is. What time is it?*

Vladimir looked at the phone. "I guess I am going to Medellin."

TWO

After leaving behind the chaos in the Medellin's airport, Alejandro relaxed in his bedroom suite. He watched the unfolding news on the TV set. He decided to work out the adrenaline off and stretched his tall frame on the carpet. After doing fifty push-ups and a similar amount of crunches, he took a quick shower, put on fresh clothes and called the charter company. "Is this Joe?"

"Yes? Who is it?"

"Alex Calwel."

"Don Alejandro. Are you okay? Have you seen the news?"

"What? No. I left when the plane took off. What happened? Are my wife and my friends safe?" *I must make him think I don't know anything.*

"Everything is at a standstill right now. No one can get in or out of the airport. It's a madhouse. Ambulances, police, firefighters, soldiers crawling all over the place."

"Good God. No. Are they hurt?" His voice dropped to a whisper, keeping the farce.

"No, no, I'm sure they're already landing in Santa Fe."

"Damn, you scared me." Alejandro snickered in silence. "When was this?"

"It looks like the FARC is back in action. A bunch of people killed. One of the guys at the terminal told me that a big fish, some politician, caught a bullet."

"They catch the killer?"

He ignored Alejandro's question. "A baggage handler told me that the largest coca producer near the

Venezuelan border and all his bodyguards were shot dead. No one really knows." His voice went up several decibels in his excitement. "There's been nothing but sirens since you left."

"Any suspects?" He said.

"I don't believe so. You are all very lucky. You could have been caught in the crossfire." Joe exhaled and swept his short pudgy hand over the few strands of hair on top of his head.

"Could you arrange a flight to the ranch for me? I want to leave for *Los Cielos* right away." Alejandro watched the news with the sound on mute. "It's too dangerous." *And I don't want to become a suspect.*

"Today?" Joe asked in disbelief. "The airport is in lockdown."

"See what you can do. Take the hotel number." Alejandro read it out loud.

"I will let you know immediately, Don Alejandro." Joe hung up and rushed to the front of the dusty, empty office, squinting at the bright sunlight, he peeked outside. He opened the door but kept his short, heavyset frame half way inside in case more bullets started flying.

The annoying ring of his desk phone called. He locked the door and walked back to the end of the long and narrow room.

THREE

The roaring engines covered their conversation from the others, not that it mattered.

"Victor sent Hugo to beat up my son." Teresa said.

"Your son knew Victor before you went to work for him?" Virginia was surprised. She held her friend's wrinkled, slim hand.

She nodded. "My son tried several banks, seeking a business loan and failed. Too young or something to that effect, would not finance his venture. He then heard that Victor made short-term loans to shop-keepers and other small businesses."

Virginia thought that Camilo looked very much like his mother. Slim, with longish black hair. He sat by himself in the front, glued to the window. Teresa's words brought her back.

"Stubborn and independent like his father was. Instead of coming to me, he went to that dreadful man and asked him for the money to get his business going."

"Oh, Teresa." There was sadness in Virginia's voice. She touched the corner of one of her eyes and brushed a tear away.

At first, everything was going well. But a large wooden liquor display he'd built and shipped to the U.S. was delayed in customs for several weeks and the company held payment."

The copilot rose from his cramped seat in the cockpit and walked over to them, interrupting their conversation. "We'll be landing shortly, any one cares for a cup of coffee?" He held a large thermos in one of his hands. His eyes were drawn to Virginia and he held his gaze on her. *She has to be one of the most beautiful women I have ever seen.*

"I would." Teresa raised her hand.

His stare interrupted, the co-pilot poured coffee on a Styrofoam cup, and brought it to her. "Sugar?" He handed a wood shaker and a sugar packet. His eyes strayed to Virginia. He admired her oval face, long black lashes and beautiful almond shaped eyes. "Miss?"

Virginia smiled and shook her head.

"Thank you." Teresa took the coffee and turned to Virginia. "Camilo explained the problem to Victor and asked him if he could fall behind in his payment for about a week. He had gone to Miami and had sat down with company executives since the problem was of their own making."

The copilot went back to the cockpit.

"So why would Victor want to harm him then?"

Teresa didn't answer but went on, "the company agreed but payment to vendors was every other week. His payment would be delayed and there were no exceptions."

"I don't understand." Virginia raised an eyebrow.

"Victor told Camilo not to worry, but then sent Hugo anyway to remind others who owed him money."

"What a…" Virginia sighed.

"That's why he's paralyzed. I almost lost him."

"You must have been desperate." Virginia patted her newfound friend's hand.

"Quit my teaching job to care for him. I all my savings on doctors."

"Something told me that he is an evil man. I hate him, I hate him."

"I was so afraid he was going to do something monstrous to you." Teresa said.

"Would have killed myself first."

"But you were so helpless, not knowing who you were or why you were there."

"If it hadn't been for you and the others...you all took a big chance in trying to help me and, and convincing Andres to talk to Alejandro. I still can't believe he's my husband."

"I hope your amnesia goes away soon."

The small plane lurched and both women held tight to their arms rests.

"Uhh, that was quite a little bounce." Virginia smiled at Teresa. "I can't remember what my house looks like. I hope this...memory thing, whatever it is, goes away soon. Alejandro told me that if my problem persists he's going to take me to see a specialist." Virginia looked back and glanced at Andres. "He is worried about his mother. He's very attractive. Don't you think? How did he end working for that man?"

"Andres? He looks like a *futbol* player." Teresa smiled and turned to watch him staring out the porthole. "I'm glad he was able to bring his mother." The ailing woman rested on the opposite seat across the aisle from her son.

"I'm going to talk to my husband. There must be something that can be done to people like him, so sadistic and vile. They must not be allowed to get away with things like that."

"Sometimes it seems only the bad guys win." Teresa's voice ended in a whisper.

Virginia shook her head in dismay.

"Had to sell my house..." Teresa grieved. "I begged him to let me take my son to the U.S. for an operation that hopefully would restore his ability to walk."

Furrowing her brow, Virginia said. "He didn't want to help you?"

"He said I had to settle the debt first." Teresa pushed some loose gray strands around her right ear.

"How awful. That man is the most despicable human being. No wonder his wife is so-"

"I ended up selling the house for a pittance. Later I found that Victor was behind the whole thing. Hired a fake buyer and demanded I work for him to pay off the remaining balance," Teresa sighed and continued, "But room and board takes any money I have after paying his outlandish interests."

"Don't say anymore. The important thing is that we are out of there and together." Virginia put her arm around Teresa's fragile shoulders and hugged her in a deep gesture of affection.

FOUR

His cell phone buzzed. He gave an annoyed look at the phone. *Victor calling this early?* "I got to go, I have another call, go ahead and call me later with the details." He pressed the disconnect button of the desk phone and picked up his cell. "Victor?"

"It's me, Claudia. Victor was shot dead this morning. Call Eric and tell him."

"What?" Jolted by the shocking news he jumped of his chair. He was at a loss for words. "This is not a joke, right?"

"No, some mother-fuckers killed him at the airport."

"Are you sure? What have you been told?" He stared pacing the large room trying to gather his thoughts.

"His bodyguards bought it also." She spat the words.

"Damn." Fabian stopped walking.

"You pay good money to have men protect you and what difference does it make?"

"And it happened at the Medellin airport?" Fabian restarted his aimless walk.

"The son of a bitch had left for the plantation two days ago." Her eyes blazed with fury.

"The army found the factory? Are you sure it was him?"

She went on. "I found out he had a hooker in my own fucking house." She shouted.

"Right under my nose. He's lucky he was killed because otherwise I would have cut his balls off with a dull kitchen knife. *Malparido. Hijo de puta."* She went on yelling expletives.

"Claudia, stop. Settle down. Tell me again, but stop the histrionics, okay?"

She let out another swearword. "When he was gone, I went into the guesthouse and I found a puta living there. I knew something was going on."

"Tell me about Victor. What happened?" Fabian groaned, exasperated.

She ignored his question. "Can you believe what that mother-"

"I don't care about that shit now." H growled. "Don't start again. Damn."

"How soon can you be here?"

"I'll make arrangements...will you tell me about Victor? Shit."

"I told you he was killed at the airport. Gunned down. Don't forget to call the Cuban or whatever he is and tell him to get his ass here. We need to talk." Claudia hung up.

He remained pensive for a few minutes.

What bothered him was, how was it possible that Victor had been ambushed at the airport?

Security was very tight. There were armed soldiers inside and outside. And he reasoned, the mostly deserted two lane highway to the airport, with plenty of curves and hills would have been more practical and allow for an easier and faster getaway.

Whoever had done it had superb intelligence regarding Victor's whereabouts. Fabian felt at a loss for answers. It had to be a set up. But who? Calwel? He had his doubts whether the man was dead or alive. As far as he knew there had never been proof positive the man was dead. It the rancher was alive, he had turned out to be more resourceful than Victor had anticipated. But no, Calwel was supposed to be dead or was he? The question kept coming back. Notwithstanding if he was dead or alive, how did he find out about Victor's return? He shook his head perplexed and went back to his reverie.

Okay, he thought to himself, the perpetrators had accomplices at the airport to be able to get away with it; which meant that it could not have been the rancher. Unless the man planted someone in Victor's cocaine plantation. No, that didn't sound credible.

Therefore the only conjecture that made any sense was that men had been following Victors' activities. Still, no one knew when Victor was returning. Would the conspirators have had enough time to set up an ambush in a matter of minutes? Not likely, but only if he willingly accepted Claudia's assertions. Another thought crossed his mind. What if it was Claudia the one who masterminded the plan to kill her husband? Could she have planned it? Was she that conniving? He wondered. She certainly knew when he was returning. Did she have the resources, the people to put together a plan to kill Victor in a matter of several hours? If it was Claudia, she was a masterful, thieving, calculating bitch. A better actor than anyone could imagine.

So, who had killed Victor? He had no answer. *I need to dig in deeper to discern what happened. Everything was running smoothly.* Fabian walked to a wet bar encased in a wall-to-wall oak wooden cabinet. He peered at the bottles and chose a *Dalmore,* forty-year-old single highland malt Scotch whisky and poured himself a healthy amount.

FIVE

"We will be landing shortly." The pilot turned around and surveyed his passengers. "Please, make sure your seatbelts are buckled."

The twin-engine six passengers *North American Sabreliner NA-265-60* circled the small Santa Fe airport twice. The pilot lined up with the runway, revved-up the engines, dropped the wheels and touched down with a small bump on the asphalt driveway. The plane taxied down to the one story airport building.

The pilot shut down the engines and waited for the propellers to stop before disengaging from his seat and getting up. He was middle age and had the beginnings of a potbelly. Coming out of the cockpit, he looked at his passengers. *I never have seen these many so happy to land, even when we have had bad weather.* The thought made him smile.

He cranked the handle. The door opened outwards, went down slowly, becoming a ladder. He thanked the passengers as one by one they began disembarking

Waiting with a handful of men behind him, Hernando watched the airplane's door open and a stairway deploy from the aircraft. Virginia stepped out, shielding her eyes from the morning sun with one hand. She strode down the narrow steps helping an older woman walking behind her.

After reaching the tarmac, they stopped and waited while an airport attendant climbed up the steps carrying a four-wheel collapsible chair. Seconds later, the baggage handler reappeared. He held the back of the contraption with upmost care. A man sat in it. A strapping youngster assisted him, carefully holding the other end. They descended one step at a time.

Next, the attendant went to the cargo hatch, opened it and took out two sturdy wheelchairs. The youngster helped the crippled individual switch chairs and returned to the plane, disappearing inside.

The rancher realized that the man in the chair was actually young. *They both are about the same age I think.* No longer able to hold his enthusiasm, Hernando took off his hat, showing a balding pate and rushed to the small crowd gathering in the tarmac.

A minute later, the teenager came out carrying an older emaciated woman. He managed the steps with caution and positioned the woman on the empty wheelchair, then wrapped a blanket over her legs and stood behind her.

Two men walked closely behind Hernando.

The rest of the group remained at a discrete distance.

For some reason, the men reminded Virginia of cowboys from a western movie. They were all carrying belts with gun sin holsters.

"My God! I can't believe it. It's you! Elena is dying to see you and going crazy keeping the secret. Nobody knows. Alex made us promise."

Virginia nodded graciously but remained unsure.

"I can't wait ti see Gabriel's face when he sees you. God have mercy on us all. This is really a miracle. But let me look at you!" Quitting his monologue, he gave her a bear hug and a peck on the cheeks. He stood back and grabbed her arms with both hands. "You look stunning."

Virginia smiled uncertain. She didn't remember the man although Alejandro had mentioned that Hernando and his wife were their best friends and that he would pick them up to take them to *Los Cielos*. "Excuse me, somebody is calling me."

"Go ahead, take the call while I welcome all these good folks." Hernando began greeting the rest of the new arrivals.

Pushing back her long black hair, Virginia put the cellphone to her ear.

The two ranch hands standing behind Hernando stepped back and joined the others. Their faces, serious and somewhat disjointed.

"You must be Teresa, right? Virginia's fierce supporter." Hernando took her hand.

Smiling timidly, Teresa introduced the young man in the wheelchair. "This is my son."

"Camilo at your service." He was amused by the excited baldheaded man that looked like would jump out of his boots at any moment. And shook hands with him.

"Yes! You are one of the heroes, Hernando said, "Alex told me all about you."

"And that's Andres and his mother Amelia." Teresa introduced him to the athletic youngster and his visibly ill and aging mother.

"Pleased to meet you." Andres held Hernando's hand in a firm handshake.

"Ahh. You are the one who saved Alex's life. Give me a big hug man." Without giving Andres a second, he clutched him in his arms. He then took Amelia's hand slipping out from under the blanket and held it gently on his own. She gave him a wan smile.

"Señora, you'll find our land has very good recuperative powers." Stepping back, he opened his arms and exclaimed excitedly. "Delighted to meet you all!"

Alex had told him all the things they had done for Virginia and for him.

"I am indebted to all of you. I'd do anything for those two people. There's no one like them in the world." He gushed with pleasure.

Virginia took advantage of the momentary distraction. "Hallo?"

"Everything all right, love? How was your flight?" *Damn, I love hearing her voice.*

"Excuse me? Who is this?" Virginia asked distractedly, her attention still focused on Hernando's excited discourse.

"It's me, your husband, or have you forgotten already?"

"Oh, I...I am so, I guess all these things, my escape...finding me, my amnesia...and saving my friends. I don't remember Hernando. He and his wife are our best friends, right?"

"Yes, my love."

"I'm so happy. I can't wait to see you, please come right away," Virginia said.

"Does that mean you miss me?"

"How long is it from here to the ranch? Oh God, I can't wait to see Gaby. You should have let him come. Oh my God, my son. How long to the ranch you said? Alex. Can I call you Alex?"

Alejandro laughed. "My love, you can call me anything you want."

"Don't laugh, please, I'm serious. How long will it take to get to the ranch?" Virginia wiped her teary eyes.

"It depends, about an hour and a half more or less."

"That long?" She said.

"How was your flight?" He asked her again.

"Fine my love." She giggled. "My, I'm already flirting with you, and I don't know you."

Alejandro chuckled.

"I don't want to stop talking with you. I need you here, please, please, come soon. You make me...feel safe." She whispered the last few words. She thought about the attractive, tall man who had rescued her the night before...her husband. *God, please give me all of my old memories back.*

"Alex...Alex, how far to the farm? Oh, you told me already, it's just that I want to see Gaby so bad that it hurts."

Hernando and the others stepped away to give Virginia a smidgen of privacy.

"When am I going to see you?" Virginia asked, a gentle smile floating in her face.

"I'm hiring a charter to fly me to the ranch."

"How soon?"

"Something is going on at the airport and no one can get in or out at this moment. I guess you were the last to leave." Alejandro said.

"What happened?"

"I heard it was a terrorist attack but somebody said it was a narco killing. So, who knows what happened? I have the TV on in my room but they're not saying much yet. They are not letting the reporters get close to the passenger terminal." *I can't tell her, not yet anyway. I had never killed anyone before this nightmare began.*

"Alex? Alex? Are you there?" Her voice filled with concern.

"Oh, sorry my love. Yes, I'm here."

"Were you still at the airport?"

Hernando overheard the questions and shifted his attention. He remembered seeing something on a TV set at the airport, but hadn't paid it any notice, wanting to rush to welcome Virginia.

"No, no, I left a few minutes after the plane took off. I got in the car and came back to my room here." Alejandro exhaled quietly. *Liar, sweetheart, I will tell you soon.*

"Please, I don't want anything happening to you. I just found you. No, that's not true, you found me. God knows where I would be if you hadn't shown up. Be careful and come home."

"I will, I will. We'll be together soon." Alejandro exhaled, "promise."

"We're getting ready to leave with Hernando." Virginia shielded her eyes again. "I like him."

"Let me talk to him love."

"Hernando, Alex wants to talk with you." Virginia handed over her cell phone.

"Hey, Alex. Where are you? When are you coming back?"

"At the hotel. I'm arranging my trip back."

"Do I need to send someone for you?"

"No, don't bother. I'll be flying straight to the house."

"By the way, Virginia looks wonderful. You're a lucky man. And to think we had given up on her. This is great."

"Hernando, if it hadn't been for you, who knows if we would be having this conversation. I'm thankful to God for having friends like you."

"A few days ago you were almost dead, your wife missing, your son running from murderous thugs and now we're all together again." Hernando smiled.

"By the way, at some point the news will reach you that Victor and his bodyguards were shot dead this morning. It happened just minutes after Virginia left."

"What?"

"The police have not released his name to the news media, but I don't doubt they will have to do so soon. She doesn't know."

"Jesus!" Hernando exploded but then turned around and lowered his voice when he realized Virginia and the others were giving him odd looks. "Were you involved?"

"She doesn't know anything. I'll tell her at a more appropriate time."

"I see." Hernando said.

"We'll talk later. If she asks you, you only know what I told her, okay?"

"But of course. I can't believe it. Damn." *How you survived it all, I'll never know. Someone else would have lost it. You never gave up, even when faced with the worst fate anyone could imagine but damn, you came through.* "Anything else? I think we are ready to go."

"Thanks, take care and see you soon." Alejandro said.

"And don't worry about your gorgeous wife and her friends. They'll be safe and home tonight."

The connection ended. He handed the phone back to Virginia. "So? Ready to see Gaby and be home again?" He grinned.

Everyone started heading for the building.

Virginia and Hernando remained a few paces in back of the pack.

"I..." Virginia stood ramrod still.

Hernando stopped too and looked at her, perplexed.

A wide smile appeared on her face. "Hernando!" She yelled and ran to him, giving him a huge hug and kissing him on the cheeks.

The older man almost fell back from Virginia's unexpected assault.

"It's you. It's you. Where is Elena? Zuri? Mirta?" She was laughing and crying at the same time. Big tears pouring down her cheeks.

"Yes, Virginia, it's me. Your memory is coming back?"

She could only nod, overwrought by the sudden emotion.

A gentle but sad smile appeared in his face.

The others, walking ahead, and following the men carrying their meager belongings, heard Virginia's outburst and turned around. Their faces, showed bewilderment at first, then amusement and then realization.

Teresa ran back and hugged Virginia, laughing and crying too. "Thank you Lord, thank you."

Virginia smiled, even though tears were flowing profusely. "Yes, Tere, Hernando and Elena are our best friends and neighbors. Let me make the proper introductions." Virginia wiped her face. She was transformed, sure of herself, no longer confused. She felt giddy, relieved and jubilant. "I have to call him. Oh my Alex, Alex. Love, I remember you real well now. How could I have doubted that you would rescue me?" Virginia made a pirouette on the tarmac.

"Come, young lady, let's take you home." A grinning Hernando said and put his arm over her trembling shoulders.

She remembered her other friends, the people who helped her run the household. They were her employees but she considered them family. "How are Mirta and Zuri, Juan, the others?"

"Virg...it's a long story, we'll bring you up to speed later." Hernando stood by, not sure if he should say anything. *Coming home is going to be so sad when she finds out about the massacre, but I know Gabriel will bring her incredible joy.*

"I'm so happy to see you." Virginia put her arm through Hernando's waist. Her face radiated an intense feeling of happiness. How is everybody else? Why all the armed men? Oh, my God. Those are Daniel and Jimmy." She disengaged from Hernando and rushed forwards. "I'm so sorry. I didn't recognize you before. Come here, let me hug you."

The embarrassed ranch-hands walked shyly towards her.

Her face was like a painting depicting her raw emotions. She wrapped her arms around them and kissed them both. "What must have you thought of me? Please forgive my stupid brain."

The young men, big grins on their faces mumbled their thanks.

"Ah...where is Rolando?" Her face darkened and a slight tremor shook her core.

They all noticed her sudden change.

"A lot of...of awful things happened while you were gone, but let's celebrate this happy occasion and let's give Alex the good news. Your memory is back," Hernando had a sad smile.

"Yes, yes." The thought of talking to Alejandro again made her lightheaded.

SIX

Still reeling from the news that Victor had been killed, Fabian called the man in charge of running his distribution network.

"My Colombian partner hung his tennis shoes. Get going with the planned shipments across the border. I'll have to fly to Medellin soon to sort this mess out."

"*Sin problema, jefe.* Are you still coming today? Anything you need before you arrive?"

"Yes and no. I may go straight to Colombia after we meet. I am afraid this is something I have to figure out by myself."

After retreating to his office, Fabian called Claudia again and managed to get more details. Afterwards, he turned on the computer and clicked on *Caracol*, the Colombian website with news feed. The images on the screen showed trap covered bodies and the demolished front end of a car riddled with bullets.

A news report went on about an Escalade with rear fender damage found on the airport parking lot. The police had not disclosed who the dead were. But the identity of the car's owner was already an open secret. All the damaged autos had belonged to Victor Draco.

There was rampant speculation that the alleged drug dealer was one of the men sprawled and covered by a plastic sheet on the curb. After satisfying himself and corroborating what Claudia had told him about the murder, he turned off the computer and glanced at his

Hublot watch. *Bullocks, it's already past noon. I better call Eric.* He punched the numbers.

"Eric, I have bad news." He went on and told him what had occurred.

The call didn't last long and Eric closed his cell phone. "Excuse me, I need to…I'll be back in a minute." Fabian's call had shaken him. *What the hell? Victor? Damn.*

Lillian gave him a look that had could have killed him. "Sweetheart, something wrong?" Her frosty voice made him more anxious. "Lunch is about to be served. Our friends are hungry after the tennis match, and no one likes to eat lukewarm food." She smiled at the two couples in sport clothes having drinks around the round glass table. Behind them, the wide sliding doors opened to the balcony offering a stunning view of Miami's skyline.

"Sorry babe, go ahead and start, I'll be back as soon as I can." His face looked gaunt and pale, his forehead glistened with sweat beads.

He rose from the table and walked away. *Claudia called him this morning? And now he tells me?*

Eric entered his office and locked the door. He picked up the phone and pressed the speed dial button.

Fabian, expecting Eric's call, grabbed the phone when it rang.

"I'm in my office now, I couldn't talk, there was a bunch of people around"

"I figured as much." Fabian said.

"What the hell happened? Why didn't you call me before?"

"Eric, cool your knickers. I only found out a short time ago when Claudia called. She's half mad right now. Doesn't know what she's going to do. She yells one moment, laughs the next, then screams and blabbers about some woman Victor had sequestered in the guesthouse. The woman beat her and tied her up, gagged her and escaped. I don't believe any of it."

"You got to be shitting me." *Is that why I saw a maid taking a tray to the guesthouse when we were in Victors' playroom? I give it to the man. A lover right under his wife's nose? I didn't like him but shit, he wins the prize.*

"Oh, and one more thing that I could not make sense of. One of the maids ran away, killed a guard and stole a vehicle. Most maids here do not even know how to read or write, never mind drive a car. So I know it wasn't the maid. She has definitely gone bunkers. Mind you, I'm giving you the revised version. It was a rambling conversation punctuated by fits and starts."

"What are you going to do?" Eric put his hand on his forehead trying to comprehend what his partner was telling him.

"I ended calling her back to get more details. I'm heading for Medellin. You should come down too. I'm still trying to put together this puzzle. I think, this may have been an inside job."

"Is that what you think happened?"

"Conjectures; that all I have." Fabian said.

"What do you think really happened?" Eric wiped his upper lip.

"For a moment, I wondered if it had something to do with the killing of the gringo. Does that does make any sense?"

"You don't think he's alive, is he? And if he is, how the hell would he know about Victor's travel plans?" Eric said.

"I know, and if I believe Claudia, he came home after the cockup in his house."

"Do you have any one in mind? I mean Victor had lots of enemies."

"He was at one of the plantations and flew back this morning but that was not his plan."

"Unbelievable."

I want to go there and see what happened for myself, plus there's the issue of who is going to take charge. This is a major budge. Blimey." His tone became bitter.

"Do you think she'll help me with my money problems?" Eric said.

"We need to pause and reconsider what has occurred and what possible consequences it might have on our mutual business interests. I am certain his rivals will try to muscle in and wrestle the business from her. Any ideas?"

"All I know is that I, I, need more cash. I'm too rattled now to think clearly. I guess I better catch the first flight to Medellin I can get. This is a real mess."

"A real snafu, another of your Yankee expressions. You should really consider owning your own plane." Fabian scoffed.

"Yeah, right, as if I didn't have enough problems with the bankers."

"I told you guys to think this thing thoroughly before committing to it. I made it distinctly clear that I am able to transport all the shipments across the border but you and Victor wanted Calwel's land."

"Fabian, you just said it yourself. You're not sure that's what happened. How could Victor's killing be connected to Calwel? You, you don't really know?" Eric's face flushed. "We did agree to proceed and get rid of Calwel. Right? And well, he's dead. Right, right?"

"I am not so sure anymore."

"Victor killed him. He told us." Eric's voice became strident. "We need to continue working the land deal. I need it. Anyway, I have guests waiting. I'll see you in Medellin." Eric slammed the phone down. He regained his composure and stepped out of his office.

Asshole, he thinks that fake English accent makes him superior. Such a snob, I had my own jet too. He grimaced. *Masoni and his backstabbing partner made me get rid of it.* He went back to mingle with his guests.

"Ah, you're back." Her sparkling green eyes softened up. "I asked the kitchen to wait a few minutes. I hope your delay hasn't messed up the main course."

"Please forgive me." He smiled at his friends sitting around the table.

"We already had the Portuguese grilled octopus appetizer Ortensia made. It was delicious. We are drinking white wine sangrias. Would you like one?"

"I apologize but I had to take this call. Sweetheart, please go ahead, I'll skip the starter."

Eric sat down, but his mind was whirling with worrisome thoughts. *Shit, if the business goes down, I am in a real hole. Maybe I can get that stupid bitch to buy one of my condos.*

****

After every one left, Vivian followed Eric to their bedroom. "You ruined our lunch, you know? I was trying to impress Vivian but you were so morose and disinterested. Everyone noticed and left as soon as they could." Lillian was parading back and forth across their large bedroom foyer. "You hardly spoke at all. Every time I asked you a question, I had to repeat myself. God, what will they think of me?" She stopped in front of him. "Well?"

"Well what?" Eric sat on the bed, he had taken his shoes off and seemed distracted.

"See? That's what I mean, you're not paying attention. Damn, Eric, what is wrong?" Her straight long red hair bobbed up and down. Her freckled face showing frustration.

"My Colombian partner was shot dead today. I need to fly to Medellin right away."

"What? How? No, no. You're not going. You want yourself killed?"

"Fabian is on his way there. I have to go." His sullen face stared at her.

"Baby, please, don't go. I'm sorry I yelled at you, I didn't...why didn't you tell me sooner?" Her green eyes became moist.

"Nothing is going to happen to me. No one knows me. Fabian will pick me up. He knows his way around. Relax, everything is under control." *Just when I thought I had it all figured out, Victor screws up. Asshole.* Eric walked into his walk-in closet and grabbed an overnighter garment bag. "Why don't you make yourself useful and get me a drink while I call the Platinum desk. The flight to Medellin leaves around five thirty."

Lillian started for the stairs. "Vodka Gimlet?" She asked him on the way down.

SEVEN

A balmy, cloudy seventy-seven degrees welcomed Fabian when he arrived at the Federal de Bachigualato international Airport in Culiacan. Ash clouds from the Popocatepetl volcano had delayed his flight from Mexico City.

A driver and a bodyguard were waiting to take him to meet with his local cartel chieftain.

The guard opened the passenger door of a black SUV with heavily tinted windows. Fabian entered the car and half hour later they about reached the iron gates of Vicente Ferrera's imposing French chateau. He looked out the window and marveled about the incredible amount of water the beautiful landscaped grounds had to consume to be in such immaculate shape. The Escalade circled the twenty-car driveway bordered with sculpted topiaries and stopped at the mansion's entrance. Vicente, alias *El Carnicero,* The Butcher, waited for the car to stop and opened the passenger door before any of his men had a chance to do it. *"Ah compadre*, you finally arrived."

"I had a little bit of a delay. How are things?"

He gave Fabian a hearty embrace. "Good, good, join me for a tequila shot? A sangrita?"

The young kingpin was wearing a long sleeve dark green, silk shirt, black pants and green boots matching the shirt. Considering how hot and humid the day might become, the clothes were somewhat over the top. He was short, unassuming, slightly overweight and clean-shaven, with short, spiky hair.

Vicente grabbed Fabian's arm and escorted him through an expansive marble floor foyer to a large backyard. A spacious tiki-bar offered shade.

Smoke spiraled upwards from a gigantic brick grill. A cook, manning large cuts of meat, turned over the pieces with a long spatula. He glanced at the arriving individual while mopping his forehead.

"How you like that?" Vicente pointed and the cuff of his shirtsleeve slid back. A flashy Rolex watch and a diamond solitaire glinted in his pinky finger. "A suckling piglet for us."

"Tell me, how are the mules working out?"

Vicente had a large network of people transporting the drugs across the border and distributing through the U.S. Border States.

"You're going to need more people. Any problems with the border patrol and the DEA?"

"Ay compadre, los pendejos Raramuri Indians are stubborn like the real mules. They know all the hidden trails, the places to hide the drugs and where there isn't any police checkpoints."

Fabian was handed a piece of grilled pig-skin.

"They don't want to work for us and I need their paths to move the stuff faster and avoid the *Zetas and the Federales."*

"Are you working with El Chapo?" Fabian chomped on a savory piece of meat.

"I always let him know when we're making a transfer and give him his cut."

"Can he do anything about the Zetas gangs?"

"Oh, he's keeping them away but you never can be too sure."

"I'm going to Colombia soon. Things are becoming complicated. Is Cuauhtémoc around?" Fabian wiped his mouth and hands with a cloth napkin offered by a servant.

"He should be in Ciudad Juarez checking the last shipment that came from Venezuela. I have another shipment coming Guatemala on its way to Tuxla."

"See if you can get a hold of him. Call him now."

Vicente made the call and handed the phone to Fabian.

Cuauhtémoc, it's me. I want you to find me a village in the Canyon." Fabian went on with a set of instructions.

The cook brought two large platters with several cuts of meat but Fabian ate sparingly. With business concluded, he headed back to the airport. On the way out he placed another call to his Miami partner. "Eric, I'm going to see Claudia-Lucia. Have you made any plans yet?"

"I'm working on it."

"Jolly good mate." Fabian had spent his childhood in England and had picked up a proper English accent. "I'll see you there, then?"

"Any news on the Calwel business?"

"Not a pip but with Victor's death, I do not fathom anything happening soon. We can discuss it after we have a good chat with her. Cheerio." Fabian hung up.

EIGHT

Herding the sheep away from one of the canyon gullies, the young Indian boy saw the glint of metal in the distance. He left the lambs in a make shift corral and ran to the village to sound the alarm.

The dusty hardscrabble settlement was in the middle of nowhere. Its proximity to *Parque Natural Barranca del Cobre* could be considered the only reason for its existence. A barely existent dirt road led to the nearest highway, Interstate Forty-Five in the state of Chihuahua, Mexico.

Before the villagers had a chance to run and hide, an array of trucks arrived, forcing the old folks, women and children to seek refuge in the small church. They cowered inside the tight confines of the adobe house of prayer. Twelve young men carrying vintage hunting rifles took positions at the hamlet entrance.

Before long, the thunder of a fusillade followed by an unnerving quiet brought more laments and despair to the congregation.

The village's young men tried to defend their turf. But they were overwhelmed by the superior firepower of the bandits. Ten bloody were placed impaled around the rim of the local water-well. It was the macabre result of the valiant but in vain effort of the defenders attempt to protect isolated settlement.

Sweating and gasping for air, the people of the community waited in the confines of the small church.

The children were gathered around the one-foot high platform of the church's sanctuary. Scared and thirsty, they screamed and begged for their mothers.

High on a wall a sad Christ effigy looked at them from its six foot cross, to the side of the altar area, sitting in a niche, was a three-foot tall statue of the Virgin of Guadalupe.

The priest ventured outside.

The roaring engines of seven pick-up trucks running circles around the church, and raising a cloud of dust and chocking air, scared the huddled mass even more.

A short distance away, facing the small plaza was a black GMC truck.

The frail old man wearing a dark brown robe tried to walk to the SUV but the fast moving trucks would not let him step across. He pleaded. "Please don't harm us. My flock is simple peasants. They are unarmed and they are women, children and old folks. I beg you."

Behind the church doors, the desperate cries for help and high-pitched wails increased but it was to no avail.

The constant revving of the engines, the unceasing heckling and coarse laughs from the *Caballeros del Norte cartel* members, kept the people inside the church shaking in despair.

"Please!" The old priest cried. "They are frightened." His please went unnoticed in the deafening noise from the trucks.

****

"*Patron,* everyone is inside the village church." Cuauhtémoc, sitting in the back of the *Cherokee,* cell phone in hand, told Fabian.

Smoothing his well-kept mustache with his fingers, Fabian Negreto asked. "Anyone got out?"

"No, the heads of those who tried to fight are now decorating the village. What do you want me to do with the rest? There's an old priest begging for their release."

Fabian relaxed in a deep cushioned lounge chair in his plush penthouse. The tall, high rise sat on top of a hill in the exclusive Reforma-Lomas neighborhood. The view from the floor-to-ceiling living room windows offered a splendid landscape of the city's vastness. Today was one of those rare days when smog did not cover Mexico City with a brown-gray fog. A favorable wind had pushed the poisonous air out of the city and a cobalt blue sky radiated through. He stretched his arms and smoothed his already well-groomed hair. His eyes strayed from the scenic panorama and he stared at the speakerphone. "You know what to do."

"The women and children too?" Cuauhtémoc's face remained impassive while watching the spectacle in front of his eyes.

"How many altogether?" Fabian said.

"Maybe ninety, one hundred, one or two, plus or minus." Cuauhtémoc deadpanned expressionless. "Probably twenty-five, thirty women, a few really old and about forty, fifty kids. It's the whole village." He passed a bottle of tequila to the men in the front seat.

Cuauhtémoc, of strong Aztec heritage, was short and burly, with bronze skin and stiff hair, a wide mouth, flat nose and a hairless face. Fabian, on the other hand, was light skinned and of Castilian ancestry, tall, with a tight build. A slightly hook nose, eyes set apart, manicured eyebrows, perfect teeth and pulpy lips gave him an aristocratic air.

NINE

Leaving the comfort of the car's air conditioner, Cuauhtémoc waved at one of the trucks making another round around the small edifice. The *F-150* left the maddening circle and drove towards him, leaving a cloud of dusty hot air behind. The dirt-encrusted driver's window came down and a loud *ranchera* song blasted the copper-color man's eardrums. The driver grinned and turned down the radio. *"Diga jefe?"* A long black droopy mustache hid his upper lip.

"Grab the priest and tie him up. Splatter the walls with fuel and set the place on fire."

"And the ones who try to get out?"

"Anyone who tries to get out?" Cuauhtémoc slid his index finger across his short, bulging neck.

The driver laughed. *"Que comiense la fiesta!"* His companions joined in the laughter.

The side window went back up and the truck turned around. When it reached the isolated building, the pick-up stopped and three men sitting in the cab, jumped down and joined Flaco. The diminutive priest was seized by the cuff of the robe and was dragged down the stone steps. The frail old man continued begging to spare the lives of his people.

The wild group started tying a makeshift cross together.

Flaco grabbed the old man and hit him in the stomach. The old priest collapsed on the dusty ground writhing in pain.

Barely able to speak, the old priest went on. "Please, I beg you. I'm a poor man, this is an insignificant church and we are all humble people. Take me but please let the others go. They haven't done anything to you. Pleas-"

His words were cut short. A dark skinned thug pummeled the priest's face with his boot. The sickening crunch of broken bones and splattered blood announced the death of the man-of-the-church. The goons laid him on the log, tying his arms to the horizontal piece and his legs to the vertical pole. With that task completed, the rudimentary cross was plunked against the front doors.

The rest of the mob began taking out large plastic containers.

An eerie silence penetrated the walls. *"Padre, que pasa?"* A plump weather beaten woman called from inside.

From inside the church, someone asked in a low voice. "Everybody, quiet, shhhh."

"Don Ignacio?" A girl of about eight years pulled the sleeve of an infirm timeworn elder standing next to her. "Are they gone?"

The mothers tried to shush their children. The heavy, asphyxiating air hung over them.

Another aged man, walking with a cane, stepped to the church's entrance, and glued his face to a tiny sliver of light that broke through the closed, thick doors.

A wide plank went across the doors, preventing anyone from getting in, or getting out.

"Virgen de Guadalupe, salvanos!" He made the sign of the cross and turned around, his eyes wide with fear. *"Han crucificado al padrecito.* And are pouring gasoline on him."

In seconds, an acrid smell accompanied with heavy gray smoke filtered through the closed doors and windows. The wailing and screaming began anew.

Soon after, long fingers of reddish, orange, bluish flames began to seep in.

"Open the doors!" A hysterical old woman shouted. "We'll burn to death!"

Piled against the doors, coughing, spitting, and tearing from the burning smoke, the men and women bawled and screamed.

The children's wails were drowned by the multitude of noise. A cacophony of shoving feet and arms pounded the doors as the men and women pushed each other in a futile attempt to escape the death trap. Smoke began covering the hapless crowd, making them cough and irritating their eyes and parched throats. Pieces of burning wood and adobe rained down from the roof on the hysterical crowd.

Some of the older folks fell down and were stepped on by the frenzied and panicking mob.

Outside, the thugs jumped up and down, laughing and drinking, crashing their empty bottles against the flames licking at the walls.

The church doors suddenly opened but a hail of bullets chopped down the first few that tried running out of the engulfing blaze.

"Get back, get back, they are shooting us." An old man shouted and turned around.

A burst of gunfire pierced his back and he fell. More bodies piled over him. The fire sucked in the air through the four charred wood windows and partially open doors.

The desperate cries coming from inside the whitewashed church were followed by horrendous screams when the roof started collapsing on top of the powerless victims. The wailing stopped.

A deafening silence covered the smoking rubble. Only the crackling sound of burning wood and the explosion of adobe mud shattered the stillness.

The sweet, sick smell of burning flesh swirled upwards. The makeshift cross holding the pastor's cadaver broke in half, and his charred bones were scattered here and there.

Watching mesmerized for a few seconds, the murderous gang started whooping, dancing and shooting at the fire in a horrendous and obscene celebration. They high-fived each other and passed bottles of tequila and mescal shouting amongst themselves. The throat burning liquors were guzzled, the empty bottles thrown into the eerie sight.

Cuauhtémoc walked closer to the smoldering inferno, and satisfied, shouted, *"vamonos."* He climbed in his truck.

The men ran to their vehicles yelling and laughing.

A barking pack of dogs came out of the empty huts. In a running frenzy they went after the speeding trucks.

None of the men saw the small pair of eyes staring at them from the rubble. When the girl couldn't see the trucks anymore, she snuck out around the crucified Jesus on the cross. The icon had fell over the altar, making a crude lean-to. A piece of wall was still attached to the back of the cross and had sheltered her from the worst of the flames. She stood up next to the altar. Soot covered the eight-year-old face.

Burns covered her cheeks, arms and legs and ashes had turned her black hair to a dirty gray. Her clothes were singed and threadbare.

She held a baby swaddled in a coarse Indian blanket in her arms. Stepping carefully over the ruins, she stood in front of the Virgin of Guadalupe still in its niche, and made the sign of the cross. Somehow that piece of wall had not collapsed in the fiery inferno.

With the crying baby cradled in her arms, the little girl wandered aimlessly.

The village dogs, upon hearing the baby's cries, ran in her direction, yelping, yapping and barking, their tails wagging.

She entered one of the small shanty houses dotting the empty village and placed the wailing baby on a thin mattress lying on the dirt floor. The dogs had remained outside. The darkened room felt cool compared to the hot air outside and she shivered.

Outside, one of the scraggly dogs scratched its hindquarters, sniffed the air and then lurked towards the town's well, its head close to the ground.

The pack quieted and shadowed the apparent leader.

A jug, half filled with water, sat on a rickety table by a small wood fire stove.

Smoldering coals spread a light white smoke. Picking a tin cup, she poured water on it, drank a little and went back to the baby. After wetting a finger she put it to the baby's mouth.

The infant stopped crying and greedily sucked the finger. Repeating her action a few times, she stopped when the baby smiled and made cooing sounds. She then stood up, turned and stared blankly at the harsh glaring light from a midday sun through the open door.

Outside, the dogs were barking, yapping, snarling and howling.

Twisting around, she looked at the baby. She closed the door and barricaded it with a rustic chair. She lay next to the tot, wrapped her arm around him and hugged him tight. Then closed her eyes.

TEN

"So, Rafael, is this the same man you saw in the tape from the pawn shop?" The captain watched the video feed with her two assistants in the security room of the second floor of Medellin's Airport.

"Chief, I'm not one hundred percent sure but the physical appearance and that baseball cap are definitely about the same."

"Can you see if any of the airport cameras captured a good likeness of his profile?" She addressed the uniformed man sitting in front of the console.

The employee clicked some keys and another video appeared. A tall man was seen coming down from the second floor but he was adjusting his hat, impeding the camera from getting a clear shot. A moment later, the full shape was in plain view, except for the baseball hat blocking the face.

Karina and the two young detectives watched over the shoulder of the security man. "Stop. Good. He's got to be the same man who shows up shooting everyone outside the pick-up area of the airport." She rubbed her chin with a closed fist.

The man pressed another key. The view in the monitor was enlarged but the face remained partially concealed and sunglasses further cloaked the killer's face.

"Go back. There have to be other pictures where we can see his face...what's your name?"

"Federico Tamayo, Señora."

"Thank you Federico. Rafael will stay to assist you. See if you can find a better picture. Go back at least three hours or more. He has to show up coming into the airport. Sebastian, come with me. We'll pick Daniel on the way there and pay a visit to the widow."

ELEVEN

The car dealer picked up the phone. *"Alo? Medellin Luxury Car, Bartolomeo speaking; how may I help you?"*

"This is Claudia-Lucia Draco. I need three SUV's today. All black. Can you arrange it? It will be a cash deal."

"Three you said?" His mind was going at full speed trying to figure out the commission. "That...that will be more than three hundred thousand dollars." *Draco she said? His name is all over the news.*

"Can you deliver or not?"

"Yes, yes...I'll start working on it right away."

"Will the cars be ready by...?" She looked at her *MB&F MoonMachine* watch. "...Five this afternoon?"

"For sure. May I have a number I can call you at, Señora Claudia?"

She gave it to him. "The sooner the better, you understand? Do you have any armored models? If you do, add them to the list. If not, I want all three done. I need them reinforced right away. My men will be there at five to make the pick up. Find out when the cars can be altered." Claudia hung up.

Her phone rang again. "What is it?"

"Vladimir here, Señora Claudia. I'll be there in about two hours. One of the planes just landed to take a load. I'm going with the pilot."

"I'll send somebody to pick you up." She hung up and then dialed the number for the intercom. "Is that you, Mario?"

"Si, Señora."

"Vladimir is coming. I want to see him the moment he gets here."

TWELVE

Captain Karina Martinez and her two assistants arrived at Draco's address. A group of workmen were busy repairing a wire mesh entryway. Two burly security men holding machine guns stood by the roadside. Several men in a jeep blocked the paved road that led to the palatial estate at the top of the small hill.

One of the men approached her vehicle, "what do you want?"

"I'm here to see la Señora Draco." She showed him her police shield. "What happened?"

"Wait." He disappeared into a cinder block cabin.

"I guess he's getting instructions..." She looked at the young detective sitting next to her and then glanced through the rearview mirror at her second assistant in the back seat.

****

The house phone rang. Claudia picked it up. "What is it Mario?"

"No Señora, it's Demetrio. There's a policewoman and two men down here to see you."

"What? Nooo, noo, tell them I am not seeing anyone now. Send them away. Shit. I'm in no mood to see no cop now."

The man left the hut and approached the driver's window. "La Señora is not seeing anybody right now."

"Is there a problem? I can come back with a search warrant...there will be at least a dozen agents with me."

"Un momento." The man ran back to the small kiosk. A minute later he was ordering the men in the Jeep to move it and waved her in. The men stopped working and ogled the people inside the car when it drove by.

"Now that's what I call a fortress," Daniel said. They were nearing the high walls surrounding the estate.

A crew of landscapers was busy clearing the skirts of the hill from brush, small trees and stones.

"Do you think that high wire fence goes around?" Daniel turned his head, seeking an end but the barrier disappeared behind the curves of the rise. "Probably, right?" He answered his own question.

"Daniel, do you have the police report?" She glanced at him through the mirror.

"Yes, Captain." He was wiry with an incredibly black mob of wavy hair.

"I want you to raise questions if her answers do not correspond with the report."

"What do you want me to do?" Sebastian asked without looking at his boss, his attention focused on the upward incline. His youthful appearance gave a false impression of innocence.

"Just keep your focus and watch the body language. Make sure you keep an eye on the service folks. We may want to come back for more questioning later."

"If I didn't know better I would say that's a prison." Sebastian, sitting next to her, mused. He was slim, with an easy smile and eyes that glinted with mischief.

They reached the wide driveway facing a set of reinforced steel garage doors. Two cameras, at opposite ends on tall poles scanned the area. "Go, press the intercom. This is bullshit, they know we're coming." She said.

Sebastian got out but before he could reach the doors, the whirling grinding noise of the doors opening stopped him. He returned to the car.

THIRTEEN

Four SUV's reached the wide stone arch. Big iron letters, hanging from thick chain links spelling *LOS CIELOS*, welcomed them. A gentle cooling breeze swayed the grass and tall pines, and made the letters clang softly.

A young ranch hand, rifle in hand, appeared from behind one of the arch columns. Recognizing Hernando, he waved and then did a double take. His eyes went wide and his mouth opened but no sound came.

A slim feminine arm came out and beckoned him. "Dario."

"Señora Virginia." He ran over to the side of the car and crouched. He started laughing and slapping his knees in joy.

Hidden by a clump of trees higher up, another armed ranch hand stepped out. Dario's loud laugh annoyed him. *Why is he laughing? What's so funny? We lost so many friends. What's wrong with him?* He thought he heard his boss's wife but he knew it was impossible. She was dead. *Such a wonderful and beautiful woman and so caring.* He shook his head in an effort to dislodge the sad memory from his mind.

"Is that Manolo over there standing like a grouchy log?" Virginia goofed with Dario.

"Yes, mum, the one and only." He grinned from ear to ear.

"Well, let me out. If he's not coming down to greet me, I guess I'll have to go up and pinch his ears. He must be getting lazy in his old age."

She clambered down from the Chevy. "Manolo, is that how you welcome your friends? Can't even say hallo?" Virginia's melodious laugh sang in the open space.

The young man could not believe his eyes. He and the others had aided Alejandro, spending days nonstop looking for her to no avail. He blinked several times, still uncomprehending, watching the svelte woman limping towards him. And then he was stumbling downhill, holding to the tree limbs to catch himself from falling. He was shouting, yelling, crying, the hat flew off his head as he ran downhill to meet her.

The men of the army patrol, a few feet up the incline, wondered what was going on.

"*Señora! Señora.* You are alive! You are. Blessed Virgin. She is alive." He stopped short of hugging her. The man had the biggest grin anyone had even seen.

"Why are you stopping there, can't you see I can't walk?"

His laughter was contagious and Virginia's party started laughing too.

"Are you going to make me beg you for a hug?" Virginia took two short steps, opened her arms and hugged Manolo, who seemed to be still in some sort of shock. "We thought you were-"

"I know Manolito, I was, I really was. But Alex found me with the help of some new friends."

"*Oh Señora* Virginia, everyone will be so happy. I can't wait to meet your friends and thank them. This is a miracle."

"They are in the car, come, I will introduce you to them." Virginia took his hand. "Then I have to run uphill to see Gaby."

"Everyone will be...ahhh, I don't know how to say it. Happy. No, more than happy."

Virginia hobbled back to the car and made the introductions. Manolo's effusiveness was contagious.

"What happened to your leg?" Both Dario and Manolo asked in unison. Even Hernando had missed it when they were in the airport but now he saw it too.

"It's a long story. I'll tell you some other time." Virginia became serious for a moment but her disposition changed almost instantly to one of giddiness.

The *Suburban* began climbing the winding road. Tall pine trees on both sides of the road imbued the scenery with a touch of a peaceful, idyllic setting. Virginia caught sight of the soldiers.

"Hernando, what's the military doing here?"

"An attack to *Los Cielos*. It happened a few days after you were dead. Although...Alex and Gaby never doubted you were alive. But everything indicated you had drowned in the river. I think Rolando was involved in your disappearance. Zuri and Gaby hid in the jungle for several days."

A flood of emotions arrested Virginia's blissful disposition. Her mind buffeted by a whirlwind of despair. She wanted to speak but she couldn't utter a sound. She stared at Hernando, her mind trying to comprehend, to assimilate what her friend had told her.

In the back of the truck, Camilo, Teresa and Andres heard the grim news for the first time. Their solemn faces witnesses to the new revelations.

Coming out of her mortification, Virginia stared at the road ahead. Her eyes swollen with tears. "I'm coming home, and I have lost some dear friends but I have you all now."

****

Staring from behind the wood partition in the covered corral, Gabriel heard the cars but didn't pay any attention. His focus was on the foal born that morning. He watched the spindly animal trying to get up with Marcelo and Jimmy. "He is so shiny. And look! He's trying to walk."

"Yes, Gaby, I think he's going to be a great horse one day." Marcelo said.

"What are we going to call him?"

"We should wait until your dad comes home and ask him. What do you think?" Jimmy looked outside. Four cars had arrived and people were getting out. His jaw dropped and he blinked twice. "Gaab... Gab."

Gabriel's focus was fixed on the small newborn.

Marcelo, standing with the help of two crutches, placed one of them against the wood fence and put his hand over his brow to look. Elena was running down the front steps. Zuri wasn't far behind. "What is...?" Then he saw the hobbling woman. He tried to talk but couldn't say a word. He thought he was seeing ghosts.

"Gaby! Gaby!" Virginia shouted. "Where are you? Elena, Zuri!" She cried.

A chill ran through him. Was that his mother's voice? For what seemed like an eternity Gabriel stood still, then spun around and saw her. As if propelled by a powerful wind, he shot out of the barn and ran. "Mami! Mami!"

Virginia, hearing his voice, pivoted in his direction, and she too started running, oblivious to the pain in her leg. She fell on her knees, her arms outstretched and crying his name.

"Daddy found you. He told me he would."

Mother and son hugged each other. She kept kissing his wet cheeks, while his arms enlaced her neck. "Mami, you came back. I love you mami. I love you." He stood a few inches away from her as if making sure his mother was there for real.

She held him close and caressed his hair and face while Gabriel kept his small hands on her face. They hugged each other again. Both crying in unison, elated in happiness.

The others stood still, hypnotized. Not one eye was dry. Even the men shed tears at the profound reunion of mother and son.

Had the earth stopped turning? Were the sounds of the forest silenced?

"Gaby, I have missed you so much, sweetheart."

Virginia held him close to her breast, afraid she might lose him again.

"I knew you would be back, I knew it." He cried, holding her as tight as he could.

Finally Virginia stood up, wiped her face and turned to look at the assembly of friends watching them in rapt fascination. "Come Gaby, I want you to meet my new friends." She proceeded to limp towards the crowd with Gabriel's hand held firmly in hers.

Zuri and Elena reached them. The three women embraced each other. Gabriel's arms circled his mother's waist.

FOURTEEN

The chaos in Medellin's airport finally subsided as the authorities regained control. A platoon of soldiers, armed to the teeth, was visible in every crook and cranny. Passengers were being patted down at the entrances. Car trunks were opened and luggage and packages were being inspected on the spot. Long poles holding wide mirrors at one end were shoved under the cars to search for hidden explosives. Sniffing dogs, their leashes held by their masters, strolled around the cars.

His hotel room phone rang distracting him from watching the live news on the TV set.

"Don Alejandro, José here. I just got clearance for private flights. I called Federico and he can fly you this afternoon. Can you come around noon?"

"The sooner, the better. I have been watching the news. I want out of here." Alejandro smiled to himself. *I'm getting to be a good actor.*

"I'll call the pilot right away." *These rich guys are all the same, no balls. But he's a frequent flyer and a good tipper.*

****

"Checking out, Señor Calwel? Was everything to your satisfaction?" The desk clerk took Alejandro's room key.

"Yes, Martin." He faced the young man at the checkout desk waiting his turn. He'd seen the nameplate on the jacket. "Thank you. Just wish we had been able to spend a few more days enjoying the city. Maybe next time...is it okay if I leave the rental car with you? Can you call *Hertz* to come for it?"

"But of course, Señor Calwel. I'll let the concierge know. We'll take good care of it." He handed Alejandro the credit card statement.

"Can you call me a taxi please?"

The man clicked his fingers to get the bellboy's attention.

"Please, come with me." The bellboy escorted Alejandro to the hotel entrance and whistled a taxi.

An hour and a half later, Alejandro's taxi reached the private section of the airport. Security was almost as tight as in the general boarding area. Heavy traffic clogged the two-lane street. An army checkpoint inspected every car and truck entering the area. Drivers and passengers alike were being asked to show their ID's. And all truckloads were being searched.

"Tell you what, I'll walk the rest of the way. Let me pay you now. I'll make it faster on foot." Alejandro picked up his garment bag and exited the taxi, heading for the not too far hanger-office one story building.

****

The small Piper coup began to descend on the large lawn that surrounded the century old mansion. The pilot touched down and steered the airplane towards the large front portal of the gracious house. Built in the early nineteen hundreds by Alejandro's grandparents and added onto it by his parents later on, it resembled a southern estate. Faded brick walls and white washed stone pillars gave it an air of subdued elegance and well-worn age.

A large group began to gather out in the porch. Prominent in the center, Gaby and Virginia. The rest of them stood around them in a close-knit bunch. Loud talk and laughter could be heard as the plane's engine was turned off and the propeller slowly came to a stop. Both pilot and passenger jumped down. Alejandro went around the aircraft's tail and rushed to embrace the two dearest people in his life.

Mother and child ran to meet him but Virginia's limp held her back. "Go ahead Gaby." She let his hand go. "I'll follow you, I can't run as fast."

In seconds Alejandro reached Gabriel and lifted him up in one swift move. He ran towards Virginia, making his son laugh with delight at being bounced up and down.

"My love, I got my memory back, I remember you." She exclaimed breathlessly and opened her arms to hug him and her son in a fierce embrace. She trembled with emotion. Alejandro used his weaker arm to hold Virginia by her waist, while Gabriel wrapped his small arms around their necks.

Everyone, including the men, shed more tears.

FIFTEEN

"We're having more company." A limousine was fast approaching. "Sebastian, when we stop at the entrance, stay outside and see if you can get a look at whomever is coming in that car." Karina said.

A minute later, they arrived at a large, circular port-de-cochere and stopped in front of an imposing entrance. A dozen steps led to two magnificent dark wood doors, at least ten to twelve feet tall, if not higher. A man waiting at the bottom of the steps opened her car door.

Sebastian got out of the car and slowly walked towards the back of the car, stretching his arms and yawning out loud. But his eyes were fixed on the luxury car parking in front of a large two-story building that housed a huge garage. He guessed that it could easily fit a dozen cars. The building's plain façade was a stark contrast to the sumptuous mansion only a few hundred feet away.

A deeply tanned, blondish man with an unkempt beard stepped out of the limo.

Another man came out from the garage, spoke with the newcomer and pointed towards the main house. Both men hurried inside the cavernous dark carport.

The young detective took a mental picture of the man's features. He brought a small notebook out of his suit pocket and scribbled in it.

Karina and Daniel, in the meantime, seemed to be having a private discussion. Her back was towards the impressive entrance. She too scrutinized the new arrival. *I'll compare notes with Sebastian later.*

Daniel saw a gray hair man open the doors and start coming down the steps. "We're being summoned by the Doña." He mouthed to Karina in a barely audible tone.

The man, wearing black pants and a white long sleeve shirt, buttoned at the top, reached the small party. *"Señora, me acompaña?"*

"Boys, let's go." She made a sour grimace and looked at the short, round man waiting for them. "We are ready."

The grand-round foyer's high glass cupola made the visitors gape upwards. But the twelve massive bronze sculptures of the Zodiac signs circling the walls brought their eyes back down.

Two burly men seemed to be finishing setting down the massive pieces. Karina thought that if the sculptures were meant to overwhelm, it was accomplished.

They stopped in the middle of the large room ogling open mouthed the whole ensemble. "Close your mouth, Sebastian." *If I ever had any doubts regarding the rumors of Victor's illicit wealth, this is proof. No wonder so many fall for the mirage of reaping a large fortune, not realizing that it will be short lived at best.*

The old man snorted. "This way please." The manservant opened two high polished mahogany doors and they entered a wide rectangular hall. At the end of the room, square center in the middle of a large light cream-colored sofa, sat Claudia-Lucia. A large nude self-portrait hung on the wall behind her. The hands demurely covered her private parts and long cascading blond hair discretely hid the areolas of her breasts. The highly suggestive imagery of the painting was unmistakable.

In stark contrast to the naked woman in the painting she was wearing a tight black silk dress that covered her from head to toe. A single strand of white Japanese pearls hung over a collar that extended to her jaw line. She made no effort to stand up.

Approaching Claudia, Karina offered her hand. "My sympathies over the untimely death of your husband."

"I can't understand why you have to come now. Don't you people know what I'm going through? I'm in mourning. I hope this doesn't take long."

Her two companions kept stealing glances at the disturbing erotic watercolor. They stood ramrod still across from their boss, who sat down in one of two smaller sofas facing each other. A low glass coffee table in the middle separated them. She turned sideways to face Claudia. *Damn, these guys are losing their concentration.* "Hmmm, Sebastian and Daniel are my associates."

Both men faces turned red and each one mumbled something about her loss.

Gazing at the two young detectives, Claudia coyly accepted the condolence. "Sit down." She motioned with her hand, and flaunted an enormous flawless diamond ring.

What happened to her fingernails? Looks like she broke half of them. Karina was getting wary with the whole theater set in motion in front of her. *I have to get their attention back to what we're here for.* Her throat cleared again but this time a little louder.

The two young detectives avoided Karina's blazing eyes.

Sebastian stole another glance at the nude and then kept his eyes focused on Claudia's face, just below the eyes. He was making a superhuman effort to concentrate.

"Señora Draco, I'm sorry to disturb you." Karina said.

"Yeah, right. What gives you the right to barge into my house when I'm still trying to cope with my husband death?"

"But it's very important that we talk to you right away. We'll try to make this short. When did you find about your husband and where were you at the time?"

"I was here, where else? As a matter of fact, I was damn asleep when your morons called me. They wanted me to go to the mortuary to identify Victor. I didn't want to go but how the hell was I going to know for sure? Cowards, killing my husband when he couldn't defend himself."

"Do you know where your husband was coming from?"

"He has many ranches all over the place. I don't bother with those things." She made a dismissive gesture with her hand. The retrieving sleeve uncovered what looked like a rather exotic, expensive watch.

"But this particular time, did you know where he was going or coming from?"

"I already told you, I don't know."

"Do you suspect anyone in particular? Someone who could have been after him? We heard there was a disturbance around here. Police reports mentioned that early last night shots rang in the area. And three of your husband's men were killed a few blocks down below. And we were able to identify a charred SUV that belonged to your husband. And then this morning, sadly your husband meets a tragic death."

"You damn well know that my husband has many enemies. I mean, had." She sniffled. "People are jealous because he is...was a very smart man. He made money the honest way, not this bullshit of being involved in drug trafficking. Was he ever arrested? Of course not, because it's a lie." She finished in a shrilling tone.

"I understand. But can you tell me what happened here? Those men doing repairs at the bottom of the hill...does it have anything to do with all the shooting that went down here last night?"

"No! Nothing happened here. The work had been planned a long time ago."

"Are you sure?"

"It must have been someplace else. Why don't you send your men to bother the other neighbors instead of wasting my time?" Claudia touched her nose.

"So...you claim that you have no idea who may have been after your husband?"

"Of course not! I'm no gipsy card reader."

"What about a man named Hugo? He reported to your husband, did he not?"

"How would I know?"

"Hugo tried to kill another man at a hospital in town. Apparently, it was the second time the victim was almost killed in a matter of days. Your husband had nothing to do with that either?"

Claudia's ears perked up. "Huh? Who was that? I mean at the hospital?"

"I can't tell you that. Did you know a man named Rolando? I heard some rumors that he had recently switched jobs and had come to work for your husband. Did you know him?"

"I...no. My husband has many people working for him. Do you think I know everybody that works for him?"

"You won't mind if I ask around. I will have to talk to your help and the security people."

Shit, sooner or later somebody is going to tell them that those two idiots worked for Victor. "Hugo? Oh yes, I remember. Victor fired him. A fat lazy bastard, if you ask me."

"And Rolando?"

"Rolando? Now that I think of it, he did come to work for Victor, but he only worked here for a few days. I thought he didn't like his job and had gone back to his old one."

"I see. You won't mind then if my men stick around for a while and ask a few questions from the servants and the security that work here, right?"

"I...I need to talk to my husband's lawyer. I'm not talking anymore. This meeting is over." Claudia rang a small silver bell and immediately the gray-hair little round man showed up. "Take these people out." She stood up and sashayed away. Her tight dress clinging to every curve in her body. Sebastian and Daniel's eyes followed her every movement.

"I will come back with a subpoena, just so you know." Karina said.

"You can do whatever the fuck you want. As if I give a shit." Claudia didn't bother to turn around and walked out of the room.

SIXTEEN

His biggest concern was the cash flow needed to keep his tottering real estate empire afloat. Eric had spent most of the three plus hour flight to Medellin mulling over Victor's sudden demise and the effect it could have on their business over the course of the next few days. If the coca shipments dried up, he was fried. The insistent and annoying banker calls asking for a meeting to resolve his past due debt were irritating him to no end. He knew that he would not be able to stall much longer.

Walking out of Medellin customs and immigration, he started looking for Nené, the big man with the small child face, but couldn't find him. He noticed the waiting crowd was subdued instead of its usual boisterousness.

The strong and heavily armed military presence made everyone around the airport cagy. *Hmm, I wonder if this has to do with Victors' murder this morning.* He glanced at his *Breitling* watch. *I need to get my own private plane again. It's already past nine. It will be midnight before I get to bed. Fabian is probably whore mongering and the business is going to shit.*

"Eric, Eric, over here." The voice came over from behind a throng of people waiting at the exit. Fabian's sleeked black hair and thin mustache came into view. Three men surrounded him.

Are these his bodyguards or did Claudia send them? Eric didn't recognize any of the faces. He waved.

"Meet you at the exit." Fabian and his companions strolled towards the end of the barricade that separated arriving passengers from those waiting.

One of the men took Eric's luggage and the foursome walked out together to the curb. A big black *Mercedes 550* approached them. A suburban followed behind. The chauffeur opened the rear door and Eric followed Fabian into the car.

Two men dressed in what looked like police uniforms and riding *Kawasaki* motorcycles appeared from nowhere and moved in front of the cars. One of the men blocked one of the two-lane street while the other one went ahead followed by the small caravan. The motorcycle men kept blocking one traffic lane and then the other so that the two cars could speed away unobstructed. Once the limo and its follow up car moved into the cleared lane, the motorcyclist that had blocked the roadway, would move ahead and obstruct the other lane.

It forced motorists to slow down and clear the path for the cars to advance at a rapid pace on the two-lane highway.

The riders went on switching back and forth the many curves and a series of deeps and rises, maintaining their momentum until the caravan reached Medellin's outskirts, and slowed down.

Colombia's second largest city, with close to four million people, seemed to beckon them with its bright lights dotting its surrounding hills.

After going through a series of hitch backs clustered with high-rise apartments, commercial buildings, several hotels and two large malls, they began to climb a curvy road. Here, the houses were more sparse and luxurious. The motorcade led by the two motorcyclists stopped in front of a high wire fence.

Eric looked at the two high intensity spotlights that lit a tall wire fence. "Any more news about what happened?"

"Nothing more." Fabian's thoughts were on Claudia and how she would react to her being relegated to nothing more than a passive partner.

"I told her about my cash flow problems and suggested she come to Miami and invest in my companies. She liked the idea."

"When will she make the investment?" Fabian moved slightly in his seat, changing his posture.

"Soon, I hope. Those damn bankers are after me like hound dogs. No, they're more like hyenas. I need money." Eric licked his lips. *How about you giving me a helping hand, you fake English prick?* "I don't know what else I can do for now."

"Let me know how it works out."

"You think she'll be in a better mood? I don't want to deal with a mad woman." Eric frowned. "That looks new. I don't remember seeing those high beams, and looks like they are reinforcing the cyclone fence."

A man came out of a shelter, machine gun at his side.

"They are buttressing the fence since the presumed maid escaped in one of the cars. Can you believe that?" Fabian snickered.

"The men in the bikes...they aren't policemen, are they?"

"No, they wear uniforms that make them look like the real thing." Fabian said.

"I wonder how Victor got away with that." Eric nodded to the man looking at him through the window.

****

Both men were ushered to what until recently had been Victor's private office.

"I hope this doesn't take long. I'm tired..." Eric got up and made a sweep of the room looking for the wet-bar. He walked around stretching his legs. "Where the heck is she? Victor never made us wait."

Both men were standing, impatient. Their annoyance visible in their faces. The waiting time had seemed longer, and worse, no one had come to ask them if they wanted anything to eat. They had taken over the bar and were on to their second whiskey.

Twenty minutes later Claudia-Lucia entered the office.

"About time." Fabian made a move to kiss her face but the look in her eyes stopped him.

"What's wrong now?" Fabian said.

"I'm sorry about Victor's-"

"Sit, both of you."

Eric defied her and remained standing. *I need to show her who is boss, although I don't want to antagonize her if I'm going to ask her to help me. I guess I better.* After a few minutes he sat down reluctantly.

"The cops were here today, some mother-fucker detective and her two lapping dogs were here asking a bunch of questions." She scoffed. "And then as if I needed more shit, Vladimir arrived from the plantation about the time they were leaving." She paced back and forth. Her high spike heels made her seem taller, but the staccato noise on the highly polished wood sounded most unpleasant. Tight black leggings covered her shaped legs, a long white cashmere sweater, covered her from the neck to mid thighs and buttocks. It too fit snuggly, accentuating her large breasts, small waist and round gluts. She finally stopped, pushed her hair back in a coquettish gesture and smiled. For the first time, her face softened, enhancing her beauty.

Eric and Fabian relaxed.

"Can you take me through what happened in the last twenty-four hours?" Fabian said.

Eric sat in a wide cushioned leather armchair that swallowed him, he moved forwards.

Starting with Victor's trip to the jungle factory, she recounted the events of the last two days. "I spoke with Vladimir and he agreed to work for me and run the plantation and manufacturing process. There's one small problem but it's not a big issue."

"What problem?" Fabian looked at her suspiciously.

"Victor kidnapped a chemistry professor about three years ago and had promised the man to let him go back to his family."

"So? What's the problem?" Eric said.

"I'm getting a drink." Fabian got up and walked over to the wet-bar.

"Victor told Vladimir to have the prisoner train a couple of men with the promise to let him go afterwards. We're going to kill him when the others learn the process." Her eyes kept going back and forth between the two men.

Fabian looked at Eric. They had already discussed who would take over for her dead husband, but Claudia's statement now made it clear she planned to run the business.

"Are you sure you want to get involved?" Fabian crisscrossed his legs and relaxed on the soft leather chair. "We could find someone to run the business and you could keep enjoying all this." He made a sweeping gesture with his arms.

"Do you take me for an idiot?"

"We are only thinking of your well-being-"

"Well-being my ass. There's a fucking brain inside this pretty head. Why do you think I married the old fart? I'm in charge now and I'm not letting this go, I'm going to be the coca queen of Colombia. Are you in or out? Make up you minds. I can find someone else real quick to take over for both of you."

"Relax Claudia, if this is what you want; then it is." Eric padded his upper lip with his index finger several times. "All we want is to make sure the business is running smoothly. With all that has happened, Fabian and I thought that it would be best for you to keep a low profile, especially with the police sticking their noses-"

"I can handle the police. You keep your end of the bargain and everything will continue as it was before." She pointed at both men with her index finger.

"Jolly well then, I guess there's nothing more to discuss tonight." *I hope she does not do a cack up of everything.*

Eric checked the time and covered his mouth with his hand to hide a yawn.

"Actually there is. I'm having problems with some of the investments and need an infusion of capital to grow the money laundering." He didn't say that the biggest problem was his own finances.

"How much of a problem?" She said.

"Eric hoped that once Victor acquired the...what was his name, Calwel? The land."

Eric clarified. "We discussed with Victor using the property as a front, making it seem it was part of my assets. It would allow me to make more investments that can be used to launder funds."

"I see." *I don't understand this mumbo-jumbo bullshit.*

"I would register the property as mine and use it as collateral to get more funding and invest in businesses that work with lots of cash. I'm having a hard time converting all those bundles of money into legitimate funds without raising suspicion. I can't go to the banks and deposit hundreds of thousands of dollars without a legitimate cover-up."

"Where is the ranch or whatever it is?" Claudia-Lucia's interest had perk up.

"It's a very nice spread somewhere in the northeast and from what I understand it butts with the shore line somewhere. And there's a river that crisscrosses the property and reaches the Caribbean." Eric became animated. "Victor thought it would make it a lot easier to transport production and the land could be used to plant more coca. He had sent some men to take care of things...if you know what I mean."

"Is that the *Los Cielos* place I heard Victor talk about? She lied. "So, Calwel is the man Hugo went after, hm, I see." Claudia gestured to Fabian to serve her some wine. "Did Victor finish him off?"

"That's my worry. And I don't know how to find out. Is Victor's death and the man who owns *Los Cielos* related? It is a puzzle. This is a nice wine." Fabian read the label on the bottle. It was a *2006 Pierre Damoy Pinot Noir.*

"Victor had expensive tastes." She smiled and moved her arm down her figure. "Of course, if he hadn't been hiding and fucking that puta in front of my eyes...."

"Please not now." Fabian brought the wine to her. "Let's stick to business, okay?"

"If he had not been fucking her right here, in my house, he might still be alive, right?"

"Did you not tell me that he was holding her for some kind of ransom?" Fabian took a gulp of wine and let the taste linger in his mouth.

"Maybe she is *El Quimico's* wife." Eric said.

"Yeah, right, and if you believe that, I'm the bastard daughter of the Queen of England. Tell me more about that ranch."

"Before we get into that, I need suggestions."

"About what?" She said.

"On how I can get my hands on a couple of million dollars." As usual, Eric was losing his patience. "Real quick."

"What about the place that you were talking about?" Claudia said.

"Calwel's place? *Los Cielos?*" Eric glanced at Fabian. "It will give me the façade I need to foil the bankers and the feds. Otherwise, it's a slow and I mean, slow process getting all that cash flushed into legitimate businesses."

"It was an unmitigated and resolute disaster." Fabian shook his head.

"But that was because you men always want to be more macho."

"It was a good...it still is a good idea." Eric said ruefully.

"Confronting him head on? That was stupid. I don't know the man but with a little patience we can find a better opportunity. Victor's macho personality got the best of him and the motherfucker paid with his life." Claudia crossed herself. But for her, the gesture had nothing to do with religion.

"I don't have much time." Eric exhaled.

"Look, relax, I'll invest in your business." Claudia eyed him. "How much do you need to get yourself out of the hole?"

"A minimum of five million to balance the cash flow."

"Work out the details. But don't try to screw me or your ass is mine."

"It is becoming late, Eric. Can we reconvene here tomorrow? Claudia?"

"Fine, fine," she said. "I'll have the limo drive you to your hotel."

"Let's go Eric. Tomorrow we can discuss infusing more cash into your business."

Eric nodded disappointed.

"Follow me, I'll get the driver." Claudia strode ahead of them, her hips undulating in a seductive manner. The knock, knock of her spike stilettos echoed on the Spanish tiles. She led them through the immense round foyer with the bronze sculptures.

SEVENTEEN

Virginia's parents waited outside the customs and immigration area in the private section of the Benito Juarez Airport in Mexico City. They saw Virginia, Gabriel and Alejandro from behind the glass doors that separated arriving passengers and waved.

"There's grandma and grandpa." Alejandro picked up his son, so he could see them. Virginia swayed her hand and smiled broadly.

Her parents waved back, big smiles on their faces.

Ahead of the family, were two men in front of the customs and arrival desk. One of them had curly, sandy colored hair, a slight pouch and fair skin. He was speaking with a taller, pale man with black hair and a trim mustache.

After putting Gabriel down, Alejandro began sorting out the various custom forms and their passports. He stood behind a thick yellow line painted on the cement floor, but then raised his head. A man, wearing a dark ill-fitting suit, stood up from behind his desk and brought something to the attention of the two men. There seemed to be some sort of confusion about one of the men's papers.

"*Señor*, you need to fill out an immigration form. You're American but flew in with *Señor* Negreto from Medellin, Colombia, right? You didn't fly there through here. You need a visa entry form and you'll need it when you leave Mexico. You understand?"

The taller man spoke with a Mexican accent "I invited my friend, to come back with me. We were in Medellin on urgent business. A friend of ours died and we were there to pay our respects. I don't carry immigration forms in my plane. Don't you have any?" He handed his and Eric's passports. Between the documents, neatly folded, were several one hundred dollar bills.

Alejandro appeared distracted sorting out their papers but was listening to the conversation. Virginia, behind him, was distracted talking with Gabriel. He kept his head down pretending to untangle the forms but caught a quick glance of the two men. *Didn't Andres or Camilo tell me that one of Victor's associates was Mexican?* He attuned his ears to listen and watched out of the corner of his eyes the officer taking the men's documents and saw the bills.

"Oh, I understand *Señor* Negreto. Wait a second." Surreptitiously, the officer made the bills disappear in a side pocket.

He waved at a woman standing nearby and shouted. "Juanita, can you bring me an entry visa form?"

The two men were now speaking in English. Alejandro heard a distinct British accent.

Fabian took a furtive look at the man a couple of feet behind them but the bloke seemed distracted with the forms. "With Claudia-Lucia's investment, things will be right side up." Fabian glanced at the government employee and continued talking with Eric. "The bankers will leave you alone and you will not have to fret anymore."

"There's no other way. Not until we get that land. If Victor hadn't..." Eric wiped his upper lip.

A gnawing uneasiness hit the pit of his stomach. Alejandro's neck stood up.

"I'll fill out the form for you." The officer had a thin white form with a light pink back.

"Thank you, then we can leave, correct?" Fabian addressed the man rubber-stamping the two-page document with the entry date.

"Yes, el Señor Santos has a thirty day visa. Welcome to Mexico." The officer smiled at Eric. "*Y disculpe la molestia Señor Negreto.*"

Both men left in a hurry, carrying two-day suiter garment bags.

Alejandro kept his eyes on them and when they exited turned towards Virginia. "It's a good thing we came to visit them."

"I'm so thrilled." She smiled happily.

"It was so hard to tell them you...had disappeared, I didn't know what else to say to them. Your poor dad, he was so distraught. Your mother, thank God, she had faith. Like Gaby, she never accepted it. Neither did I." His eyes watered and he took her hand and kissed it. "They never heard the rest of it. Don't know half the story."

"I can't even begin to imagine."

"When they heard you, it was like...you gave them new life."

"They kept asking when we were coming to visit them. This visit will do wonders for dad."

"And after a couple of days, we'll take our little vacation. What do you think, Gaby?" Alejandro ruffled his son's hair.

The smiles in Virginia and Gabriel's faces were more than enough proof for Alejandro. "I'm going to take you to see Copper Canyon."

"Dad, daddy, daddy." Alejandro looked distractedly at Gabriel.

"I heard it's bigger than the Grand Canyon. I'll work out the details."

"*Señor?*" The dark-olive skin, diminutive man was waiting and waved him over.

"I have the forms all sorted out." He grinned at the customs official and gave him the passports and immigration forms.

The bureaucrat checked their passports; then with a puzzled look addressed Alejandro. "Are you with the same party? Were you all at the same funeral?" His head turned to the two men that had just disappeared through the sliding doors.

"What funeral?" Virginia said.

"They arrived from Medellin. And you flew in from there too." *Well, they look like a nice family. Yeah, and these are the ones who get through because no one suspects them. I wonder if they are carrying drugs. I'm going to alert the major.* "Un momento por favor." He pressed a hidden button under his desk.

An officer pacing the aisle saw a small light turn red on the side of the desk. He approached them. "Good morning. May I see your passports please?" He eyed Alejandro, then Virginia. *Beautiful woman.*

"Something wrong officer?" Virginia asked.

The man behind the desk shielded his mouth and said something to the standing officer.

"What is the purpose of your visit?" The man in uniform asked.

"My parents live here and we wanted to see them and maybe do a little sightseeing."

"We're going to *El Parque Nacional Barranca del Cobre.*" Alejandro added.

"Where is your luggage?"

"There, the airport attendant is bringing them right now." Virginia pointed to several suitcases. She looked at her parents across the way, waiting anxiously behind the glass panels, and waved at them again.

"We need to inspect your plane and your luggage. Matias have Juanita take the *señora*, and you take Mr...." he looked at the passport, "...Calwel with you."

About to ask what was going, Virginia stopped, knowing better.

"Señora, bring your son." The man in the dark suit signaled Juanita at the same time. The woman promptly walked to him. "Check the lady. I'm taking her husband."

"Venga conmigo."

Virginia took Gabriel's hand and gave Alejandro a worried look.

He followed them with his eyes. They disappeared behind the door of a windowless room.

"Take off your blouse and hand me your brassiere. I need your pants too." Juanita had already demanded Virginia's jacket and was in the process of inspecting it. She was feeling the slightly padded shoulders. "I may have to cut these open. You won't mind, will you?" She made a dismissing smirk and took a small pocketknife out. *Rich bitch, you can afford a new one.*

"Is that really necessary?" Virginia said in a soothing tone even though she was angry but knew better than to antagonize the woman.

Alejandro, staring at the windowless room, heard the major's voice. "I'm sorry, what?"

"Follow me." The man looked suspiciously at Alejandro.

"Officer, I don't understand. Is there a problem?" Alejandro stared at the diminutive man.

The man opened the door of an adjacent room. "Take off your clothes."

Damn, they think we're bringing drugs. "Including my underwear?"

"No, you can leave those on...for now. Someone will be with you in a few minutes."

****

A loud knock on the door startled both women and made Gabriel jump off of his chair. A voice shouted from the other side of the closed door. "Juanita, stop everything. There was a mistake, please let *Señora* Calwel out right away." The officer hurried to the next room and opened the door.

Alejandro had already taken his shirt and pants off when the door opened abruptly. *What now?*

"Mil disculpas Señor Calwel. There was a terrible mistake. Please put your clothes back on." The man looked like he was going to have a heart attack. He looked pale and anxious. He closed the door and took a handkerchief out of his back pocket to wipe his brow.

Virginia finished buttoning the blouse and put her jacket back on. The woman opened the door for her and she came out holding Gabriel's hand. He had not spoken a word and now gazed at his mother with an inquiring look.

Another door opened and Alejandro emerged. "I think we are free to go."

The major stood nearby looking very uncomfortable. He withered when he saw Alejandro approach him. *Puta, me van colgar por los huevos.*

"Major, you only did what you thought was right." Alejandro smiled, offering his hand.

The officer thanked him profusely and escorted them to the sliding doors. He yelled at the officers inspecting the luggage, "stop, close the bags and bring them over."

The glass doors opened and Virginia was in front of her parents in an instant, hugging and kissing them profusely. Gabriel and Alejandro fallowed suit and shortly after, the daughter, lacing her arms around both parents walked with them to the building exit and to a long black limousine parked at the curb. Everyone got in and the car took off.

Her parents sandwiched their grandson between the two of them and were asking him all kinds of questions about the flight, the ranch, his pony and his school friends.

Virginia sat next to Alejandro in the opposite seat. "Sweetheart, is something wrong? You seem a little distracted," Virginia squeezed her husband's hand, "not that what happened wasn't upsetting."

"No, my love, just that after everything, and I know that our home is well protected with the soldiers there and all that, but you know how it is..." *I have to find out who those men are; if what I think I heard is correct and that comment about the land...what else could they have been talking about?* "Don Emiliano, did you have anything to do with the officer's sudden change of mind?"

"I realized something was very wrong and made a call to an old friend and told him what was happening. He told me he would take care of it."

Jorge G. Reyes S.

EIGHTEEN

Alejandro called Andres and Camilo and asked them what they knew and remembered about Victor's partners. After the phone call he went to see his father in law. "Do you think your friend could find out who were the two gentlemen that preceded us at the airport?"

"Oh, something the matter?" They were sipping coffee while seated in large plump cushiony chairs in the patio of the two-story Spanish mansion.

"They were coming from Medellin."

High arches offered a shelter area with a beautiful and pleasant garden ensconced in high walls. It offered privacy and deadened the ever-reverberating rumor of the vibrating and pulsating city.

Virginia's parents' home was in the swanky and distinguished *Polanco* neighborhood. The community, one of the oldest and plushier sections of the city had once been a quiet and quaint neighborhood.

It had morphed from a peaceful oasis in the middle of the twenty two million people megalopolis into an amalgam of high raise condominiums, five star hotels and office buildings.

Alejandro raised his eyes from the beautiful Spanish mosaics floor and fixed his eyes on his father in law. The older man still retained some of his once handsome looks. His mostly gray hair was combed back. He had lost some weight and his face seemed more lined with vertical streaks but his eyes had not lost their keen and perceptive look.

"Let's say that I'm curious. I'm thinking of expanding. They were obviously businessmen. I would like to make their acquaintance or at least know who they are for future business possibilities."

"I will call Aureliano and see if he can do me another favor." Virginia's grandfather had once been the Cuban ambassador to Mexico. He had resigned his post and decided to stay in Mexico when Castro's rhetoric took a left turn.

His son, Emiliano Jr. held dual citizenship. Cuban and Mexican. But he had never gone back to his country of birth in honor of his father. As long as the Castro regime held power he would not go back to Cuba. Virginia's father, educated in Mexico had later gone to Harvard where he had become friends with Aureliano Domingues.

His best friend's father was the patriarch of a prominent Mexican political family. The man held a high position in the government.

Both friends had been very successful in their careers, although Virginia's father had retired already.

NINETEEN

Cradling the baby in her arms, she entered the last shack foraging for food and found a paltry amount of oatmeal. She watered a little bit with water and fed the baby. They had survived the last several days by scavenging the village's ramshackle huts. She meticulously closed the door to make sure the dogs would not get in, and carried the rest of the pottage in a small sack tied around her neck.

When she came out with the baby, the dog's leader growled at her and the others started imitating him. The hungry pack went on a furious ruckus, snarling, barking and yelping.

She stepped back in and slowly closed the door.

A large mixed breed with floppy ears wandered off to the water-well and jumped to the lip to bring down one of the heads. But the gruesome body part fell down the well with a sickening splash. The other dogs turned around, their attention shifting.

With their focus of attention gone, the dogs headed for the dilapidated burnt church, and began scratching and digging in the ruins for food.

After waiting for what she thought was a long time. She re-opened the shack's door and trying not to make any noise, ventured outside. She glanced back at the sleeping baby resting on a thin mattress. The last rays of the sun were disappearing behind the canyon walls and soon the temperature would drop. Her eyes swept the area trying to see where the dogs were. She stayed glued to the wall and peeked out of the corner. The dogs were resting in a tight knit group near the church's hulk.

Retracing her steps, she went to the mattress where she had laid the baby, grabbed a blanket, kneeled over and wrapped it around the tiny human life. The baby's face was clean and she swaddled him in the blanket.

Lifting him with great care, she wobbled to the front. The door made a faint squealing noise. She attuned her ears but there was no sound of the dogs. She ventured out further, one step at the time. There was a faint rustle caused by the evening breeze over the scant trees and the pines dotting the area. She chose a trail that meandered close to the creek.

Sleeping peacefully, with the baby cradled in her arms, she looked back at the humble house where she had lived with her parents.

Walking, ever so slow, looking back every few steps, she trudged on. The evening shadows were beginning to blend and hide the land features.

If anyone had seen her, all disheveled, wearing the same grimy smudged and singed dress that she had on that fateful day; the person would have been appalled. Her face was mucky with dirt and her hair was a tangled mess.

She didn't know how long she'd been alone with the baby but there was no food left and she couldn't go to the well for water. She had not spoken one word since the event.

But she kept the baby unsoiled and she always made sure to gently wipe his mouth and face of any food with a soft piece of cloth that she immersed in soap and water. She always threw away the water afterwards and kept a small basin filled from a wide, tall *jarron* that sat on the kitchen floor of the cabin.

TWENTY

Word reached Claudia-Lucia that some local chieftains were trying to muscle into the business by taking advantage of the vacuum left by Victor's sudden demise. But she had other ideas in mind. She called Mario into her office and gave him a short list with four names in it.

The second name on the list, a man named Pablo Matacon, was having dinner at an exclusive gourmet restaurant a few blocks from *Parque Lleras.*

Mario, dressed in a conservative business suit, and two companions arrived at the famous eatery around nine thirty. One man stayed in the driver's seat of a brand new black Escalade. The car still showed a temporary license tag. One of Mario's companions, a thug nicknamed Cuchilla, took out a cigarette before entering. He too wore a suit, although his appearance and demeanor made several late arriving patrons scurry by him real fast. A long pink corrugated scar went down from the side of his forehead to his jaw line. His small eyes, thick eyebrows and neck made people avoid looking at him.

He scanned the outside of the restaurant and approached a man resting against the side of a shiny black Mercedes Bens sedan. "Do you have a light?" Cuchilla showed the other man his cigarette as he put it between his lips.

The man, at first suspicious, relaxed, and brought out a lighter from his pants pocket. He lit it up and offered it to the waiting man, cupping the flame with his other hand to keep it from being snuffed. His eyes, attracted to the small flicker glowing in his hands, missed Cuchilla's move. Before he had a chance to react, a long knife was slicing upwards from his stomach to his sternum. When it reached the bone, the man with the cigarette dangling from his lips, pushed the knife in deeper. The other man's eyes looked up in pain and exhaled a breath of death.

Cuchilla held him up before he could fall down by the side of the car. The dim lighting of the dead end street helped him camouflage his actions. The man in the Escalade opened the door but no light went on in the big car and hurried to Cuchilla's side. In one swift motion they opened the MB's passenger door and shoved the dead man inside. The driver hurried back to the car. Cuchilla remained outside smoking.

Mario and his male companion sat at a table on the edge of the intimate outdoors patio. It offered them a view of Matacon, his girlfriend and the two bodyguards. They were the only people sitting outside since the evening was nippy.

Medellin is known as the city of eternal spring.

A small fountain by a wall gurgled happily nearby. A young woman with long blond hair and succulent lips was crushing her breasts against Pablo's arm. She was whispering something in his ear. He smiled and nodded. Her hand was caressing his leg under the tablecloth.

The drug lord's guardians sat at a nearby table, chatting quietly.

Mario's companion got up and went to the men's room. A few seconds later, he emerged but instead of a suit jacket he was wearing a long apron and a bow tie, making him look like one of the waiters. In one hand he carried a small round tray. He stopped by his table, dropped his suit coat and picked the champagne bottle on the table. Next, he walked to the patio and approached Pablo. The man's girlfriend was giggling. She said something to the drug-lord and pointed towards the bottle.

"That's not for me, shoo." Pablo made a dismissive gesture with his arm.

"But this is." From underneath the tray came out a pistol with an attached silencer, and fired rapidly. The bodyguards hardly realized what was going on. The stunned woman automatic response to get up and scream was muffled when the waiter shot her in the forehead, turned towards the bodyguards and shot them at point blank in quick succession. He dropped the gun in the small fountain, turned around and marched casually towards the restaurant exit. Mario followed close behind.

Staring puzzled at the departing waiter, the wife of the restaurant owner-chef, who took care of welcoming their patrons, spoke. "Hey, wait. Who are you? I have never seen you before. Wait."

The man paid her no attention and continued out to the exit. Mario got close to her, his mouth covered, "I heard someone complaining about their food in the patio," and left for the exit.

When Mario and his companions reached the Escalade, loud screams were heard coming from inside the restaurant.

****

Four men in a SUV and a dozen more in two *Wagoners* waited in another section of town. The trucks were partially hidden in the large shrubs covering both sides of the road. The hillside, one of the many features of the city was somewhat different.

Only a few sparse houses surrounded by high walls dotted the hill.

Just before midnight, the headlights of several cars approached the zigzagging road.

The crackling noise of a two-way radio broke the silence. "Confirmed. It's him." The quiet returned. The man, who received the call, jumped out of one of the *Jeeps* and hurriedly unfolded a rubber strip with steel spikes imbedded in it. At the same time, his cohorts exited their wagons and lay in wait on both sides of the hilly street.

Sitting in the middle backseat of the *Range Rover*, Arnaldo Escobar was enjoying the company of his two gorgeous lady friends. He was pouring champagne right and left to his scantily clad companions.

The lead car shifted gears as it headed up the upcoming high incline. Escobar's SUV slowed down, maintaining its distance.

The four tires of the head-car blew up. The driver screamed. "It's an ambush!"

The second car made a screeching halt.

Arnaldo fell forwards, the bottle crashing against the back of the front seat. The bodyguard sitting next to the driver took out his gun.

Rapid fire erupted from both sides of the road. Arnaldo yelled at his driver, "put it in reverse, hurry." Those were his last words. A rocket-propelled grenade hit the expensive SUV head-on. The impact of the explosion lifted the car off the road, crushing its occupants against the roof. They joined the other four dead men in the advance truck.

The assailants ran back to their cars. When they reached the first crossroad, each car took a different route.

TWENTY-ONE

After spending three days in Mexico City, Alejandro and his family headed for the Benito Juarez airport national terminal to board an *AeroMexico* flight to Chihuahua. They had gotten up at dawn in order to avoid the city's chockfull traffic nightmare.

Two and half-hours later they disembarked after an uneventful flight. Alejandro held his wife's hand and she in turn held Gabriel's. The weather was a pleasant and dry seventy-one degrees and much warmer than evenings in *Los Cielos*. "We'll check in the hotel, have lunch and then head for the Pancho Villa museum."

"Who?" Gabriel asked.

Turning his head towards his son, Alejandro told him about the famous legendary Mexican war hero and revolutionary figure. "I guess you could call him kind of a Robin Hood."

"Really?"

"Yep, he seized land from those who owned vast spreads and redistributed it among the peasants and his soldiers. He robbed trains and printed his own money to fund his revolutionary efforts. He even invaded the United States."

"He did?" Gabriel asked, his eyes wide.

"A famous U.S. Army General named, John Pershing, came into Mexico trying to find Villa and take him back to New Mexico. But his nine month search didn't ferret out the peasant leader and with the U.S. entering World War I, he had to return."

"So, what happened to Pancho…Villa?"

"He entered politics and it's rumored that one of his opponents had him killed. We are going to see the house he lived in. Do you want to go?"

"Yes, yes."

Virginia smiled bemused at her son's excitement.

"And tomorrow, we'll take the train that will take us through the canyon. I'm thinking of getting off at one of the stops, rent a four by four and take a little excursion into one of the many rock formations."

"Is that safe, sweetheart? Dad told me the cartels roam around this area." Virginia said.

"I'll ask, if there is any danger or risk; we'll stay in the train."

"Good idea."

****

Three black *Chevy Suburban* stopped by the curb a few hundred feet behind where the taxi was picking up Alejandro and his family. Mid way into entering the cab, Alejandro noticed a small group of men stepping out of the trucks.

To his surprise, one of the men was the same individual in front of him in immigration days earlier. More remarkable still was that the man was wearing a well-tailored business suit and looked incongruous and out of place in the group. Accompanying him was a short brawny man with unmistakable Indian features and a young man wearing orange color boots and matching shirt with gaudy designs and a big cowboy hat. Alejandro looked through the rear window. He addressed the taxi driver, "Wait a minute, don't go yet. I think I saw a friend back there. What is that building a few hundred meters behind us?"

The driver, Virginia and Gabriel looked back. "Which building *señor*?" The driver said.

"That one back there." Alejandro pointed.

"Ah, that's the private section. People who own or lease planes."

"Wait here. I'll be right back." He stepped out.

"Where are you going Alex?" Virginia asked him perplexed.

"I want to make sure it's my friend, someone I known for a long time...I think." He scrambled at a fast clip towards the building entrance, and slowed down when he reached the glass doors. He glanced inside. Fabian was in front of a counter, his back sideways to the doors, holding a cell phone to his ear. The other men talked among themselves, waiting.

Alejandro made a one hundred and eighty degree turn and went back.

Virginia and Gabriel stared at him from inside the taxi. "You lost him?" Virginia said when he got in.

Alejandro smiled at them. "Not really sure it was him. Maybe it was someone else I've seen before." *I'll come back and ask the man behind the counter.*

"He was the same man that was in front of us at the airport, dad."

"You may be right Gaby. That must be why I thought I knew him." *When did he notice him?*

TWENTY-TWO

"**A**nd where can I find Mr. Calwel you say?" A secretary translated to Gianni over the phone.

She explained to Mr. Hoffman, the lawyer handling Mr. Murphy's affairs, what the ranch's caretaker was saying. Mr. Calwel was on vacation with his family in Mexico. "Thank you, she said in Spanish, "if you talk to him, please let him know Mr. Hoffman needs to speak with him. *Hasta luego.*"

"Did he tell you how long he's going to be away?" The lawyer asked. He was tall, slim, with an aristocratic air and receding gray hair. He had a booming voice but a pleasant angular face.

"The foreman was not sure, but he thought they would be gone for at least ten days." Margarita answered.

****

When his cellphone vibrated, Alejandro thought it was his father in law. There was no caller ID. *"Suegro, como le va?"*

"Doo...Alex, its Gianni, how is Gaby and Virginia?"

"Gianni?" Alejandro's brow creased. "Is everything all right?"

"Yes, yes *jefe*. Nothing for you to worry about. The army is planning on leaving next week. By the way, a Señor Josman, or Jof..man. Wait, he left me his name and telephone number. Ah, here it is. The name is, H..." He spelled it out and gave Alejandro the phone number. "He wanted to talk to you; something about a message for you in somebody's will. He asked me if you knew a Señor Morffi?"

"I'll call him later." They stayed on the phone for a few more minutes. Alejandro asked him about Zuri, Teresa and Camilo, Andres and his mother. *Murphy, Murphy...*He looked at his watch. *Hmm, it's after six, I don't think I'll find anyone in the office now.* He went looking for Virginia while Gabriel waited for him in the suite's living room. "Let's have dinner. We have to get up early again tomorrow. The train leaves at six but we can have breakfast in the dining room car. There will be a short stop in the city of Cuauhtémoc. There is a significant Mennonite community there. And the area is supposed to be Mexico's largest apple-producing region."

"What are Menno...no?" Gabriel had problems pronouncing the word.

Virginia glanced at her small son.

"How did I know you were going to ask me that? They are very devout Christians and are very committed to peace. Their leader was born in Sweden a long time ago. They are very good farmers and wear what we would consider old-fashioned garments."

"I see..." Gabriel didn't seem too convinced the first stop would be that exciting.

"And we are going to eat in the train while it's moving?" That seemed to get him thrilled.

"Yes, and they have very good breakfasts. After that, we'll get off in the small town of Creel and rest there overnight. We can take an excursion and see some of the canyons and waterfalls. We'll rent a car and visit *Divisadero,* which is right by the edge of Copper Canyon. The *Raramuri* Indians live there in isolated villages. When we're finished touring, we'll get back in the train and end up on *Topolobampo* Bay on the Sea of Cortez. That's in the west coast of Mexico."

"Real Indians, dad?"

"That's right." Alejandro blinked at Virginia who seemed as interested as Gabriel. "But first the train goes through a long tunnel."

"Ohh."

"Actually there are eighty-nine tunnels and some thirty-seven bridges. You think you're going to like it?"

"Wow. That's a lot of tunnels."

TWENTY-THREE

Meeting for lunch in the otherwise empty restaurant, the two drug lords took furtive looks around them. The place, normally closed at that hour, was open only for them.

"Have you heard anything?" The barrel chest man, with sweat beads glistening on his forehead, glanced at the door. Four guards kept watch. Two by the kitchen entrance and the other two stood by the front door. The mobsters had agreed that their personal bodyguards would be paired with each other, that way they could also look on each other.

"I checked with my contacts in Cali. No one knows anything, who the hell can it be?"

Both men sat in a way that their backs were against the wall.

Outside, half a dozen men were guarding the place but Salomon was edgy. The uneasy alliance between the various factions had been fractured. Any attempts to muscle into one another's territory were considered treason and a declaration of war.

None of them wanted that. There was more than enough cash to go around. But Victor's sudden death and the two recent killings had them on edge.

The ring of a cell phone broke the silence, making Salomon jump. He felt his jacket. Roberto, his counterpart had gone for his too in an unconscious gesture.

"It's mine," Salomon said. He took the cellphone out of his pocket. There was no ID. He showed the screen to Roberto. "Alo?"

"Are you enjoying your lunch with Robertito? I know the two of you are wondering what the hell is going on."

Putting his hand over the mouthpiece he whispered to his partner in crime. "It's a woman and she knows we are meeting."

Roberto swung in his chair and stared at the thugs guarding the place. The men reacted nervously, their hands on their guns. "Anyone out there?"

The four men shook their heads almost in unison.

"Who is this?" Salomon said.

"Claudia-Lucia Draco. I'm running Victor's business now. You have two choices; work for me or else...the same goes for Roberto. Finish your lunch. Come to see me afterwards. If you don't; be ready to face the consequences." She hung up.

"That bitch just threatened me and hung up." Salomon got up, his face red.

Roberto stared at Salomon. His hands rested on his beer belly. "What did she say?"

The still livid Salomon recounted his phone conversation. "Can you believe the balls of that *puta?*"

"What are you going to do?"

"I'm going to go see her. By the time I'm done with her, she will wish she never called me."

A man knocked on the restaurant's door. Both men turned towards the door at the same time. "I think it's one of your people." Salomon said.

"Let him in." He motioned to one of the men holding guard by the door.

"Don Roberto, the warehouse was robbed. The shipment is gone."

"What?" A phone rang again. But this time it was his cell. The fast running events of the last twenty-four hours had him jumpy. Annoyed, he flipped it open and answered.

"It's Claudia-Lucia. Don't worry about your inventory. I'm keeping it safe. After all, we're going to be partners soon."

"Why would I want to do that?" He stammered, not believing the woman had the audacity to confront him. He swallowed a shot glass of *aguardiente* before continuing. "You, you don't know who you're messing around with. Salomon and I can stamp you out with the flick of a finger. You're *loca*, woman, *loca*."

A loud laugh came though the phone. Claudia, sitting in the luxurious chair that had once belonged to her dead husband, rocked back and forth. "Do you want to test me, Roberto? Do you think the half dozen men you and Salomon have outside *Crepusculo* can protect you? What happened to Arnaldo?" She mocked him. "His car blew up. Maybe there's a gas leak in the restaurant and it will go boom in a matter of seconds. Maybe you and Salomon should hurry up and get out but oh, wait a minute. Do you have armored cars? Only one way to find out."

Roberto gulped, cold sweat beads began forming on his forehead.

Salomon stopped pacing and stared at the front and back doors of the restaurant.

Their bodyguards kept a fidgeting watch.

He gave a questioning look to Roberto and whispered to the men staring out the doors to be on alert.

"What happened Roberto? The cat ate your tongue?" She said. "If you work for me, there's nothing to worry about."

Wiping the sweat off his face with a handkerchief, Roberto looked at his partner.

"Otherwise, you can kiss your pretty ass goodbye. Which is it going to be?" She interrupted his thoughts of how to get out of the cat and mouse game he was now in. "Salomon has the same choice. And don't even think that the two of you can run me over. You'll never make it to your homes today. I need an answer, now." She shouted the last word.

Before Roberto could relay the jest of the conversation to his associate, Salomon's cellphone rang again. He looked at the ID and almost smiled. "I have to pick this up." He said in an apologetic tone.

His lover, a twenty some aspiring TV actress and part time model spoke on the phone. "Salo, there's a couple of men here. They said you sent them to protect me, but I have never seen them before. When I asked them about Pacheco and Rafael, they said you had asked for them. Is everything okay?" She smiled at the four men sitting in her living room. They smiled back at her.

One of them even asked for an autograph and inquired about having a picture taken with her. She had acquiesced graciously. Her maid took a picture with all the young men around her.

"Mi amorcito." Salomon stopped pacing mid-stride, he was panicking, no longer sure if he was in control of anything. His eyes showed fear and cold shivers went down his spine.

"Hold it for a minute, Claudia." Roberto blocked the phone mouthpiece with one hand and spoke to his counterpart, "what is it?"

But Claudia-Lucia's voice brought him back. "Is Salomon okay, Roberto? Tell him his girlfriend is in good hands, nothing is going to happen to her. I wish I could have been an actress but I don't have the talent."

Roberto's mouth hung open.

"She has Carolina." Salomon said in a dejected tone. "Tell her we'll be there." He looked at the *El Colombiano,* one of Medellin's largest newspapers, and picked it up. The front-page showed pictures of the assassinations with lengthy pieces about the two suspected kingpins. He opened the inside page where the report went on to expand on the recent killing of Victor Draco and his security detail. The extensive coverage also included the massacre in a ranch of a well-known and respected rancher and several failed attempts on his life.

TWENTY-FOUR

Crying inconsolably, eyes shut, the baby struggled inside its blanket. She put him down on the sandy ground, wetted her fingers in the creek's waters, and dipped two fingers in the gruel. Then she put them in the baby's mouth to quiet him down.

The little girl was hungry too and had been drinking water to assuage her stomach but she could not fool her hunger any longer. Her step slowed, her feet hardly moving off the ground with each stride. All she really wanted now was to lie down and sleep. She went up a slight incline and after walking aimlessly for about half an hour reached a dirt road. She didn't notice it, not that it mattered. No one had been on the road since she had left the burned out village two days before. Behind her, a rugged and beautiful canyon rose between the pines and oaks.

The high and distant *Piedra Volada* waterfall served as the backdrop for a painter of nature settings.

****

Creel, better known as the Gateway to Copper Canyon, is peaceful and picturesque. And considered a popular tourist spot with a variety of overnight accommodations. It has the look of a two hundred year old logging settlement. It is almost eight thousand feet high, in the middle of a valley, with pine forests surrounding it.

Alejandro took his family to the motel where he had booked the reservation. An older woman took them to a well-appointed bungalow. Afterwards, they walked around exploring the city of around six thousand people.

A *Jeep Rancher* was waiting for him at the rental car agency.

"We're planning to head to *Batopilas* Canyon tomorrow," Alejandro said.

"Beautiful place, sir." The manager of the rental agency said. He had a round face and thick eyebrows,

"How early should we get going?"

"There's a lot to see and it will take you a while to get there. Once you leave the highway the road gets rugged. I suggest that you leave early. Wear warm clothes." The attending middle age man took out a map, and using a yellow magic marker, traced the route they should follow.

"Is it safe? What about all the cartel violence one hears and reads about?" Virginia followed the map's pinpointed route.

"Not around here ma'am." This area is very safe." He gave her a reassuring smile.

"That's good to hear. Thank you." Alejandro picked up the map. "How about we do a little sightseeing around town? Any particular place you'd recommend for a nice meal?" He pocketed the map in one of the inside pockets of his hunting vest.

Holding hands, the three left the rental agency and soon found an Indian souvenir store where Gabriel bought several trinkets.

Meanwhile, Virginia bought a lunch basket and plenty of bottle water for the next day excursion.

****

A rising sun was barely edging the hills when the family headed out of town. The crispy dawn was cool and dry. They followed the signs towards the *Batopilas* abandoned mining town and then headed down a rough road that took them to the Hidden Cathedral. The scenery was spectacular.

Gabriel was fascinated with the wide variety of cactus. He remarked that it was very different from the mountains of northern Colombia.

The *Jeep* climbed a steep curve and then Alejandro went down on another dirt trail. The setting was breathtaking. Strange looking boulders with picturesque names like the Valley of Breasts, Frogs, Mushrooms and the last one, the Nuns. Far in the distance they could see a high cascade.

"Do you think we can drive to that waterfall?" Virginia pointed.

"It will start getting dark soon and there are not too many markings letting us know which way to go. I'll drive for another half hour. Let's see if this trail will take us closer."

"This is so beautiful." Virginia said.

They took off on the dusty almost inaccessible trail. Alejandro had to continuously shift down to first and second gear. Rocks and deeps in their way had to be carefully skirted to avoid a mishap.

"Something happened." Gabriel said.

"What was that sweetheart?" Virginia turned around facing Gabriel in the back seat.

"I think something bad happened."

"Why do you say that?" She gave him a perplexed look.

"What's that?" He pointed at the windshield.

Vultures were circling in the clear blue sky somewhere further downhill.

The scavenging birds were an ugly memoir of the wreck. He remembered when he and Zuri had come upon the horrible sight. They had spent a whole day trying to find their way home after spending the night hiding from the assassins.

Virginia and Alejandro fixed their eyes on the path ahead but they were still too far to see what had brought the birds to gather there.

"Probably a dead animal." Alejandro creased his brow.

Another curve and the faint trail seemed to go somewhat straight for another mile. They were approaching the place where the vultures had flocked together.

"I think I see it. Looks like a small dead animal on the side of the road." He went slowly around a deep depression on his right side. Virginia watched from her side with some apprehension. If they fell in, they could have a difficult time getting out.

"Does the cellphone works here?" She said.

"I don't know. We're off the beaten path so it may be difficult to get a signal. But the man at the counter knew where we were going." He skirted a large stone and shifted gears.

"But this is so isolated and this road…well, I wouldn't even call it that. Maybe this was not such a hot idea. Should we turn around?" She glanced around nervously.

"Dad, let's see what the birds are after."

"Ugh, Gaby, why would you want to do that?" Virginia shook her head.

"Look, the road seems to go uphill. There's a stream on my side. We'll go up to the top, take some pictures and turn around."

The vultures scattered, some taking flight, others hopped on the ground, a few flapped their wings and three disregarded the intruders and attempted to get closer to what looked like a pile or a mound.

"That's not a dead animal, mami." Gabriel sat in the middle of the car, gawking.

The birds scampered when Alejandro pressed the car's horn. Virginia kept her eyes on the inert bundle coming up ahead from her window.

Alejandro drove slower, the dark shape was on Virginia's side.

She stared at the bundle. "Oh my God." She put a hand to her mouth.

Gabriel moved to the right side of the car; his eyes wide with concern.

"What is it?" Alejandro asked his wife, his voice low and concerned. The trail pits and holes forcing him to concentrate on the driving.

"Daddy, it is a person."

"Stop, Alex, stop please." She put her hand on his arm unable to keep her eyes off whatever it was.

The car slid down another foot before he could stop. Alejandro shifted it into neutral and put on the parking break. "Stay here."

Stepping out of the car he thought he heard the soft whimper of a baby. His dark brows drew together in a deep frown. The birds had moved away from the dark bulk but remained at a close distance. Everything was terribly still, terribly quiet.

Kneeling, he started trying to unwrap the small bundle. A blanket seemed to be hard-pressed and held tight against the hapless mass. Carefully, he pulled one end out and let out a loud groan. "Virginia, come here, quick."

A small girl in a fetal position, one arm shielding a baby in a protective embrace faced him. One of her hands held the blanket in a tight grip.

Virginia felt the hairs on the back of her neck rise when she heard Alejandro's somber tone.

With gentle care, he dislodged the baby from her protective embrace.

The girl moaned feebly, eyes closed, oblivious to what was happening, and started babbling about heads and fire, a church, wild dogs. She kept shaking her head, incoherent.

Opening his eyes, the baby looked up and gurgled. His small mouth puckered and then smiled. He handed the precious bundle over to Virginia and kneeled down again.

His arms went under the little girl and picked her up, trying not to scare or wake her up. She was not much bigger than Gabriel and light as a feather. She started trashing but he soothed her. "Relax, you are with us now, nothing will happen to you, shhh." She calmed down and went back to a state of unconsciousness. "How was she able to carry that baby?"

Husband and wife stared at each other. "We need to take them to a hospital right away."

Nodding, Virginia spoke to her son, "Gaby, move to the front. Alex, let me settle in with the baby and you lay her on the seat with her head resting on my thigh."

****

The return trip was agonizing. Alejandro wanted to speed up but the ruts, potholes and broken uneven surface impeded him from going any faster than ten or fifteen miles per hour at best. He kept glancing back at Virginia through the rear view mirror.

Her sad face conveyed more than enough to constrict his heart. He kept attempting to communicate with his cell phone but there was no signal yet.

Another moan from the little girl brought Virginia's gaze to her. Her lips parted.

She attempted to moisten her burnt lips but her tongue was swollen and dry. A faint croak escaped from her throat.

"Gaby, take a bottle and give it to your dad so he can open it." Holding the sleeping baby next to her chest, Virginia freed her other hand and tipped the water bottle over the girl's parched lips.

Coughing at first, she went on to swallow the water drops wetting her lips.

"Gaby, can you take one of those napkins and moisten it with a little bit of water?"

The boy did and handed back the wet cloth to his mother.

She caressed the sunburnt face.

A soft whine left the girl's mouth and she opened her eyes. Staring wide-eyed and scared, her immediate reaction was to get up, but Virginia's arm and soft voice soothed her. She closed her eyes and went back to the void dreamless world where she had found refuge. But this time she had the image of a beautiful woman and a boy looking at her. She let out a soft sigh.

"How is she doing?" Alejandro asked.

"Went back to sleep. I wonder how long she's been without food and water. Whose baby is she caring for? And where are her parents, her family? How did she end up in the middle of nowhere?" She wondered how the baby was kept alive and fed. She unfurled the blanket a little and saw a small sack on a cord around the girl's neck.

She held the little satchel up but the baby impeded much movement. "Gaby, I need help."

He turned around. His mother held what looked like a small Indian handbag.

"What do you want me to do, mami?"

"I'll stop." Alejandro said.

"Help me take this off her neck and see what's inside."

Unbuckling his seat belt, Gabriel went back through the center console.

He stood in front of his mother and untangled the cord from her neck.

"What's in it?" Virginia stared at her son.

"I don't know." He showed her the open sack.

"Corn meal?" Okay, close it."

"Shall I continue?" Alejandro said.

"Yes, please. Why don't you call the rental car agency and tell them what we found. The police should be contacted."

"I think that's the highway up there." Alejandro took out the phone and called. He told the attendant what had happened and that they needed to get in touch with the police. Shortly after he hung up, he received a call. It was the Creel police.

Re-telling the story a second time Alejandro and the policeman agreed to meet at the clinic. The officer gave him directions.

Alejandro closed his cell phone and gazed at Virginia through the rear-view mirror. "They want me to take her to the town's hospital."

They exited the dirt trail and were now on an asphalt two-lane highway speeding towards Creel. The GPS kept reminding him to continue on. Not that there was any other road he could take to the *Clinica Santa Teresita*, the Catholic institution that cared for the Indians in Creel.

Both baby and girl seemed to be sleeping peacefully in the confines of the air-conditioned *Jeep*. The soft rumbling of the engine and the road motion were like a calming soporific.

TWENTY-FIVE

T he two naked women danced listlessly on a center platform. A rowdy group stood by the bar counter drinking and whistling. Their noisy and loud chatter and a bad sound system made the sound of a popular *ranchera* almost impossible to hear. Not that it mattered to the dancers or the men haranguing them.

The men were celebrating another successful run across the border. The cocaine shipment was already on its way to Chicago. The rundown joint near the crossing between *Palomas, Chihuahua* and Columbus, New Mexico was one of the many watering holes the men used.

One old man sat at the far end of the bar. His scraggly beard and unkempt hair, lanky frame and stoop shoulders made him indistinguishable from many of the other low-life in the place. His trembling hand brought to his mouth what looked like another shot of cheap tequila. The raucous members of the *Caballeros del Norte* gang missed his keen eyes. He wasn't old but his well-disguised get-up would have fooled even the sharpest eye.

His ears perked up when one of the gang members made a boisterous claim about him being the one who had set the church on fire. Another man shouted that if it hadn't been for him, all the Indians would have escaped. He stood up groggily and made it look like he had a machine gun at his waist. His boozing body told him to stop babbling.

"That's what happens when you refuse *Los Caballeros!* No more *aldea de San Benedicto.*" The low life lush said.

"Time to go you drunken bastards." The fake laugh of the one who seemed to be their leader, sounded worried.

The men, pushing and shoving each other, walked out.

The bartender asked who was going to pay.

One man with a lopsided face turned around. "You are." He laughed and joined the others.

"Hijos de puta." The barkeep mumbled under his breath.

The scraggly looking customer stood up, left a one hundred peso bill on the carved, tainted bar surface and walked out the door. He squinted under the bright sun, and watched as the last of the trucks sped onto the two-lane highway. He took out his Blackberry typed in the numbers and letters of the license plate. He speed-dialed a number.

The automatic response came on. "Hey Jacinto, it's me Panchito. Have you heard anything about the burning of a church in an Indian village?" Pancho was a Mexican-American DEA agent. Jacinto was his counterpart in *Ciudad Chihuahua.* "I overheard a conversation. I think they were *Caballeros*. Here's the license plate number of one of the trucks." He spelled it out. "Call me if you hear anything." He took one last look around and headed towards an ancient looking Chevy Impala. When he started the engine, it roared with surprising strength.

TWENTY-SIX

C reel's outskirts came into view and Alejandro let out a burst of air through his lips. In a short time they would arrive at the complex. A man wearing a police uniform stood outside an official police car near the entrance.

Parking near him, Alejandro waved at the officer while dismounting and walking around to the passenger rear door. Gently, he picked the small girl and took her out of the Jeep, her head resting on his chest. She was still asleep.

Virginia opened her door and climbed out too, holding the baby in her arms.

The rugged looking, bronze skinned officer approached Alejandro, who was already on his way to the hospital entrance. A nun in white garments waited by the doors.

The policeman followed close behind. Virginia walked behind them. Gaby stood by her side.

"Both need food and water. I think the girl is dehydrated. I found grinded oats or something similar that she may have fed the baby." Virginia said when she approached the nun.

The head nurse took the infant from Virginia. A young looking thin, short man wearing a doctor's robe appeared out of nowhere. His large eyeglasses gave him an odd owlish look.

"Doctor, I'm going to check the baby now. The girl is unconscious and dehydrated." The nun said.

Standing by a stretcher where the girl now laid, Alejandro was answering the questions asked by a matronly looking nun, who appeared to be the in-charge nurse. She had finished checking the girl's pulse, heart rate and now was looking for any physical signs of violence.

The police officer was speaking with someone on a walkie- talkie. He asked Alejandro to repeat what he thought he had heard the girl mumble a second time and asked him for identification. Virginia gave him Gabriel's and hers.

"I'm reporting this to Chihuahua. They may know what to do and have more resources." He went to a desk phone and dialed a number he read from a pocket notebook. While on the phone he asked Alejandro a few more questions and repeated the answers on the phone. "Can you stay until tomorrow in case we have more questions? It would be very much appreciated, he says."

"I...guess." Alejandro looked at Virginia.

She nodded.

"We were planning to get back on the *Chepe* tomorrow and continue our trip to the west coast. I'll have to see if I can keep the rental an extra day and re-arrange our passage." He glanced at his watch. "I think they have closed for the day." It was almost seven o'clock.

****

Long after Virginia and Gabriel had gone to sleep in the rustic but clean and pleasant bungalow, Alejandro remained awake, troubled by the events of the day. He kept wondering about the little girl. He pondered the same questions Virginia had asked. Where were her parents? Where was the village she came from? Why had she taken the baby? How come no one had been looking for them? Where were the people from her village? What was the meaning of the words she blurted out while semi-conscious?

He hoped that come morning, the mystery would be cleared. He walked towards the fireplace, stirred the coals and threw in several logs. Flame sparked with yellow-gold flares.

Rubbing his arms, he went back to bed to join Virginia.

He stopped first in his son's bedroom. Gabriel had kicked off his blanket. He put the quilt back on him and went to his room.

TWENTY-SEVEN

J acinto was finishing for the day when he saw a blip on his old *IBM* desktop. He opened the e-mail and read about some tourists finding a young girl and an infant off the beaten path. But a cryptic comment about heads, a burnt church and wild dogs caught his attention. He remembered his conversation with the DEA agent. He clicked the name of his colleague and forwarded the brief message.

Francisco, aka Pancho, Rodriguez was attending a meeting of field office heads at the DEA, El Paso Intelligence Center (EPIC). New intelligence obtained through wiretapping and covert agents from the FBI and U.S. Customs Services indicated that rumors about more tunnels being built between the two borders were getting stronger. More than one hundred and sixty had been found before they had become operational. Additional information with the cooperation and support of their Mexican law enforcement counterparts reported that stronger ties were being cemented between Colombian and Mexican cartels.

Pancho sensed the buzz of his *BlackBerry*. The meeting was basically over. He and a fellow agent stationed in Eagle Pass were chatting about stories of new infighting going on between the *Zetas* and the *Caballeros del Norte* cartels. Their biggest concern: that the cartel war would spill over across the border. If local gangs affiliated with either faction started fighting, the lives of the residents of the border towns would become more perilous.

Excusing himself, Pancho looked at his cellphone. He read the short message. "I need to make a call." He walked away and punched the agent's name. When the numbers showed up on his screen, he pressed the call button. "Jacinto, it's me, Pancho. Wass up?"

"You got my message? I have a special interest in this. I was born in Creel."

"No shit."

"I still have family there." *And I have a safety deposit box that no one knows about with all the info you have provided me.*

"Well? How about you and I make a little trip to Creel, courtesy of the U.S. government?"

"Cuando?"

That was one thing Pancho liked about Jacinto: he never gave you any *mañana* bullshit. He was always rearing to go. He didn't know how he managed his bosses but he never said no, or I can't, or maybe later.

"How about you drive over in the morning and we take a little flight down there? I'll get a chopper or a plane. Can you get up real early?" Pancho chuckled.

"Go fuck yourself." Jacinto laughed out loud. "What time?"

"I'm thinking sunrise, is that okay with you?"

"I'll be there. You bring the *Starbucks*. I'll bring the buñuelos."

"See you man." Pancho hung up and walked over to his boss's office to tell him what he was planning to do.

"Fine, keep me in the loop." Howard dismissed Pancho with a wave of his hand.

TWENTY-EIGHT

The small news item in one of the inside pages of *El Universal* reported that a group of tourists had found a small Indian girl near death and an infant. The article went on to explain that it was somewhere in the vicinity of Copper Canyon. The newspaper clip continued on about the good Samaritans who brought the two children to Creel. The nuns at *Clinica Santa Teresita* were taking care of them now. The local authorities were investigating from which of the scattered and secluded villages she was and how she'd come to be found in a deserted road.

The tittle of the article caught Fabian's eye. The newspaper, one of Mexico City's mayor dailies, continued on detailing that local officials didn't have any more information but had asked the tourists to stay around for further questioning. The local chief of police reiterated that the family that had discovered the emaciated little girl was not suspect. They had only arrived in town the day before in the train from Chihuahua.

He finished breakfast and folded the publication but something, like a small itch that doesn't go away, kept nagging at him. If the government sent the marines instead of the army or the police, who were regarded as unreliable and susceptible to bribes things might get uncomfortable. *That was my mistake, I should have thought about it before I sent him. Well, what the hell, who gives a shit?*

The Mexican Navy marines, although small in numbers compared to the other Mexican armed forces, were considered mostly incorruptible and were starting to make headway in the fight against the narco-traffickers and other criminal gangs.

****

Pancho and Jacinto landed in Creel's small private airport.

The local head of police was waiting for them. The two men could be considered handsome in a rough sort of way. Both were deeply tanned, broad shouldered, and walked in slow long strides.

They wore weather beaten baseball caps. The DEA agent had a long droopy mustache and long hair. He could be confused for a thug motorcycle rider while Jacinto's clean-shaven looks made people feel at ease.

The policeman walked up to them, offered his hand and introduced himself. "I spoke with you yesterday."

Both men appraised the policeman.

"Domingo, right?" Jacinto said and shook hands. "This is my friend Pancho, he looks dangerous but he's really a pussycat." He laughed lightly.

"And if you believe this poor excuse for a policeman, I can sell you my baseball cap for two hundred dollars." Pancho's easy smile and open demeanor made Domingo relax. He usually didn't deal with law-enforcement agents from other jurisdictions.

As a matter of fact, this was the first time he remembered having to deal with any.

During the short ride to town, Domingo told them the little he knew. "Where do you want to go first?" He asked. "We can go to the clinic or visit the family that brought the girl and the baby."

"How about we stop for a quick breakfast first? Let's make the gringo pay." Jacinto laughed again and patted his friend's shoulder, seated in the front of the car next to Domingo.

"I'd like to talk to the family first. I mean...after I feed the hungry freeloader sitting in the back seat."

Domingo caught on to the easygoing banter between the two agents. It made him feel more at ease as each minute passed. He chuckled and parked in front of a restaurant on the main street.

TWENTY-NINE

Medellin's police force was on full alert. The recent assassinations of rumored top guns in the cocaine trade were bringing the kind of national and international attention the City did not covet. It had been attempting to clean up its image for years. The recent drug related murders were undermining its efforts to erase its past violent fame as the place where Pablo Escobar was born, lived and died. A vibrant metropolis with a spring like weather year round, fabulous shopping malls that could compete in an international scale, and excellent cuisine, was being tarnished by the latest spate of ugly killings.

Karina presented her report to the police commander. In it, she went at length over the details of her visit to Victor Draco's enclave and her meeting with Claudia-Lucia. "I'm going back to interview the people that work for the widow."

The commander squeezed his lower lip with two fingers and nodded in reflection. "And you think it all started with Draco's killing?"

"Actually, the more I think about it, the attempt on the wealthy rancher, what's his name...? Calwel."

"What does he have to do with this? The man isn't from here."

"But that started a cascading effect, except I haven't been able to link it all together. It may have been just coincidence. And yet...one of Victor's henchmen tried to kill the man at the hospital."

"I remember, I gave the approval for the ambush but a sharpshooter killed the hoodlums involved. Calwel never told us who tipped him off but it had to be an inside tip. And several days later some of Victor's men were killed near his palace, right?"

"Yes, I met him briefly at the hotel. It was...after he had left the hospital. The army brought him here for medical care. He was pretty bang up. His ranch was attacked and the house caretakers were all murdered and he barely survived. His wife died or drowned before the attack. Do you think Calwel could be the one?" Karina frowned and waited in silence.

"Well...I wouldn't dismiss him outright but yes, this all happened too fast for him being the mastermind. Keep digging, I want this city calm. One thing is the normal small fry drug related killings. The fuck-ups in the bad sections of town and another thing are the killing of prominent citizens even if allegedly they are drug lords."

"But-"

"We can't have these kinds of incidents happening where rich people live. See what you can find when you meet with Victor's service and his widow." The commander smoothed his mustache and picked up the phone. He looked at his subordinate. "You can go."

His insensitivity made Karina angry. She left the office without saying another word, found Sebastian at his desk and asked him to grab his jacket. "We are paying another visit to Mrs. Draco. Any news about the airport's mystery man?"

His boss was upset, he could tell. Her face was angry. "There was one man."

She stopped and twisted, almost colliding with Sebastian. She had an annoyed look in her eyes. "What?" She snapped.

"There were a few tall men seen entering the airport. But we found them in other shots nowhere close to where the shooting occurred at the airport entrance. By the way, the man we were shadowing? Alejandro Calwel?

His physique fits the profile. He was seen going into the airport with a large group. I think one woman may have been his wife. I didn't recognize any of the others."

"His wife? Didn't we read that she had recently drowned?" Her eyes flicked up to meet his.

"Yes, that's what was reported about a month ago but she certainly looked like his wife. The woman was limping. But if she's dead, then I don't know who is the ghost in the film. Unless...she has a twin sister. By the way, Calwel wore a sling on his arm. The killer did not. Also, he was not wearing a hat."

"Interesting... find out who the woman is. If it's his wife, how come he never said anything? And, what was she doing in Medellin?"

"She found out he had been hurt and went to see him?"

"Yes but what about the reports about her disappearance? Was that cleared up? I don't remember reading anything about her being found alive. Look into that and let me know. And who are the others? Damn it, I hate it when there are so many puzzles and I have no answers."

Her young detective assistant nodded in agreement. "I called his home and asked to speak with him. They told me he's out of the country."

"Did you ask to speak with his wife?" She said.

"No, I didn't think of it at the moment."

"What's wrong with you, Sebastian?" She slapped his arm.

He gave her a sheepish look.

"When we finish at Draco's, I want that information in my desk when we get back. I also want to know where they were going and where they are now..."

THIRTY

His eyes gazed at the electronic board showing the scheduled departure, so far it was still on time. Eric called Claudia to confirm he was leaving at around ten thirty. He was watching the news in one of the lounges at the Admiral's Club and sipping a *cubanito* coffee. As usual, he had arrived at Miami's International almost two hours before flight time. Today, he would sit down with Claudia to go over their new business venture. She had promised him an investment of at least five million dollars. He knew that most of it was laundered money but the certified check could be deposited without problem. It came from a reputable Colombian bank. Other than the five working days waiting time, the money would be deposited in his bank account and with that, the bankers would give him some much-needed breathing room.

An appraisal with the accountant confirmed what he already knew: the partnership had already delivered millions of dollars. He knew it could be more but there were only so many companies that would easily fit the handling of significant amounts of cash without raising suspicion.

Often times, the laundering was made at less than its dollar value to make the money legit. Filtering thousands of dollars through various cash businesses was tedious and required careful consideration. He had to. Export businesses, bars, restaurants, laundromats, bakeries, carwashes and other sundry businesses that took in liquid cash couldn't skim or overstate expenses to the IRS.

The government agency reviewed these enterprises against similar operations throughout the country. A commercial entity that reported exorbitant amounts of cash transactions and too many loses would raise suspicion.

His biggest problem was to not overextend his hand in any particular business. Whether a business was profitable or not made very little difference. In reality, it was better if it had real losses because more cash could then be reported as income to make it look profitable.

And once a restaurant or a bakery, or any of the slew of retail ventures they had bought, began to show profits, they could parlay it into a for sale business. A business broker, similar to a real estate broker, would be contacted to market and show the enterprise. A misguided novice would look at the ever-increasing monthly income and would be jaded by the appearance of a venture that was taking off after prior years of measly returns or loses.

The proof was in the ever-increasing income taxes being paid.

Changing neighborhood, better service, a new menu, all these items, whether true or not, would be ticked off as the reasons for the business change in fortune. But the reality was, the enterprise was nothing more than a front for money laundering. The hapless investor would mortgage their house, spend their savings, quit their job and obtain a large commercial loan from a lending institution.

And in less than a year, the business more often than not, would end up in bankruptcy. The merry-go-around was basically fool proof.

He was thinking of setting up several electronic exports company. Use the dirty money to buy laptops, cellphones and tablets and export them. They could sell at heavily discounted prices and turnover the money quickly. And last they could also have large amounts of money wired from presumptive overseas sellers to pay for fictitious purchases.

THIRTY-ONE

From the restaurant to Alejandro's cabin was a short five-minute drive. He was waiting on the portico, seated in a rocking chair and holding a large ceramic coffee cup.

A rising sun was beginning to get rid of the morning chill. The temperature was expected to remain in the low seventies, with perhaps a passing drizzle but otherwise it was going to be a regular sunny day.

Stopping in front of the small house, the three men came out of the police car. Alejandro stood up and stepped down from the porch. He and Pancho were about the same height, Jacinto was a couple of inches shorter and the policeman was no taller than five foot four at best. The men greeted each other, a few pleasantries were dispensed with and Alejandro asked them if they wanted to come in.

They sat around a small round table. "How is the girl doing? Can we see her before we resume our vacation? My wife finished packing and my son is raring to go." Alejandro said

"I don't think that would be a problem, right chief?" Jacinto glanced at the policeman.

"No, not at all."

It didn't take long to account for what had happened the day before. The men took advantage of Virginia's presence and asked her a couple of questions.

"Alejandro, would you like to follow us to see the girl?"

In a few minutes both cars were parking in front of the complex. One of the sisters showed them to a large room. There were six beds but only the little girl occupied the room and she seemed to be asleep. Intravenous fluid was being fed through a vein in her arm.

The nurse opened the curtains and let some sunlight in.

With the men in tow and Virginia and Gabriel a step behind, the nurse checked the girl's pulse and put her hand on the girl's forehead. "You want me to wake her up?" She asked in a low murmur.

"No, don't," Pancho said, "we'll wait a few minutes and if she doesn't wake up we'll come back later."

Virginia came to one side of the bed and gently took the little girl's free hand in hers. She nodded at Gabriel, who took a small stuffed doll out of a canvas bag and put it on the bed.

Freeing one of her hands, Virginia took the doll and put it underneath the girl's hand.

The small group stood around the bed. Their solemn faces said it all.

Big, beautiful eyes of a deep almond color looked at Virginia. They exuded a deep sadness. Her face transformed when she saw the men. She trembled and closed her eyes tight.

"Te traje una muñequita. Como te llamas?" After hearing Virginia's soothing voice she opened her eyes again.

"How are you feeling?" She said softly and showed her the doll.

Her hand grabbed the cloth doll and she peered at it. *"Donde esta el bebe?"* She asked.

"The baby is fine. The nuns are taking care of him for you." Virginia smiled.

"Can I see him?"

"I'll bring him to you when he wakes up and you can hold him for a little while." The nun said.

"How is she doing?" Jacinto asked.

"She had a fever last night but it's gone now. She cried in her sleep and kept shaking in the bed. She's being treated for dehydration and she's undernourished. The ends of her hair are singed and there were burns on her face, arms and legs. I don't know how she managed. It had to hurt."

Pancho and Jacinto looked at each other.

"Have any more information come your way regarding what you sent us?" Jacinto asked the police officer.

"No."

Smiling at the little girl, Virginia asked her for her name again.

"Maria de Guadalupe." She whispered.

"Thank you, these young men are from the police and they want to know where they can contact your parents. I'm sure they are very worried." Virginia sighed. "Is the baby your brother?"

"*No, mi mama y mi papa estan muertos.*" Her eyes became wet.

"Dead?" Virginia gently squeezed the hand that held the doll and looked at the men and her husband.

"Gaby, can you go out and ask the nurse for more water?" She gave him a tin container.

"Mami..." He was going to object but then took the metal jar and left the room.

"Why don't you continue talking to her? Maybe it's better if it's coming from you."

"If I have a question I will tell you so you can ask her." Pancho said in English.

"What happened to them *linda*?" She addressed her as *linda*; which means pretty.

"Men came into town and killed everyone in the church."

Virginia gasped and put a hand to her mouth. The men listened intently.

The nurse walked in with the baby, who made little gurgling noises. Maria-Guadalupe smiled. "Antonito!"

Putting the baby on the side free of the intravenous feed, the nurse started leaving. "If the baby starts fussing, I'll come back for him."

Little by little the story came out.

"Where is the village?" Pancho asked the local policeman. And pointed with his mouth at the girl.

"It's out of the way, there's a dirt road that goes to *la cascada* and then it forks but no one goes that way because people can see the waterfall is to the right and head in that direction. Still it's a few kilometers on a very rough road."

"We were near it but it was getting late. I was about to turn around but Gaby saw something on the road and we decided to go and inspect it. We could have easily missed her." Alejandro felt guilty that he had brought his family so close to danger.

"This is supposed to be an area free of smugglers."

"I wouldn't go that far." Jacinto said.

"Nothing of significance has happened here in a long time...other than a tourist drinking too much tequila or getting lost in the hills."

The comment put Alejandro somewhat at ease but not completely.

"Can you take us there?" Jacinto asked.

"Ahh...we are shorthanded as it is. I don't know."

"I was there yesterday, so I'm already familiar with the road. Do you have a map that can pinpoint where the village is?" He asked Domingo, "I can take them."

"Gaby and I will stay with Maria-Guadalupe." Virginia said and turned to smile at the bed-ridden girl.

"I'll see you at the cabin." Alejandro kissed Virginia and ruffled Gabriel's hair.

THIRTY-TWO

Several hours later they were in the rented jeep with Alejandro at the wheel. Not much was discussed. Alejandro asked a few questions about other places to get off and on the train on the way to the Pacific. They asked him about Colombia, and the violence there, and what did he do for a living but he never mentioned what he had been through.

"I think this is the where we found her yesterday but as you can see, this is pretty bare. I recognize the creek down the embankment making a curve down there, but there may be other similar locations, so don't bank on it. How far are we supposed to be from her village?"

"Based on this map...I'll say that we are a good thirty to forty kilometers but you must be wrong, how could she have walked this long and with a baby?" Jacinto shook his head.

"Hmm," Alejandro glanced at the gages.

"What is it?" Pancho asked.

"If we don't find it soon, we'll have to return tomorrow. We could run out of gas before we make it back to town."

"Okay." Pancho pushed himself forward and checked the gas gage from his back seat. "Keep going and when we drop below the half tank mark, we'll turn around." He pushed himself forward and touched Jacinto's shoulder, sitting next to Alejandro in the front. "You agree, *hermano*?"

"You don't want to do a little bit of work pushing this thing back to town? It's almost downhill all the way." Jacinto tried to make some light of the already gloomy trip. He didn't know what had happened to the Indian girl but the statement she'd made was almost too horrendous to be credible. Alejandro interrupted his thoughts.

"We're at less than half a tank gentlemen." He looked at Pancho trough the rear view mirror.

"I think I see some huts over there to the right. Is that what Domingo wrote in the map?" Pancho pointed ahead of them.

Alejandro glanced at Jacinto who was spreading the map over his legs.

"That may be it," Jacinto stared ahead, "if not, we'll ask the villagers."

"Something isn't right." Alejandro steered the Jeep around a deep rut. They were getting closer and there were no signs of life. Not one person had come out to see who was coming.

They heard loud barks and a pack of mangy dogs ran towards them from around a corner.

"Go the way they came from." Jacinto said.

Turning the corner he stopped. A few feet further down was a well. A few scavenger birds flew away.

The remnants of a burned and demolished church loomed behind.

"What are those things on the rim of the well?" Pancho asked.

"Shit...are those heads?" Alejandro looked at Jacinto. "What the hell happened here?" He accelerated.

"Head straight for the church." Pancho said.

The dogs followed them yelping and barking.

"Sonofabitch." Was all that Pancho could mutter when they drove by the water-well.

The strong putrid smell accosted their nostrils when they passed it by. The dogs started barking louder as they inched closer to the ruins.

They stared at a standing blackened piece of wall.

A small effigy of the Virgin of Guadalupe was ensconced in a niche. Next, they stared at a stone altar, its sides scorched. What appeared to be the top of a cross, rested on the altar tabletop. The pieces of adobe still attached to it, made an unstable lean-to.

A harrowing decomposing smell permeated the area. They noticed that most of the scrawny dogs had lacerated paws and limped when walking.

"They have been...eating the dead." Pancho held a handkerchief to his nose.

Alejandro walked over to the altar area, trying to avoid stepping over the bones scattered under pieces of adobe bricks and wood rafters.

Jacinto took what looked like a charred piece of wood and pushed a piece of roof. "There are cadavers everywhere."

"These are small bones. Children." Alejandro held the bile forming in his stomach. Under the lean-to, he could tell, were what seemed at least a dozen small skeletons.

"Who could do such a thing?"

"There are at least forty houses." Pancho made a three hundred and sixty degree turn.

"And all are dead..." Alejandro ran his fingers through his hair.

"Let's check each one." Jacinto moved away.

"Alejandro, why don't you go that way, I'll take the ones in the middle and you can take the ones on the left." He signaled Pancho.

A few minutes later they met by the jeep. The emaciated dogs had become bored and left them alone. Most of them were lying in a loose circle near the car.

"I think she was the only survivor...and the baby." Pancho's voice sounded sorrowful.

"I have the feeling that she rummaged through all the huts and when she ran out of food she took the baby with her. Alejandro's grim face spoke volumes.

"But, but, there must have been fifty or sixty people living here...at least that many...I think." Jacinto shook his head.

"Who is capable of killing women and children?" Pancho took his baseball cap off and brushed his hair with one hand.

"There's nothing we can do here. I have to call Chihuahua. You want me to drive back Alejandro?" Jacinto kept pinching the bridge of his nose.

"That's okay, if I drive I have to concentrate on the road, and not think too much about what happened here, and what that little girl went through."

"Pancho heard them talk about it."

Pancho pushed his hair back with both of his hands. "Murdering bastards," he mumbled.

"Can't you go after them, Jacinto?" Alejandro waited for them to climb in.

"What proof do I have? And they are very powerful around here. They extort people, bribe others and pretty much have a monopoly on the drug-running to the border."

"Where are the drugs coming from?" Alejandro said.

"Most of the coca comes from your country. We have intercepted some shipments and it was Colombian." Pancho jumped in the back seat.

****

Evening was close approaching by the time they made it back to Creel. The cool evening air felt more chilly than usual.

Jacinto directed Alejandro towards the police office, city hall and volunteer fire brigade building. The three men walked in with gloomy faces.

Domingo saw them get out of the jeep and went out to meet them.

A hush, like a black cloud, fell on the foyer-office as the few people still around, watched the dejected men slowly walk in.

"Bad?" It was all Domingo said.

"Do you know how many people lived in that hamlet?" Jacinto said

"I have to check, I'm not sure. I think about one hundred?"

A loud growl, more animal than human escaped from Pancho's mouth.

Domingo stepped back as if afraid the tall, husky man would eat him alive.

"There's nothing we can do for now, Pancho. First, we have to bring additional people to go through the...finding." Jacinto put a hand on his friend's shoulder.

The old policeman's eyes kept darting back and forth between the three men.

"The little girl and the baby are the only survivors." Alejandro told him what they had found.

Domingo slumped in a nearby chair.

Pancho took out his cell phone and called Howard. Their conversation was brief.

THIRTY-THREE

Seated across from Claudia-Lucia, Eric explained where the money was being invested.

"Let me be clear Eric, I'm only putting up the money so that you can get the bankers out of your ass. The moment you are in the clear, I expect my money back. I want a ten percent annual interest."

"Ten? That's...that's...I can't start paying back the interest now." He glared at Claudia. She was not as stupid as he had thought when he first met her.

"You'll pay me the first installment a year from now and twenty percent of the principal and the interest in arrears. If not, I will simply deduct it from your percentage of the money laundering."

"What about all the money I've been sending back?" Eric was flustered.

"You think I don't have expenses?" She rolled her eyes.

"I didn't say-"

"I have to pay bribes, protection, guns, cars, the harvests, the production, getting it to the border to Fabian. What? You think all those costs get paid from money that comes out when I open my legs?"

"Okay, okay, fine, let's finish this so I can go back to Miami and meet with the bank."

"My lawyer will draw the documents assigning me a minority partnership in your real estate business and I'll FedEx the documents to you."

"What partnership?" Eric blubbered, his eyes wide. He was shocked.

"You didn't think I was going to fork over five millions without some kind of collateral, did you? What do you take me for?"

"But...but, I thought we were partners."

"And we are now, legit, right? Here is the certified check for the funds. Get the fuck out of here and don't even think of double crossing me." Claudia stood up. "I'll have Marcelo take you back to the airport. Finish your drink at your own leisure. My personal trainer is here and he doesn't like to wait."

Eric was stupefied. Claudia's blow left him reeling. And the worst part was that he couldn't do anything about it. Without the money, leans would be imposed on his house, his Hargrove yacht and who knew what else the lawyers would come up with.

"Well? Let's go, you're wasting my time."

He guzzled his whisky in one gulp, grabbed the check and let one manservant escort him to the car waiting outside. His thought swirled around his never-ending dire predicament on the way to the airport. *I'll skim money from the drugs. She's not going to take advantage of me.*

THIRTY-FOUR

"**W**ho is responsible for the massacre?" Alejandro was visibly angry.

"*Los Caballeros del Norte,* they have been wrestling with the Zetas for the upper hand." Domingo, still shaken by the revelation, remained seated. He looked up at the tall man whose brooding eyes had taken a darker hue.

"The local police don't have enough resources to fight these gangs." Pancho looked at Jacinto for additional confirmation. "Unless the central government steps in and sends the army, the local guys are powerless."

His friend nodded.

"They are very powerful, we are no match for them." Domingo looked crushed.

"These *Caballeros*...who is their leader?" Alejandro rested against the balustrade that separated the office from the rest of the hall.

"Come with us." Jacinto grabbed Alejandro by the arm. "If the girl says anything, call us."

Domingo nodded and wiped his face.

Once outside, Jacinto asked Alejandro to drive away. "I took you out because we can't take any chances. Too many eyes and ears around. We have intercepted some calls. Their local leader is named Cuauhtémoc. His boss is a rancher in Culiacan but we're sure he is not the top man."

Turning a corner, Alejandro drove at a slow pace.

"See that canteen ahead? Let's get a drink. You want to call your wife? Tell her you'll be out a little longer. A few days ago we stopped a truck full of cocaine coming from the border. Usually there's more than one driving a truckload. One man drives while the other acts as his bodyguard."

Alejandro listened quietly.

"They never drive without an escort who communicates with the driver and his accomplice via walkie-talkie. We were lucky." Pancho said while Alejandro parked in front of the bar.

They walked in and found an empty table at the far end, sat down and called a waitress over. After the plump woman took their order and left, Alejandro spoke. "What do you mean by lucky?"

"The lead car broke down in an area controlled by the Knight Templars cartel." Pancho said. "The bodyguard stayed to help fix the car. They were afraid that if the KT found the drugs, they would be kidnapped and killed. There's fierce competition between the various outlaw groups."

"When we questioned him, he told us the plan was for them to catch up in about an hour's time," Jacinto continued, "If not, he was to wait outside Tuxtla Gutierrez, at one of the highway's fast food shacks. We were doing surveillance around the border with Guatemala in a helicopter when we caught sight of them. We stayed high up to avoid being detected."

"So what happened?" Alejandro said.

"We landed about ten kilometers further up the road and stayed hidden until the truck came into view and we stopped it," Pancho said, "to make a long story short; we told him he had to work for us or else. He's still our snitch."

The three men walked up to the counter. There was hardly a soul in the place. They ordered beers and took the bottles with them to a table in the farthest corner of the bar.

"So...how is he helping you? Why can't you arrest this guy and his boss?" Alejandro took a big gulp from the bottle.

"Vicente, also called *El Carnicero* is taking orders from someone with deep political ties. He is, what we call in the States, a person of interest. But we have to tread very, very carefully. The man is very astute. We haven't been able to obtain enough evidence to indict him."

"He travels frequently to the US and to Colombia in his own Lear jet, which makes it more difficult to keep tabs on him." Pancho said.

"That's funny, well not really. Let me tell you..." Alejandro told them what had happened to him and the two close encounters with a Mexican man who owned his own plane and had some heavy Colombian connections.

Jacinto and Pancho looked at each other. "You got to be shitting me." Pancho remarked after Alejandro finished his story.

"My father in law was going to try to find more information about the man."

"You could be our link to get this bastard." Jacinto said.

"I already told you what happened to us. I can't put my family in danger again. No way."

Both men looked at each other and nodded.

"Where do you want me to drop you?"

"Nah, go ahead, our car is not too far. We need the walk anyway." Pancho gave Alejandro a friendly pat in the back. "We'll see you later, okay?"

"How long are you staying here?" Alejandro asked.

"I already contacted the Distrito Federal. Tomorrow a contingent is arriving from Mexico City to run a forensic evaluation of the village massacre," Jacinto said, "if you could stay another day or two, your wife also. She seems to have made a connection with the little Indian girl...I know we are screwing up your vacation, but we can really use your help."

"You know where to find me." Alejandro grumbled.

"Count on it." Pancho and Jacinto shook his hand before he left.

****

A note that Andres had called awaited Alejandro when he entered the empty cabin. The Miami lawyer had tried to reach him again, and a phone number was included. Virginia had added that she and Gabriel had gone to see the little girl, and would wait for him at the hospital.

He looked at his watch. *I wonder if I'll find anyone, it's already past six. Well, I'll leave him a message that I'll try again tomorrow.* He called the number.

"Mr. Hoffman's office." A soft female voice answered after the second ring.

"Hrrm, this is Alejandro Calwel, I understand Mr. Hoffman has been trying to contact me?"

"Mr. Calwel? Yes, let me tell Mr. Hoffman, wait a second, please."

After a short delay, a deep man's voice spoke, "Mr. Calwel, thank you for returning my call." Carlos Hoffman proceeded to explain that an old client of his, John "Jack" Murphy, had passed away and had left a request in his last will regarding Mr. Calwel.

"I'm not sure I knew the gentleman. Can you enlighten me?"

"It seems he had your permission to prospect for oil in your land...does this ring a bell?"

"A while back? I think I remember an older gentleman came to see me. A geologist, right?"

"Yes, well, I'm not sure if he was in terms of education but he certainly had the experience. Anyway, he apparently found enough proof of possible oil in the area."

Zuri told me that she made torches when she and Gaby were hiding in the cave. She had found a small oil pool. "I see...please continue." Alejandro said.

"His letter explains the kind of rocks and ground surface he encountered in your land."

"Hmm, I see."

"He writes that he did some shallow drills to obtain core samples. Mind you, I'm not an expert."

Mr. Tagliari, Petroleum Oil Exploration, the company in New York, was he working for them? "Did he say where?" Thinking of that day made his heart beat faster and a deep sadness invaded him for a moment. He shook his head trying to shake the awful reminders of those terrible days when Virginia disappeared.

"Yes, he wrote down where he thought the company should begin further testing. Something about using shock wave equipment and electronic sniffers. But the letter says he never told the company. I think there was some disagreement between him and his bosses in Houston...or New York...I'm not sure. He wanted you to have this information."

"Thank you Mr. Hoffman. I appreciate you're going all this length to find me. What's the next step? I'm on vacation with my family."

"When can you be here? I complied with my client's wishes. He asked me to personally hand over to you detailed information about the area he thought has the oil deposits."

"Can it wait a few days?"

"Of course. You have my number. Call me when you're ready. Have a good night."

"Thank you, good night to you too." Alejandro pondered about his conversation and about the information vested on him. *Well, now is not the time, I better get ready and find Virg and Gaby.*

THIRTY-FIVE

"W here is Cuauhtémoc?" The young kingpin was taken aback. Fidel seldom talked to him with such bluntness. "As a matter of fact, he's here with me. You want to talk to him?" He handed over the phone to Cuauhtémoc.

"Si, Señor Negreto?"

"There were survivors. The nuns at the clinic in Creel are taking care of them. You didn't finish the job. Some tourists are involved. Get rid of them too. Make it happen fast. I want the whole region scared shitless."

"I will." But Fabian had already hung up. Cuauhtémoc shuddered slightly.

"Everything all right with the boss?"

"No, something about someone from the village survived. I need to take care of it and some tourists."

"Let me call a friend, find out what she knows. Maybe I'll even pay her a visit. It's been a while. I can fix you up if you want."

"After...first I have to deal with the leftovers."

****

The flight landed in Chihuahua around midnight. Cuauhtémoc would have preferred spending the night in Culiacan and leave in the morning. But knowing that Fabian was upset was enough inducement to keep going.

Two *F150's* and six members of his gang were waiting for him at the airport.

The city was asleep when they arrived. Cuauhtémoc was able to doze off a few times during the three hours plus drive. They woke up the proprietor of a small by the hour hovel and each one got a dingy room.

Cuauhtémoc didn't bother to take off his clothes and laid down on a rickety bed with a thin mattress that had seen better times. He set up his alarm watch for six. It would barely give him two hours of rest but he wanted to get a good look around before deciding how to handle his assignment.

THIRTY-SIX

C aptain Karina sat in the small conference room. She was watching on the computer screen the film snippets her detectives had collected at the airport.

On another computer was the picture of the man at the pawnshop. Sebastian, her young assistant stood behind her. He had seen the films several times already. "So...what do you think?" She swiveled in the chair and faced him.

"I think they are the same man. But we still don't know who he is. Nowhere in either film can we get a good enough picture. The baseball cap, the dark glasses and the shadows don't allow for a good look at his face."

"It's like he knew where the cameras were..." She said.

Sebastian agreed. "The height and weight appear to be the same. He's about six foot four and maybe around one hundred and eighty pounds? Hard to say. He's broad shouldered and I'd say, has a solid build. But there are a million men out there fitting that description."

"And that tape from the airport is the best we could get?"

"I'm afraid so." Sebastian swayed in the balls of his feet.

"What about Claudia's people? Anyone there? Who went with you to her house?"

"Daniel, he's a little green but he did pretty good."

"So...what did you find?"

"Starting with the fact that the three men who died that night on a street near her compound worked for her husband and a SUV was found burning not too far," he continued, "There were several bullet marks on the burned out wreck."

"Interesting." She deadpanned.

"The fence fixing we saw the day we went there? We went to the junkyard and collected a few of the discarded pieces...there were signs a car rammed it. The paint chips embedded in the barbed wire? Almost one hundred percent sure belonged to the same SUV. Here are photos of the vehicle...what was left of it." He handed over several enlarged pictures to Karina.

"So she did lie to us."

"Circumstantial. She can claim she was not where it happened."

"And the people that were at the airport with Calwel?"

"Now, that is interesting. I was waiting for you to ask me-"

"Come on Sebastian, don't play games, I don't have time."

"The very attractive woman...with the limp?" He pointed at the screen. "She's most certainly his wife, unless she has a twin sister." Sebastian goofed.

"Let me see her picture." She raised her hand impatiently, her fingers beckoning back and forth. "Where was she? How come he didn't tell us? We sent people to his ranch to investigate. He feared she had been kidnapped but there was never any ransom demanded."

"I showed that picture to two of the detectives that went to the ranch to help look for her," he pointed with his index finger, "they literally scratched their heads."

"One and the same?" She asked.

"Aha, she's the same one on the pictures they were given. Here." Sebastian took another photo out of a folder.

The captain laid both enlarged copies side by side on the table. "This is...I don't know what this is, what the hell is going on?"

Sebastian handed over an amplified take. "And a maid and her physically impaired son lived in the compound.

They disappeared that night...and a young good-looking man, very athletic. No one at the compound knows what happened to them."

"Are you telling me these are the same people?" Karina stared at the photocopy.

Sebastian didn't answer her straight out but went on, "Daniel kept vigil nearby for several days and finally got lucky. He saw two maids leaving and followed them. At one point the two women went their separate ways and he followed the younger one with whom he had spoken before. He caught up with her at a bus stop about half a kilometer down hil-"

"And?"

"He offered her a ride and she took him on. Driving to her parents, he asked her if she would look at some pictures." Sebastian stopped.

"Come on, keep going. You're driving me crazy."

"She did and was almost certain that out of the five people at the airport, three were the missing maid, her son and the other youngster."

"But what the...what is the connection between these people and the man's wife and why was he taking them to the airport? Where are they now? What are their names?" I want to talk to them."

"Andres is the stud. Camilo, the one in the wheelchair is Teresa's son. He deadpanned.

"Who is the older woman?" Karina asked.

"We don't know." A chuckle left Sebastian's mouth. He was enjoying his boss's bewilderment. "They all live in the Calwel ranch now. I'm game if you want to take me with you. One of the guys who was there said the place is unbelievable."

Karina was stumped. "There are more riddles here than in an *Alice in Wonderland* fairy tale. I don't know where to start. Okay, let's break this down into manageable bites. What do we have?" She got up and went to a whiteboard. "Bring masking tape and some magic markers. The whole thing starts when Calwel's wife disappears, right?" She used one of the pictures and taped it on the board.

"Ahem. Then, a band of criminals attack his ranch and kill almost everyone. The nanny and his little boy escape and the bacrim think they killed Alejandro with the rest of his household."

"But there was a second attack, right?" She sidesteps, looks at the board and waits for Sebastian. "When was that?"

He looks at his notes, flips several pages. "Ahh, yeah, Wednesday, November fifth. Another attack to Calwel's ranch is foiled when the army intervenes and captures the *banda criminal*, the bacrim." Sebastian reads from his notes.

"They didn't question them?"

"Yes, army intelligence did but the leaders got killed in the firefight and the men didn't know much. One of them said; Dager, Daco or Dogo, he wasn't sure."

"Maybe we need to go to the jail and talk to a few of them again," she said, "it sounds to me more like Draco, wouldn't you say?"

"And here is another interesting fact," Sebastian gesticulates all excited, "one of the men caught in the attack had worked for Alejandro."

"He betrayed Calwel." Karina said.

He scribbled on the board at a furious pace as if afraid to forget an important detail. "Yes, he was in charge of the ranch security and was considered Alejandro's right hand man. Because of his betrayal, the first attack on the ranch almost succeeded. I'm guessing."

"Do we know...what was the man's name?"

"Rolando," Sebastian said, "the army took a mug shot of the dead man. Daniel showed it to the maid."

"And?" Karina gave him an impatient look.

"She told him that he looked like someone who had started working for Victor. But had only been there for a few weeks. She wasn't sure."

"Hmm, well that makes for a nice coincidence, wouldn't you say. That's a solid tie between the two events right there and it all points to Victor." The captain moved back and stared at the board. "Things are beginning to gel."

"There's more." Sebastian exhaled and waited for her to explode.

"I'm going to kill you, if you keep this going..."

"According to General Calderon," Sebastian writes as he recounts the events, "Alejandro told him that the leader was a man named Hugo-"

"He was the one who attempted to kill Calwel in the hospital. Damn," she punched the palm of her other hand, "but gets killed by a sharp shooter. Later we find out he worked for Victor Draco. And a few days later our mystery man goes to a pawn shop, buys several pistols and kills a couple of men who worked for Victor." Karina rubbed her chin.

"And now things get more interesting. Oh, shit, I forgot. The maid told Daniel that there had been rumors that someone was staying in a guesthouse behind the mansion."

"We didn't go there, did we?" Karina asked.

"No, and no one ever saw her. The service thought it was Victor's lover. But who can say, gossip?"

"How did she know it was a her?" She bit her lower lip.

"Hearsay, like I said, no one saw the guest but the maid said the cook was sure it was a she."

"Did we interview the cook?" Karina looked at her notes.

"Yes, but she didn't say much. She was uncooperative. I didn't like her."

"Well, then we have to talk to her again and put some pressure. Leave it to me. She'll talk." A mischievous smile crossed the captain's lips. "What else do we have?"

"The night when several of Victor's men were ambushed near his place? A whole bunch of other things happened. Someone stole a car from the compound."

"How was it done?"

"Beats me, the maid said that security men ran into the guesthouse and Claudia was furious. I haven't been able to corroborate any of this. The burned wreck?"

"Yes, you already showed me the pictures."

"It was the one stolen, the one that crashed the gates."

"And...so the next day all these people leave from Medellin's private airport." She pointed at the blown-up print showing the group heading for the airplane. But Alejandro stays. And a mystery man kills Victor and his bodyguards...interesting..." Karina mused.

"Right, and they are all living in Calwel's ranch...happily ever after. End of story." Sebastian scrawls a big black line with a flourish at the bottom of the notes on the board.

THIRTY-SEVEN

Rubbing his face, Cuauhtémoc stared at his watch with bleary eyes. But lacking sleep was not a mayor issue for him. He was used to it. The sun would be up in a few minutes and he needed to check things out. He got up, walked to the rusty bathroom sink, threw water on his face and then smoothed his hair with his wet fingers. Putting on his cowboy hat and boots, he left his room and knocked next door. "Get up *pendejos*, we need to get going."

He lit a cigar while waiting for his companions and stared at the deserted street and the few frost-covered vehicles, wondering if the tourist family was still in town and where they might have spent the night. His thoughts jumped to the survivor.

He had no idea of who he or she might be or how the Indian made it out alive, but he wasn't too worried. He would find out very soon.

His driver came out and blew in his cupped hands to shake off the morning cold. The rest of the crew followed behind in a grouchy state. Most of the men were about the same height, short with thick torsos, arms and legs.

They shoved their guns to the floor of the trucks.

Cuauhtémoc carried a small revolver inside his left boot. A concealed four-inch knife was hidden in the other one.

"Let's get some coffee and find out if our *turistas* are still here." They got in the cars, their breath condensing in the frigid air until the heater started warming them. A couple of streets later they reached the main road. Down the street, the lights of a coffee shop window spilled onto the street.

They parked behind one truck and walked in. Their rumpled clothes and disheveled looks made them conspicuous.

Inside the restaurant, a young Indian girl came over and handed them paper menus. She waited and took their order. Ten minutes later she was back, carrying a large tray with breakfasts and hot steaming coffee.

"What's the best way to get to the *Santa Teresita* Clinic?" Cuauhtémoc asked her.

She gave them directions and left to attend Pancho and Jacinto who happened to walk in and sat on the counter. Both men asked for coffee and *huevos rancheros.* "I guess we're not the only early birds." Pancho said under his breath.

"Yep, Domingo should be here any minute. I wonder if he heard from the D.F."

They saw the old policeman enter, the face reflected on the mirror above the counter.

Both men swiveled on their seats. "Any news from el Distrito?" Jacinto asked.

"Yes, they'll be arriving later this morning."

"How many?" Jacinto said.

"Two groups, one from the D. F. and another one from Chihuahua."

"They'll want to talk to all of us. Calwel isn't going to be too happy. Maybe his wife and son would like to ride the cable. It will give them something to do in the meantime." Pancho grimaced and turned back to his breakfast as Domingo slid into the seat next to Jacinto.

"But remember, the girl has bonded with Calwel's wife. They may want to have her hang around when they start talking to the child. She may not want to talk to them." Jacinto said.

"You're right, I didn't think about that." Pancho shoveled a big mouthful into his mouth.

At the other end of the café, Cuauhtémoc finished his coffee and motioned to the young waitress to bring him the bill. He told his men to hurry up. He'd seen the police car park outside and the policeman meet the two strangers sitting by the counter. He'd told his men to quiet down, got up and walked by the three men on his way to the men's room.

When he came back from the men's room he told his men it was time to leave. They left the coffee shop single file.

Domingo watched the group. Jacinto and Pancho noticed his change in attitude. The policeman frowned, a questioning look registered on his face.

"You know those men?" Pancho said.

"No, I have never seen them before, and they don't look like tourists." Domingo called the young Indian waitress over. "You were taking care of those men? The ones that just left?"

"Ahem." She nodded.

"Did they ask you anything? Have they been here before?"

"No."

"Did they ask you for anything? He repeated the question.

She thought for a moment, pursed her lips and frowned. "Directions."

"Where to?" Jacinto asked.

"La clinica."

The three law enforcement men looked at each other.

"What are they looking for at the clinic?" Pancho said.

Jacinto got up from his stool and walked to the front of the café to see a truck backing away and a second one turning the corner. But he couldn't get a clear view with the sun right in his eyes. He used a hand as a visor to improve his sight. "Where do we go from here?" He grumbled.

Domingo and Pancho joined him outside.

"Domingo, can you get Calwel, and bring him over to the clinic? We'll meet you there." The men walked to their car and left.

Outside, Cuauhtémoc had directed three of his men to hide in their truck by the corner of a dirt dead-end side street. "I'm headed for the clinic. This is what I want you to do." He told them, looked at his driver and the rest of the men. "Let's go."

A few minutes later, Cuauhtémoc and his men reached the end of a street that ended in a big square with the clinic taking most of one side. They parked a few feet before the street disappeared into the large plaza. The other truck continued, then made a U-turn and parked about four feet away and across from the first SUV.

Momentarily distracted by the vibrating cell-phone, Cuauhtémoc stood by his truck and listened to his men telling him that the policeman had left the coffee shop. "What about the others?"

"They left together but headed in a different direction."

"Follow the policeman, you know what to do." He pocketed his cell, took a bottle out of the truck and sauntered by the side of the car while his men waited inside the two trucks.

THIRTY-EIGHT

There was hardly anyone outside. The streetlights had gone off a few seconds earlier. The morning sun was barely up, casting long shadows and not quite beginning to erase the morning chill.

The oncoming car lights bounced on the uneven pavement, heading in his direction. Cuauhtémoc staggered into the middle of the street holding the bottle. He took what seemed like a big guzzle and walked unsteadily, ambling into the advancing vehicle.

"Watch it Pancho, I think that guy is drunk." Jacinto's attention focused on the drunkard. Pancho slowed down while leaving a message for Howard, apprising him of what was going on.

The man kept coming in their direction with an unsteady gait. They saw him take a big guzzle from the bottle and almost drop it. He was smack center in the middle of the street and with two trucks parked ahead and blocking either side of the street Pancho had no choice but to stop.

"Wait a second Howard, I got a drunk ahead." He put the cellphone down between his legs.

The man was almost on top of his left fender.

"Hey amigo, muevase, no lo quiero arroyar." Pancho opened the window and waved.

Cuauhtémoc recognized the men and turned slightly aside, like letting a bull pass. He dropped the bottle on the street and stumbled backwards.

That was the signal.

"Isn't he one of the men from the coffee-shop?" Jacinto asked, alarm in his voice. But his question was a shade too late; the car was already sandwiched between the two trucks.

The roar of gunshots came out almost simultaneously. In an instant Pancho was dead, his head blown away. Jacinto's hand twitched slightly and touched Pancho's. He let out a soft sigh and passed out. The truck continued at a snail's pace and crashed against a lamppost.

Cuauhtémoc ran to the stuck vehicle, checked inside, fired twice for good measure and ran to the entrance. The driver in his waiting truck pushed the gas pedal to the floor, making the truck jump and the wheels squeal and headed straight for the clinic's entrance. The second *F150* ran in reverse until it reached the corner, made a spinning turn and followed the first truck, braking in front of the building.

****

Alejandro stood outside the girl's room, talking to the same young doctor with the owl glasses he'd met the day they had brought Maria-Guadalupe. He had left Virginia packing, hoping that this would be the day they could resume their interrupted vacation. He felt good knowing that the good nuns were taking good care of the girl and the baby and headed back out towards the clinic entrance.

About to open the glass doors, he saw the gruesome assassination several hundred yards in front of him. He rammed a bench and a stretcher against the doors and yelled to the petrified nuns to drop to the floor and hide. He kept going and asked another nun to take the little girl and hide her. He found a rear exit and ran to the side of the building while Cuauhtémoc and his men struggled to open the blocked entrance.

THIRTY-NINE

"**M**ami, we should be with papi."

"Why Gaby?"

"I don't know, just because." He shrugged his shoulders.

Virginia gave him a curious look. "He'll be here in a short while. Come, help me pack. We are going back on the train today."

The men following in the pick-up watched the police car stop in front of a cabin. With the lights off, the truck parked about half a block away. The driver and his two companions waited.

Domingo stepped down from the car and strode to the porch entrance. He wondered whether to knock on the door, but light from inside, filtered out by the window of the cottage. He assumed they had to be up already and besides, Alejandro's rented *Jeep* was gone. Without any more hesitation he knocked on the door.

Virginia jumped at the sudden noise, went to the window.

Gabriel had already reached the window and mover the curtain. "It's the policeman."

Virginia smiled when she saw it was Domingo and opened the door. "Good morning," She smiled.

The boom of firecrackers rang on their ears. The sound didn't seem to be far away.

She jumped startled by the noise and then saw three men, guns out, running towards them. "Watch out!"

The policeman, also startled by the blasts, started turning when the bullets pierced his body. One hit him in the back and twisted him around. Another bullet opened a gap in his midsection, a third bullet went through his arm.

Virginia almost fell backwards when the officer almost fell on her. Somehow she managed to hold her balance and grabbed the injured man. Quickly, she removed him from the entrance, and laid him down behind the wall next to the door.

A hail of bullets rained on them. Shots continued to strike the cabin door and its walls. Wood splinters scratched her face and dug in her hair. She grabbed Domingo's gun from its holster, took off the safety catch, and threw herself flat on the floor.

"Kill whoever is in there," a man shouted, "we don't have much time." He ran towards the cabin, his AK-47 pointing menacingly.

She glanced out of the open door and fired.

One of the men fell down. His companions stopped in mid stride, surprised.

Another shot, and another man cried in pain. A red splash, getting bigger by the second, started tinting the sleeve of his jacket. He grabbed his arm. The fallen man lay on the dirt street motionless.

The injured man looked at his companion, who was now firing a volley at the door, windows and front wall of the cabin. The sound of broken glass added to the havoc.

"Gaby stay down, away from the door and windows." Virginia looked beside her. He was pressing Domingo's midsection to stem the blood flow.

The fallen officer held a walkie-talkie to his mouth.

When the barrage stopped, she peeked out and fired again. The bullet almost hit the leader. He heard the bullet buzz his ear, forcing him to throw himself on the dirt street.

Another bullet rang out and pebbles hit his face. "Pepe," he shouted while firing and backing out to the truck, "pull Benito to the car."

"He is dead." Pepe walked backwards and kept shooting. But his shots were going nowhere. Without his other arm to help him hold the gun, the bullets were not even reaching the cabin.

Not too far away, another salvo of gunfire reached their ears, followed by sporadic shots.

Police sirens joined the bedlam. Creel's quiet mornings had gone berserk.

"We have to get out of here." Pepe bellowed, turned around, and limped back to the truck.

The burly man put another magazine on his AK-47 and kept firing while retreating.

"Hurry up, I'm bleeding to death." Pepe whined from the passenger's seat.

Gonzalo reached the truck, backed up, turned around and sped away. Their dead companion remained sprawled in the middle of the street.

FORTY

Running out by a side door and staying close to the wall, Alejandro reached the building's corner and poked his head out for a second. The plaza was empty. Two cars were haphazardly parked in front of the building. He peeked again and then scrambled to the crashed SUV riddled with bullet holes. Pancho's head was a gory mess of brain matter, grayish and red liquid splattered all over the windshield, steering wheel and dashboard. Alejandro ran around to Jacinto's side. If one of the gang members came back, he would be helplessly exposed.

Reaching through the shattered window. He put his fingers on Jacinto's neck and felt a faint pulse. "Jacinto, hang on man, hang on. I'll be back with help." Without further thought, he opened the door, climbed in careful to not hurt Jacinto, and took both men side arms sticky with blood. On one hand he held Pancho's Glock 22.40. On the other, he carried Jacinto's Smith & Wesson M&P .40. He ran back to the hospital.

A nun, her white garment now a dark crimson color, lay dead near the front door.

Hearing screaming, loud cries, shouting, and more shots being fired somewhere inside, he went running through the hall. People were hiding and cowering behind doors. More yelling, and shrieking assailed his ears. He stumbled upon a hefty man carrying an AK 47. The blast resonated in the close confines of the passageway.

The man crumbled on the floor. A bullet through his chest. Behind the dead man, Alejandro saw a trembling nun lying over a sobbing Raramuri boy. "How many men?" He asked her softly.

She held up three fingers.

"Including this one?"

She nodded.

He kept going and turned a corner. He heard sirens in the distance. The young doctor he'd met when he brought the Tarahumara girl and the baby, laid sprawled in the middle of a hall, blood seeping through several wounds on his chest. *There's nothing I can do for him.* Alejandro heard a man's shouts.

"Where is the muki that was brought here by the turista? Where? Tell me or I'll kill another one." A man held the battered, bruised head-nun in a headlock, a cruel snarl on his face.

"Hold her." Cuauhtémoc slapped the nun. Blood streamed out of her mouth.

Facing Cuauhtémoc, the man holding the nun got a glimpse of Alejandro. "Watch it!"

Cuauhtémoc started turning. The thunder of shots in the closed in space reverberated inside the room.

Cuauhtémoc tumbled forward. Two gaping holes appeared on the left side of his chest, the Glock's bullets striking him dead. His body sagged and dropped.

"I'll kill her! I'll kill her!" The man holding the nun yelled. But he couldn't get his gun unless he released the heavyset sister.

"Let her go and nothing will happen to you. Hear the sirens? The police are on their way. You can't escape. If you kill her, I'll kill you."

The beefy dark skinned man kept looking behind Alejandro, using the nun as shield.

"Your friend is not coming. He's dead."

The sister raised her knee and crashed the heel of her shoe on the man's foot. He yelled. The sudden attack catching him unawares, made him loosen his headlock.

Her elbow went back and hit his stern. Alejandro lunged forward and struck the hoodlum's head with one of the pistols. The tenuous hold on the nun was broken. Alejandro pushed her away and pistol-whipped the man, making him fall. The thug stared at the pistol in front of his bleeding face.

Without taking his eyes off the fallen man he spoke, "Sister, one of the officers is badly injured outside in a crashed SUV. He's barely alive. Go see what you can do for him and the other wounded."

Within seconds, the clinic was abuzz with people running and frantic calls for help.

Alejandro pushed the goon deeper into the room. "We're alone. I want to know why you attacked this clinic."

"Fuck you." The man sneered.

"Let's see how long it will take." Alejandro grabbed a pillow. "You have three seconds to talk or I'll blow your kneecap. And I'm no policeman."

"Wait, wait." He pushed himself against the wall, trying to buy time. "We were sent to kill the Raramuri girl and the tourists." He eyed Alejandro with a mixture of hate and fear.

A cold shiver ran through Alejandro. "Who sent you?"

"I don't know."

The muffled gunshot pierced the silence.

The thug screams echoed in the room. He slumped on the floor crying in agony. His knee shattered.

A nun, her white habit stained with blood came running into the room. She gasped when she saw Alejandro holding two guns and a man sobbing on the floor.

"Sister, please go help the injured. Make sure Maria-Guadalupe hasn't been harmed."

Looking at Alejandro's uncompromising face, the nun made the sign of the cross and ran out.

"If I have to, I'll carry you out of here so I can keep shooting you before the police arrive. Now, where were we?" The *Glock* moved menacingly towards the man's genitals. "Your balls are next. Talk."

The injured felon raised his hands pleading, "Don't, please…I…I think the orders came from *El Carnicero*, Cuauhtémoc's boss." He pointed at one of the dead men. "He, he called me to pick him up at the airport in Chihuahua, he said something about a man named Fabian. That's all I know, I swear on the *Virgen de Guadalupe."*

"Where is this *Carnicero*?"

"In…Culiacan." He stammered.

The sirens stopped. There was more commotion outside.

FORTY-ONE

A few minutes went by and Virginia saw blue and red lights splash the inside walls of the cabin. She had made a tourniquet to stop the blood from seeping out of Domingo's arm and had taken over for Gabriel, holding a tightly packed towel against the man's midriff. Gabriel held the two-way radio to the policeman's ear and mouth. His clothes and hands were smeared with red.

"Anyone in there?" A nervous, potbellied, short man wearing a police uniform and holding a gun shouted from behind his police car door.

The crackling sound of the walkie-talkie stopped him. A child's voice came on. *"El señor Domingo esta herido."*

Virginia hands trembled. She yelled to the policemen outside. "Officer Domingo is badly hurt. We need an ambulance. Hurry up!"

The policeman, his hands shaking and his eyes darting back and forth, walked slowly towards the cabin.

"Tell them...to call the army." Domingo muttered to Gabriel. He heard other shots being fired. He knew the small Creel police department for his town of six thousand plus would be overwhelmed if other attacks were happening nearby.

The child pressed the side knob of the two-way radio and repeated the instructions.

An ambulance, sirens wailing, arrived. More sirens could be heard not too far away.

****

Alejandro hid the guns under the back of his shirt and walked out. The front of his shirt and pants were smeared with caked blood.

Two policemen, the rest of Creel's police force, were standing where Cuauhtémoc had died. They pointed the guns at Alejandro. "Stop, down on your knees." One of them shouted.

"No," a nun cried, "he is the one who saved me. All of us."

"Señor, we need to talk to you." The officer holstered his gun.

"I can't. The man back there told me they were going to kill my family and me. I need to make sure they're safe." Alejandro growled. He was not going to be deterred.

The two policemen looked at each other. "Was your family in the cabins?"

The way the question was asked made him stop abruptly. He turned and looked at the officers, a mix of dread and fear in his eyes.

"Are they-?" Fear clutched his heart.

"They are at the station. One of our officers was shot outside your cabin. Your wife saved his life."

A profound and deep sigh escaped Alejandro's lips. "Where is the police station? I saw them ambush my friends, and then ran in here. I stopped them from shooting me."

"Wait, we need to ask you more questions." The policeman seemed flustered.

"After I see my family." He walked away without letting them say another word.

The two officers shrugged and asked the sister where the injured man was. She led them to the room where the moaning man remained slumped on the floor, his back against the wall.

****

The desk phone blinking light was on, telling him there was a message. Howard sighed, took the coffee mug to his mouth and guzzled a mouthful. *Fucking early.* He pressed the message button, recognized Pancho's voice and sat down. Several seconds later he jumped out of his chair when he heard what sounded like gunshots. "What the fuck?" He said out loud. Not waiting another second he called him back. The line was busy. He tried again. No change. Howard ran out of his office. A secretary stared at him wide eyed.

"Get me a plane, like fucking now." He grunted. "I'm headed for Mexico, something happened." He continued running down the aisle while shouting instructions.

A few agents already in their cubicles at that early hour came out of their boxes to see Howard disappear down the hall.

"Make damn sure they are ready to take off when I get there. Call downstairs, have a car ready to drive me to the airport!" He shouted and slowed down to call his superior. Left him a message, telling him what he was doing. He then called his Mexican counterpart and asked him if he had been in contact with Jacinto.

"He told me he was going with Pancho to Creel. Something about the *Caballeros del Norte.* Why?"

"Call him and get back to me." Howard, almost hyper ventilating, told him what he had heard. "If I'm right, Jacinto won't pick up."

FORTY-TWO

Driving like a mad man, Alejandro arrived at the police station. Town people were milling around gossiping and wondering what had happened. He took out the pistols, pushed one under his seat and the other one under the passenger's. He ran the few steps to the building entrance and threw open the doors. A startled employee watched him with trepidation. A short, fat policeman, his wife and son, huddled in a corner, turned around when they heard the crashing doors.

"Alex!" Virginia gasped when she saw him all bloodied. "Are you hurt?" Gabriel perched on a bench, jumped down, his face distraught.

"I'm fine. He practically flew the few steps, picked Gabriel and then held Virginia in a tight embrace. "What about you two?" He kept holding on to them, afraid.

"Domingo is badly injured. Have you seen Pancho and Jacinto?"

"Yes. Pancho was killed and Jacinto...I don't know if he'll make it."

His face told her all she needed to know. "Oh Alex, how can this be? Maria-Guadalupe?"

"She's fine but the doctor who treated her, and a couple of nuns were murdered."

Her soft sobs pained the deepest core of his soul. He thought of the time when everyone told him she was dead. That had been the most abysmal day of his existence and only the presence of Gabriel kept him from going berserk. This experience was not too far off. It had only been a matter of luck or divine providence that his wife and son were not taken away. And this time it could have been for good.

He promised himself that he would not stop until he unraveled who were the culprits. Alejandro knew he might have to render answers to a higher power later on, but how could such debauchery and depravity be allowed to continue unpunished? And he might have to atone for his sins, for the killings he had done, for the killings he would have to do. But there was no other road to redemption and as long as the savage killers remained at large, his life and the ones of those dear to him would be at risk. It was either the criminals or he. Therefore it had to be them. "Who's in charge here?" Alejandro asked.

A small man with a full head of gray hair and wearing a tie and jacket approached him. "I'm the mayor. Diego Domingues y Real at your service."

"Where are the rest of the police?"

"The army is sending soldiers to help us in case there's any more trouble."

"The army, why?"

"There's only three town policemen left. Two are at the clinic and the man standing beside you." He extended his hand out. "We are overwhelmed."

"How many dead?" Alejandro put Gabriel down and shook the older man's hand.

"Besides the doctor, four nuns are dead, two are wounded. Both Domingo and Jacinto are in critical condition."

"A team of army doctors and nurses are on their way here. They will be sent to the central IMSS hospital in Chihuahua. The nuns are keeping them stable in the meantime.

"I'm going back to talk to Jacinto, sweetheart, come with me." He held Gabriel's hand.

"I can't stop you but he may be heavily sedated...I don't know...if he can." The mayor stared at Alejandro through his thick lenses.

Holding Virginia's hand on his right hand and his son on the other, he shepherded his family out of the building.

"I would like to change clothes. Gaby's too." Virginia trembled slightly as they walked out onto the street. A bright sun almost blinded them at first and all three stopped for a few seconds.

"I should too." Alejandro looked down at his clothes.

Town people milling around the entrance looked at them in horror and gave them wide berth.

Driving back to the cabin, Alejandro became aware of the ordeal Virginia and Gabriel had gone through. The thought that he could have lost the two most precious beings in his life in one swift second made him shiver. But at the same time it cemented in his mind the conviction that the men responsible had to be confronted.

****

The clinic was a chaotic mess. An army patrol standing guard outside the dispensary doors stopped them when they arrived.

"I was here helping, the head nun can vouch for us."

A soldier went looking for her.

Several minutes later, the young conscript came back with the nun. She had a swollen, black eye, her lower lip was broken and a bandage covered half her right cheek.

"Yes, he's Don Alejandro, he was the one who rescued us. If it hadn't been for him..."

The nun escorted Alejandro and his family to Jacinto and Domingo.

Alejandro asked his wife and son to wait outside and walked in.

Both men seemed asleep, their bodies covered in bandages. Intravenous fluids slowly dripping into their veins.

Alejandro approached Jacinto's bed, grabbed his hand and spoke softly.

The badly injured man opened his eyes after a few seconds and looked at Alejandro. He could barely move his head.

"Hey," Alejandro whispered, "sorry about you friend, I need your help. I'm going after the man responsible for this...can you help me find him?"

Jacinto's eyes became moist. He stared at the man standing above him. His fingers lifted slightly. "My clothes...find them."

Alejandro looked at a heap of partially shredded garments by a corner of the room. "They're on the floor."

His voice but a faint whisper said, "A key."

"You want me to look?"

The eyelids opened and closed several times.

He moved away from Jacinto and started feeling the clothes. He took out a wallet and checked it. Next he patted the pants. A small hard object touched his fingers. He put his hand in and took out a key. He put it in front of Jacinto's eyes. "This?"

The eyelids went down again and he murmured something.

Putting his ear close to the injured man's mouth, Alejandro waited.

"The bank."

"You have a safety deposit box in the bank? What bank?" Alejandro raised his head.

"Only one...in town." His voice barely audible. Jacinto let out a soft exhalation, the effort to speak and stay awake, tiring him. He wanted to fall sleep. "All the information...there. No one knows...but Pancho." He let out another deep sigh. "We were...afraid...people...paid." Jacinto closed his eyes. Then opened them, looked at Alejandro and one more time his eyes lids shot down. "You understand?" His voice but a faint whisper.

"Yes, I'll see you soon." He took his cell-phone out and called Virginia. "I need to stop by the bank...a favor for Jacinto." He couldn't see the puzzled look in Virginia's face.

"Will you be long?"

"No, it won't take me more than a few minutes. Okay? I love you."

"I love you too. I...with so many things going on, I don't want to be without you for long."

"Meet at you at the cabin, bye." He drove off and was at the small bank in less than five minutes. He walked in and inspected the three rows of teller stations and two desks on the side. On the other side were what looked like private offices.

"May I help you?" A plump fifty some woman took off her eyeglasses and puffed her hair. She noticed his firm chin and thick eyebrows. *He's not from here, I have never seen him before. He's tall, hmm, has a ring, it's always the same, the good-looking ones are always taken.* Her thoughts were interrupted by the deep, pleasant voice.

"I need to go into my safe deposit box." He showed her the small key.

"Oh? You're a customer?" She gave him a thorough look.

Noticing the name in the lapel of a somewhat outdated jacket, Alejandro continued. "Juana-Maria, that's your name, right?"

His dazzling smile almost made her swoon. "Ohh? Yes, it is." She looked at the key. "Not too many people around here use them, number nineteen. Come with me." She stood up and walked away from her desk towards the bank vault. Her coworkers watched her with curiosity.

The woman was smaller than he had thought. He followed her.

She stopped in front of a cabinet and opened a filing drawer. "Now, let's see...what's your name?"

"Jacinto Villaredonda."

"Hmm, yes, here it is. Can I see your ID please?" She gave him a dreamy stare and then looked down at the date in the card. It had been opened a while back and hadn't been used since.

"Darn, I knew I had forgotten something. I left my wallet, but I have the key. Can you make an exception today?" Alejandro smiled and pressed the key on her hand, letting it linger there. "I can come back later with it, it's just that I remembered I had to get some papers."

She fanned her flushing face with one of her hands.

"Maybe when I come back with my ID, we, can go out to lunch for doing me this favor?"

Her legs felt weak, a wet, warm sensation cursed through her body and a delicious moistness invaded her most intimate parts. She trembled and looked at Alejandro. "I'm off at one. I can be free all afternoon."

"Count on it." Alejandro dark eyes remained fixed on her.

She gave him a languorous look.

A coy smile appeared on his face.

She couldn't believe the things she was thinking of doing with him. "F...follow me please." With shaky steps, Juana-Maria led the tall, attractive man to the ancient vault; it's massive steel door open. "Here's your box, there's a small room there for privacy." She sighted and then gasped when he palmed the key on her hand and let it linger for a few seconds, but for her, felt like an eternity.

Taking the master key out of her ample boson, and hoping that he would notice them, Juana-Maria's key went into one of the slots. With an unsteady hand, she buried the second key on the other slit and twisted. The small door opened and Alejandro pulled out the rectangular metal box.

"You're very kind. Thank you for helping me out." He moved to the closet size space.

"I'll be outside, call me when you finish." Her eyelids fluttered and she re-arranged her hair.

Inside the tiny room, Alejandro opened the long metal container. A thick manila envelope folded several times held his gaze. He quickly scanned the other items, a wedding band, an old, gold pocket watch and some other documents. He took the one item that interested him and peeked into the packet, making certain it was what he was looking for. Opening his belt buckle, he pulled his shirt tail out, hid the package in his back, tucked the shirt back in, made sure the thick envelope was firmly held, closed the metal container and walked out.

The short, chubby woman waited for him outside the vault fanning herself with her hand. Her underarms were damp with moisture, even though the temperature inside the bank was a comfortable seventy two degrees.

"All done." He grinned and waited next to the empty space where the safety deposit box would go back in. When she reached him, he slid in the container and waited.

She smiled at him and nodded.

"Can I have your business card, so I can call you on my way back?"

Her hands trembled and she nodded dumbly. "Yeees, sure...come to my desk." She started searching her desk.

"Are these your cards?" Alejandro pointed at a small receptacle full of business cards with an old outdated picture of her.

She flushed again in embarrassment and flustered handed him one.

"Thank you again for helping me out of this jam. He winked, turned and left.

She watched his wide back as he walked out of the bank.

Several clerks snickered behind her back.

FORTY-THREE

A television van with the logo TV Azteca arrived in Creel. News travels fast, especially if they happen to be of the gory kind. A news reporter began talking. The news feed was being transmitted live. He started describing the small town's nineteen-century feel. Being the gateway to a spectacular nature setting. He went on describing the good works of the Catholic nuns that cared for the Raramuri Indians at the clinic. That the native Indians preferred to live in quiet isolation in secluded out of the way settlements, and were scattered in the labyrinthine canyon walls and valleys.

He went on to report the news of the savage attack on the clinic. He paused and the camera made a sweeping take of the building and its surroundings. The cameraman took a zoom shot of the two trucks still parked in the middle of the wide square. The reporter informed the public that these were the vehicles used by the gang.

He turned around and walked towards the bullet riddled SUV near the end of a street that emptied into the plaza, with the camera following him.

The correspondent pointed at the wreck while the man holding the camera made a full take of the car's inside and zoomed in on the bloodied seats. About to finish filming the grisly scene, two carloads of men arrived.

A husky man, in his mid-forties jumped off the lead car before any of the others and in an imperious manner asked them what they were doing. "Stop that right now."

Slim and tall, the reporter looked back at his beefy cameraman and made a slit sign across his throat. The man put down the camera.

The rest of the group got out of their cars a second later. The men fanned out with five of them headed towards the victims' car, two of them headed towards the awkwardly parked SUVs. One of them started inspecting one of the cars, his companion mimicked his actions and began searching the second car.

"How the hell do you guys get here so fucking fast?" The man, obviously the leader, stared angrily at the TV correspondent and his cameraman.

"You can't stop us from filming. This is a live feed, the news are already out." The handsome reporter stood his ground. He turned slightly and motioned to his assistant to turn on the camera. "Are you from the Federal District? What happened here?" He held the microphone towards the man face.

"No comments. This is an active crime scene. Stay away from here or I'll put you in jail for obstruction and destroying evidence." He knew it was an empty threat but he hoped it would buy him some time. "Escort these men out of here." He roared to no one in particular.

Two of the men working on the wreck, stopped and walked over to the reporter and his assistant.

"Fine, fine, we are leaving, but we'll be back soon." They headed back to their truck. "Did you keep the mike on?" He asked his assistant.

The man smiled.

"Let's follow them. There was a news report that recently another massacre occurred not far from here."

Before long, the news was all over the air. The lead news was that the *Caballeros Del Norte* cartel had wiped out a *Raramuri* hamlet. It was followed by the story of the drug enforcement agents, one of them working for the US and the other, for the Mexican government. They had come to Creel to find out if the rumors were true. The men were executed gang like style.

The Federal District and the State of Chihuahua had now sent a task force to investigate what the two detectives had uncovered. But the teams were now primarily focusing on who and why had the agents been ambushed and slain.

Preliminary indications pointed to a hit by the cartel group. But the authorities were scratching their heads trying to figure out why the assassins attacked the clinic. Most of the perpetrators were thwarted and killed in their nefarious attempt at the small hospital.

It was at first believed that prompt police action or a doctor had prevented another bloodbath. But unconfirmed sources who remained anonymous stated that is was a tourist and that one hooligan was alive. All the dead gangsters and the captive had *NORTE* tattooed on their knuckles. A sword made the "T" of the word. A side story from several days earlier had become the backdrop for the main story. Previously given scant notice in the main stream, the story recalled an earlier incident. A tourist that had gotten lost, discovered an emaciated Indian girl and an infant boy in an off the beaten path dirt trail.

The news media was speculating whether the little girl and the baby boy were village survivors. But so far, no confirmation or details had been obtained from the authorities, the TV reporter announced.

The cameraman zoomed in on the clinic broken doors.

"And wouldn't it be an incredible twist of fate if it is the same tourist who found the children, the one who singlehanded prevented another carnage?"

The camera showed the reporter again.

"We have not been able to identify who he is. All we were told is that early this morning he came to see how the small *Raramuri* girl and the infant boy were doing.

Instead he found himself in the middle of an attack to the clinic. Putting his life at risk, he intervened, saving the lives of most of the nuns working at the hospital. The tourist killed most of the assassins but not before the marauders butchered a doctor and three or four nuns. Amazing."

The newsman shook his head. He knew this could be his breakout to become a national TV anchor. "And in a related story, another tourist was almost killed and only the prompt action by one of Creel's policemen saved the woman's life. The officer was shot multiple times and is in critical condition here," he put additional emphasis in the here, "fighting for his life."

The TV station picture split in two, one side displaying a picture of a group of nuns belonging to the same order. The newsman remained on the other spot and resumed his monologue when he was given the full take.

"To think these poor nuns cannot grieve yet the loss of so many of their congregation and must remain steadfast and minister to the badly injured policeman." The TV reporter moved in closer to the battered clinic doors.

"I'm sure their prompt actions saved the man's life. This is Arnaldo Benitez from…" A commercial brake took over. When he came back on he reported that the authorities had sent a medical crew to transport the injured survivor to Chihuahua.

He further stated that repeated attempts by him and various news reporting organizations to obtain more details from the authorities had met with strict silence. And neither he nor the other news agencies had been able to secure from the police the identities of the dead agents and the tourists involved, nor the actual number of people killed.

He added that unconfirmed reports were now saying that it was a woman tourist who was the one that actually saved the policeman fighting for his life inside the doors of the clinic. The identity of the heroes of Creel was still unknown. The reporter made the cut sign and he and his cameraman left for their truck.

****

About to leave Jacinto's room, Alejandro stopped when five people walked in accompanied by the mother superior; who introduced him. "These gentlemen are from Mexico City and Chihuahua. They are here to see Jacinto."

"You are Alejandro? The sister told me what you did." A middle age man, about his own height, addressed him. "Were you able to talk to either one of them?" His large, thick index finger pointed towards the beds.

"No, they are under anesthesia, I'm sorry about your loss. I only met Pancho briefly but I got to like him and these guys right away." Alejandro gestured with his hand towards the beds.

"I'm Pancho's boss, *was*." He corrected himself. "From the DEA office in El Paso. His killing is a federal offense." Howard fixed his eyes on the injured men. "The U.S. will go to whatever lengths are necessary to apprehend whoever committed these crimes."

The other men shook hands with Alejandro. One of them, with a compact frame that only served to accentuate his physique, spoke. "I'm Raul, the lead man from the D.F. and I work in conjunction with Howard."

"Did you see what happened?" Husky and tall, with lots of thick dark hair and humorless dark eyes, Howard entered Alejandro's private space. Scarcely inches away.

What's wrong with this guy? Alejandro did not move and Howard finally stepped back. "I was about to leave when I saw the attack. I ran back inside to warn the nuns and went out by a back door. Then I came back and you know the rest."

"You saved a lot of lives today according to the nuns. And you were the one who also found the *Tarahumara* girl, right?" Raul said.

"The hero." Howard's comment sounded somewhat sarcastic.

"Anyone would have done the same. My family is waiting. I'll see you around?"

"Not so fast. I have a few questions for you. Do you know why they wanted to kill my men or why they were looking for you? You're Colombian and you just arrived here a few days ago, right?"

"My wife-"

"Oh, yeah, I forgot. And you're not involved in the cocaine business, right?" Howard gave him a crooked smile. "So...not possible that it had to do with your export business?"

"Is there any point to your line of questioning? I came here with my wife and son on vacation." Alejandro held his anger in check.

A soft moan rose from Jacinto's mouth.

Howard glanced at the men.

Raul was already approaching the bed. "Hey...how are you feeling?"

"Don't go yet." Howard moved next to Raul. "How're you doing big fellow?"

"Gentlemen, my family is waiting. I'm leaving." Alejandro headed for the door.

"We'll talk later. Don't think of going anywhere for the time being." Howard gave him a baleful look and turned his attention back to Jacinto.

FORTY-FOUR

The call from *El Carnicero* left Fabian extremely concerned. He had been watching the unfolding events on one of the TV networks. Vicente's man in Creel, a local policeman, had confirmed that a goddamn tourist had eliminated Cuauhtémoc and all of his men but one. According to Vicente's source, it was the same man who had saved the little girl. The tourist, whoever the hell he was, had to be eliminated, Fabian told Vicente.

"I don't care how, but do it," Fabian seethed, "I'm going there myself to make sure things are done."

Only after repeated admonishments that his presence there could end up complicating things and would be counterproductive, did Fabian renege on his idea of flying to Creel. Vicente promised him that he would take care of things.

"Get it done." Fabian raged. "I don't care how but do it. Am I making myself clear?"

"Don't worry, I'm on top of this. I'm taking care of it." Vicente hung up and made several phone calls. He finally allowed himself to relax. He knew his men would deliver. They were well aware that Mexico's central government was sending reinforcements. The original plan had been stopped because of the unforeseen mingling of a stupid tourist who had no idea of what he was getting into. That was the reason why the plan had failed. Too bad, Vicente thought. The man and his family would pay the ultimate price. He should have known better than to get involved.

****

Stopping in front of the cabin, Geriberto stepped out of his police car and ambled over to the front door. He hesitated before knocking and turned to his right, then his left. He swiveled around in a slow motion and stared behind him but there was no one around. He rapped at the front door several times and swiped his brow.

A voice from inside told him there was someone inside. *Good*, he thought. *They are here.*

Virginia pushed the window curtain slightly and peered outside. "Just a moment." She recognized him as the policemen who had arrived when Domingo was wounded. And then proceeded to open the door. "Hallo again." For some reason the officer's nervous smile unsettled her. "Hi, any news on Jacinto?"

"I need to take you and your son to the clinic." The short, round policeman looked behind her and to his sides.

"Give me a minute." She left the door slightly ajar and went back in.

Walking back to the car, he heard her telling her son to get a sweater and get ready.

Gabriel saw his mother's *Blackberry* on the kitchen counter and put it in his back pocket.

Stopping in front of a small desk, Virginia scrawled a quick note for Alejandro and left it on the kitchen counter. "*Vamos*, Gaby." She extended her hand to him and they walked to the door.

Gabriel didn't seem willing to go, she could feel that he was sort of holding her back. "Gaby, something wrong?"

"I...I, don't...know. Where are we going?"

"I'm taking you to the hospice, boy." The policeman's eyes kept darting left and right. "Your father is waiting." He almost stumbled going down the steps on his way to open the car's back door for them.

FORTY-FIVE

Opening the cabin door, Alejandro was surprised that Virginia and Gabriel were gone. There was a note on the kitchen counter.

Sweetheart;

Geriberto, the policeman came for us.

Something about going to Santa Teresita.

We're there in case we miss each other.

XXXOOO.

He stared at his watch. It was barely eleven thirty. He turned around, got back on his rented Jeep and in less than five minutes reached the plaza in front of the clinic.

Three teams of agents were painstakingly searching the two trucks and the crime scene.

Alejandro walked over to the closest truck. The Creel's police car was nowhere to be seen. "Have you seen my wife and son?"

One of the men turned around to see who had arrived. The others stopped what they were doing, recognizing him. "Aaaah, check in there," he pointed towards the building, "I haven't seen anyone come in but you never know." His head disappeared inside the truck.

His associates went back to work too.

Fighting a feeling of dread trying to filter inside his mind, Alejandro trotted towards the entrance. He saw a nun and two soldiers in the foyer. "Have you seen my wife, my son?"

The two soldiers shook their heads.

He asked breathlessly. "The policeman? Geriberto?"

"No, no one has come in since…" The nun shook her head. "But maybe they are with Maria-Guadalupe?"

Not waiting another second, he sped past the nun, almost running through the hall. Alejandro reached the girl's room.

She looked up, saw him and smiled, then continued playing with the doll Virginia had given her. Another nun came into the room. A questioning look on her face.

He swallowed hard. "Have you seen my wife and son?"

"No." The nun said.

Turning in a pivot, he ran towards the injured men's room. Howard and Raul were conferring with a couple of agents in the hall outside the room.

Howard saw him first. "What is it?"

Alejandro ignored the man's gruff tone. "My wife and son. I was told they were brought here." Fear and desperation were encroaching his soul. "By Geriberto, the policeman." He finished and let out a gush of air.

"I haven't seen them." Howard turned around and began addressing a team member.

"They are not here and they are not in the cabin." Alejandro's booming voice broke the uneasy quiet.

The startled men looked at Alejandro.

"Look, you're probably on pins and needles, considering what you went through a couple of hours ago." Raul put a hand on Howard's shoulder, to stop him from talking. He spoke to the men standing by. "Call the policeman and do a quick look around. I'm sure they are around here somewhere."

"And send someone to the cabin, he probably missed them on the way here." Howard's tone was disdainful. His face was puffy red. "You better settle down boy. Don't ever holler at me again." He gave Alejandro an angry look.

"You're lucky we're not in the States and that I'm here only as a guest of the Mexican government."

Ignoring him, Alejandro turned around and started walking away, his fists opening and closing.

"Where do you think you're going?" Howard raised his voice.

"To look for them." Alejandro did not look back and kept on going.

"Wait!" Raul yelled.

He turned around. The look on Raul's face made him hold his breath.

Howard followed, a couple of steps behind.

"Alex, may I call you Alex?" Raul swiped his face.

Alejandro simply nodded.

"Geriberto is nowhere to be found. We can't find your wife and son either."

FORTY-SIX

"Why are we going this way?" Gabriel asked his mother, sitting next to him in the back seat of the small police car.

"Hmm?" She hadn't noticed, her mind rewinding the events unfolding in the last couple of days. She looked up. "Where are you taking us? I thought you said we were going to the clinic?"

The policeman mumbled something unintelligible and turned a corner. A car was blocking the street. Then a large Honda van coming from nowhere, braked behind them. Three men tore out of the wagon and ran to the police car.

Almost simultaneously, the men yanked open the passenger doors. One snatched Gabriel and picked him up like a potato sack. The second man pulled Virginia out of the passenger seat.

The third man went to the driver's door where Geriberto waited with the window down. "Good job." A shot rang out and the policeman's head exploded into a mess of blood and grayish fluid.

Gabriel and Virginia were jostled into the van. The boy was shoved into the third row of seats and banged his head against the armrest. Virginia was thrown on the second row. The filthy and gruff looking man, who had pushed her in, sat next to her. The driver went into reverse, wheels squealing, reached the main street and shot forward, speeding out of town.

Hardly anyone noticed the gory scene but for a homeless old man lying on the entranceway of an old house.

****

"Do what I tell you and you won't get hurt." The man sitting next to her spoke with a raspy voice. He held a pistol and handed Virginia a black hood. "Put this on." He wasn't worried about the little boy and besides he only had one head-sock.

She noticed the long scar that went down from near the man's left eye socket, all the way to the side of his neck, when she put on the cloth bag over her head. Virginia tried to remain calm but feared for her son. "Can my son sit with me?" Her voice somewhat muffled by the sock. The sweaty smell of the cloth almost made her gag.

"Habla español cabrona." The surly looking man grunted.

"You don't speak Spanish?" The man sitting next to the driver spoke to them. His thickset frame hardly fit in the passenger seat.

Gabriel looked at the man's big hands and saw that the knuckles bore small tattoos.

Virginia didn't answer either.

He shifted his attention to the man's big round face and dark eyes.

"I guess they don't." The man looked ahead. "Don't stop for nobody. I'm calling Vicente." he addressed the man holding Virginia, *"la mamasita quiere a su chavito con ella."*

Gabriel touched the lump on his forehead; it hurt.

The men weren't paying much attention to him. He put his hand on his back pocket. The back of the seats in front of him shielded him from the man sitting next to his mother. With extreme care he brought out the BB. No one was watching. Softly, he pressed the green dial button and then pressed mute. He slid it into the back pocket again.

In a swift and sudden motion, the man seating next to Virginia shoved her to the side, grabbed Gabriel by his shirt collar, pulled him over the seat and dumped him next to her. *"Contenta guerita chula?"* Gabriel was sandwiched between his mother and the man with sour breath.

Virginia took Gabriel's hand in hers.

The man in the front seat took a cell phone out. It looked like a small toy in his huge hands. He had a hard time punching in the numbers with his thick fingers. *"Jefe*, we got the woman and the *chavito*. We couldn't get a hit on the man. He was in the hospital and the place is crawling with *federales."*

"That may be enough for now." Vicente said. *I can use them as bait or offer an exchange. He gives himself up and we let the wife and son go.* "Head for Chihuahua."

"Si jefe. You want me to call you when we get there?"

"Yes, and don't harm them, I need them alive for now. I have to call Fabian." Vicente snapped shut his cell phone.

"Tienen suerte, el jefe no los va a matar todavia." He laughed out loud.

Virginia was glad her face was covered. The man would have seen the terror in her expression. She felt Gabriel's small hand squeezing hers. She tightened her hand over his.

They plan to kill us. But why? We don't know anything. "Gaby, don't say anything, okay. Dad will find us." She whispered.

"Silencio, carajo." The man with the hoarse voice yelled. *"No ingles, comprende?"*

FORTY-SEVEN

Fighting the anxiety that was overwhelming him, Alejandro tried in vain to discard the possibility that they were kidnapped. His cell phone buzzed and he took it out. To his utter surprise, it was a call from Virginia. Thrilled and relieved that she was on the way to the clinic, he opened his cellphone. "Virg-" He frowned when he heard muffled sounds and did his best to listen.

There was some sort of scuffle and then he heard a man talking in Spanish. More garbled noises. He pressed the phone to his ear trying to catch what was being said. And then he was sure he heard Virginia talking, and then rustling and tossing.

The voices became clearer, still somewhat distant but definitely better. The car's engine noise didn't make it easier but the men's gruff tones helped. He heard what he thought was a one-way conversation. Something about driving to Chihuahua and not being able to kill him or were they talking about Jacinto? And then he was sure he heard Virginia again. She was speaking English, but he missed the next words. A hard, deep voice told her to shut up in Spanish. A few seconds later the link was broken.

He stared through the windshield. His world had caved in. He was in a maelstrom, unhinged by the vortex, the storm, the hurricane that had taken the most precious pieces of his life. How could this be happening again? What malevolent and cruel god had dumped this darkness in his life? He was crushed. To make matters worse, he was in a foreign country with no idea of where to go or who to go to. He shook his head and called to the depths of his soul to eviscerate the despondency that threatened to drown him in sorrow and self-pity.

Sliding his hand under the car seat, Alejandro felt the package. With increasing trepidation and despair, he reluctantly grabbed the large yellow envelope. He should be speeding out of town but perhaps whatever was in the packet might provide him with some clues or other piece of vital information. A typewritten note was attached to the first page.

If you are reading this, it means I'm dead. I believe there is a mole at the highest ranks of the Texas DEA headquarters, but I haven't been able to confirm my suspicions. My DEA partner, Pancho, is the only one I trust. He shares my suspicions. Neither one of us trust our regional departments. Be careful with whom you share these files with.

Underneath the note, the first page read FYEO, but it didn't say to whom it was addressed. *That means for your eyes-only? I think so.*

Out of the corner of his eye, he saw Howard and Raul coming in his direction. Hurriedly he shoved the package back under the seat.

"Going somewhere, Calwel?" Howard came over to his side, Raul stood by the other door.

"So, your family has been kidnapped because of a bust up drug deal?"

"Do you really think I would endanger my family? I don't deal in drugs."

"Do you owe them money, a shipment?"

"What is this shit? Why are you questioning me?" He felt like taking the gun out and shooting the man.

Howard was relentless. "You come down here and one of my best men is killed. And now your family is gone. How convenient." He smirked. "Did you set this whole thing up?"

"You son of a bitch, don't waste my time. I need help finding my family. You all know who these people are. Why aren't you going after them, instead of spewing all kinds of bullshit?"

"Alex, we found Geriberto." Raul said.

"Where? Are Virginia and Gabriel with him?" He almost jumped out of his seat.

Raul raised his hand to stop him. "He was shot dead. There was no one else in the car. The only good news is that the only blood we found was in the driver's seat."

"Where, where is the car?"

Raul ignored the question. "We are assuming the blood belongs to him. A beggar saw a woman and a child going from the police car to a grey van. The problem is that the man was pretty plastered. He reeked of alcohol. He couldn't even tell us what make it was, and it's next to impossible to search all the vans in the city."

"Is this another one in your belt, Alejandro?" Howard gave him a spiteful look. "Did you have your men kill another one of this town's fine police force?"

"Are you out of your mind?" Alejandro desperately wanted to mention the phone conversation he had just heard but the note held him back. He wanted to yell at them to help him find his family, help him pursue the people who had taken them. He was sure with their help he could find Gabriel and Virginia.

"We can start by you telling me the truth. You brought this on to yourself. Tell me what's your connection to the *Caballeros del Norte?*" A thin smile ran across Howard's lips.

No I need to talk to Jacinto first. Does he trust these men? Only if he tells me. But how am I going to talk to him? "Are you going to help me find my family?"

Closing his eyes for a moment, Alejandro fought the urge to hit the man. He tightened his hands making fists under the steering wheel. But relented and flexed his fingers, laying his hands over his pant legs. "Can I leave now? I want to check the cabin again. I haven't the foggiest idea of why these people would want to kidnap my family." He spoke with deliberate slowness. "All I can tell you is that I'm not involved in drugs. Check with your counterparts in Colombia, you will find out that I'm telling you the truth. Please, help me get my family back." He kept his gaze in front of him, not looking at either one of the men on both sides of the jeep, afraid his anger would get the better of him and make him lash out at the arrogant man.

"By the way, Pancho and Jacinto's guns are nowhere to be found. Do you have them?"

"I…no." *Please God help me. I need to find my family, I can't waste any more time, I need to save them, please.*

"What guns did you use to shoot down those thugs? The coroner is conducting the autopsies but he hasn't finished yet. If you lie, I can ask Raul to put you in jail for tampering with evidence and obstructing our mission. Is that what you want?"

"I saved your partners' friend-"

"Where are the guns Alejandro? Don't fucking lie to me." Howard's voice was at the verge of being vitriolic.

"Why don't you fuck yourself, you piece of shit." Alejandro's hand moved to the ignition switch and started the Jeep. "Unless you have something helpful to say, I'm leaving. And for your information I used the goons' own guns and threw them on the ground afterwards. They're probably still there unless your men collected them."

"And where are you going?" Howard gave him a skeptical look.

"You can find me in the cabin. If I hear from the bastards that took my family, I will let you know." He pushed the gas pedal and the car jolted forward. The two men backed away.

"I'm not going to make things easy for you, asshole." Howard yelled at the speeding Jeep.

"I think you're going too far Howard." Raul admonished the DEA agent.

"Fuck him, fuck you. I don't trust him. You should send a couple of agents to keep an eye on him. He's dirty, I'm telling you."

"Based on what, Howard?"

"If I were you, I'd put him in jail right now under the pretense of protective custody. He would not get away with any of this shit back in the States." Howard spit on the street.

"What are you talking about?"

"What's wrong with you Raul? Are you blind?"

"No, but you have been jumping all over him since the beginning. I understand you lost one of your best men and you're bitter but do you have to take it on the guy who, if anything, has saved a bunch of people? I lost people too."

"Are you getting softhearted?" Howard stared at his counterpart with a look of contempt.

"All I'm saying is that we need to give the man some slack."

"My best agent is dead. One of your policemen is dead, a doctor is dead, nuns are dead! What more do you need? And two others are fighting for their lives and you think that guy is clean? Bullshit." Howard roared. His cell phone buzzed. He looked at the caller ID and ignored it. It rang again. He turned it off.

"I'm going back to the clinic, maybe I'll be able to talk to Jacinto." Raul said.

"You mind if I tag along?"

They still hadn't had a chance to talk with Domingo, who had been in a comma since the operation. But the doctor had given strict orders that the men should not be bothered for the time being.

Howard didn't care. "Raul, don't waste any more time. The guy is dirty."

"We don't know that. What is it with you and this guy?"

"I'm sure he instructed his accomplices to take his wife and son to a safe place. We have lost any leverage we might have had on him. All he's doing is throwing our investigation into disarray. Put him in jail right now. I insist."

Glaring at his counterpart, Raul shook his head but then called one of the men. "Take a couple of agents with you and pick up Alejandro. He's back in his cabin."

FORTY-EIGHT

With a screeching halt, the Jeep stopped in front of the cabin. Alejandro looked around but it didn't look like anyone was watching him. He grabbed the thick envelope, and one of the guns and hid it all in front of his shirt. Opening the door to the cabin, he did a quick search. The hurt of not seeing his wife and son tortured his soul to its deepest core. Alejandro almost fell on his knees. An overwhelming fear virtually immobilized him but he fought off the panic that wanted to rob his will away. *I need to concentrate, I need to find out if what's in here will help me find them.*

Alejandro wiped his face and began flipping pages. When he finished, his worse fears were confirmed.

The package contained several grainy photos but there was no mistake identifying one of the men. It was the same man who had been in front of him when they arrived in Mexico, the one he had seen arriving at Chihuahua's airport private terminal. The written pages also indicated that both Pancho and Jacinto had been following the trail for a while.

On two occasions, when they thought they had Fabian corralled, he slipped the trap. Both men feared that both their operations were compromised.

Staring into the empty cabin, Alejandro surveyed it one more time to make sure he hadn't missed anything. He then drove to the car rental company near the train station. With his windows down, the smell of smoky pinewood entered the cabin. It permeated the old logging-mining town and reminded him of Virginia's words about the nice peculiar smell of Creel. Now however, it only brought sadness.

He felt helpless, he couldn't trust the people around him. He had only a vague idea of where his wife and son might be. The report talked about the mansion of a reputed cartel leader associated with the man named Fabian. In it, were two imposing pictures of a mansion in Culiacan, one taken from the air, and the other from a car.

The photos illustrated the wealth of its owner, the man named Vicente, aka *El Carnicero*. He didn't want to think why the man had earned that nickname. He had been resisting the impulse to call his wife, fearing that if she somehow had hidden the cellphone and they found it, his only tenuous tie with her would be lost. *If I don't hear from her in another hour, I don't know what I'm going to do.* Feeling as miserable as when he was told she had died, he parked the car and went into the rental car agency.

"Señor Calwel, right?" The cheerful greeting came from the chubby man who managed the rental car agency. Like everyone in town, he knew what Alejandro had done. But his smile disappeared when he saw Alejandro's forlorn eyes. "What's wrong? Your wife and son okay?"

"I'm afraid not. They were kidnapped."

"Oh, my God. What is happening to my town? How can I help?" He felt genuinely sorry for the man.

A somber looking Alejandro spoke, "I need the car for a few more days and I would like to leave it in Chihuahua. Actually, do you have a car with a bigger engine? Would that be a problem?"

"Not at all. I have a Tahoe and a brand new Yukon with a 6.2-litter, eight cylinder engine. The rental cost is twice as much as what you're paying now. But I'll give it you." He made a dismissing gesture with his hand. "No charge."

"I'll take the first one."

"How many days?"

"Make it a whole week."

They both looked out a window. Sirens were loudly yelling nearby but they couldn't see the cars. "I wish there was something more I could do for you." His voice trailed off.

"Just don't tell anyone, not even the police."

"I know you will find them. Today has been one of the most terrible days in Creel...with the exception of those teachers killed several years ago by the narcos. You have saved so many. *La Virgen de Guadalupe* will protect them and get them back for you. You'll see."

A few minutes later he was sitting in the car, feeling powerless, not knowing who to go to, or where to go. Doubts assailing his disposition, he felt incapable to make a decision. He started the truck and drove away from the parking lot.

The manager watched him leave from the office. He started praying.

If they are headed for Chihuahua, then I'm going there too. He stared driving towards the edge of the town. He felt lost, unable to come up with an action plan. The jarring sound of his cellphone snapped him from his self-pity.

FORTY-NINE

Manhandled, thirsty and scared, Virginia held on, her deepest fear? Not knowing what they would do to her son.

Rogelio, the burly, scruffy man sitting next to her, stared out, hypnotized by the monotonous road. A regional ballad blasted away but it didn't keep Arturo, the man with the huge paws, from snoring loudly, his head bobbing up and down.

"Can I have water for my son and me?" She asked.

"I need to go to the bathroom." Gabriel piped in.

The voice brought Rogelio out of his stupor. *"Hey, guey, la mamacita tiene sed y el cachorro necesita miar."*

"Me vale madre." The driver said.

"I need a break too." Arturo woke up and raked his hair with his large hands. He pushed down the automatic window switch, allowing a blast of fresh air inside the stuffy cabin.

"Ahorita carnal. There's a gas station coming up." The driver said and pulled off the highway to a roadside gas station and cafeteria. Pulling the sack from her head, Arturo admired the striking woman.

"These are the rules, before you get out of the van. You try to run away or warn anyone and I'll kill you both. Is that understood?" He gave them a menacing look that said he was not bluffing. "And you are coming with me." He pointed at Virginia.

"Rogelio, take the *chaparrito* with you. As soon as these two are done," he now stared at the driver, "you'll go, then Rogelio and I will go."

The station in the middle of nowhere was about half way between Creel and Chihuahua. It was noisy with traffic, mostly truckers with their eighteen-wheelers, and pick-up trucks, their drivers stopping for fuel, a quick meal or a pit stop.

Taking Gabriel's hand and squeezing it tight, Rogelio headed for the men's bathroom on the side of the building. Several tired looking drivers were waiting in line.

"Anyone in there?" Rogelio asked.

"Why do you think we are here?" A fat man, smelling of diesel fuel answered. "Get in line." He signaled behind him.

"I give you a hundred pesos if you let the boy in first." Rogelio showed him the bill. "He needs to go real fast."

"I too, need to go, *hijo de la chingada!*"

Rogelio had no choice but to wait in line with the boy.

It was Gabriel's turn. Rogelio pushed him forwards, "don't take too long *mocoso.*"

Gabriel went in and locked the door. The stench of the place was hideous. He pinched his nose and went to the toilet, it made him gag, but he stayed and closed the door. He peed and pressed the buttons on the BB.

"Virg-"

"Dad, I'm in a gas station bathroom. We are on route sixteen. Three men took us. One of them is waiting for me outside."

"Gaby, wait, wait. Are you and mami okay? Have they hurt you?"

"No, Dad, come for us, I have to hang up." Pressing the cellphone red button and stuffing it in his back pocket, he walked out.

Sighing with relief, but still not sure of what to do, Alejandro pushed the gas pedal and headed out. *At least I know where they are...more or less.* He looked at the rear view mirror, a fairly new car crossed the street behind him. *That looks like one of the government vehicles. I wonder where they're going.* The automobile was headed in the general direction of the motel.

His mind kept going from one thought to another while driving. He asked himself why the drug traffickers were after them? Were they looking to extract ransom money from him? But, they wouldn't be going after money if what they wanted to do were to kill him and his family. And how or why had they chosen him? He shook his head.

****

"About time. Let's go." Rogelio grabbed his neck and pushed him ahead of him.

Four disheveled truck drivers waiting in line paid no attention to the strange picture of the *freso* child and the truculent looking man.

Rogelio brought Gabriel back to the van and spoke with the driver.

"Don't let him out of your sight. I'm going to pee."

On the other side of the building, holding Virginia by the arm, Arturo approached a second bathroom with a faded sign that said *mujeres.* Virginia tried opening the door but it was locked. She looked at him.

"Hay alguien ahi?" He knocked on the door but there was no answer.

"The key must be inside." She said.

"Come." On their way to the cafeteria entrance they encountered several men who ogled Virginia. One of them gave her a vulgar compliment. *"Que chichis tienes mamacita! Hey, guey*, where did you find her? Do you have any more like her?" He laughed out loud. Virginia wrapped her arms across her chest.

A man came out of the restaurant and looked at her. *"Te la compro berraco.* How much do you want for her?" He laughed in a lascivious manner.

The women's bathroom door opened and Virginia went in. Once inside, she locked the door. Her mind was a whirlwind of thoughts. Could she escape with Gaby? Who could she tell? The men were watching every move she made. She agonized over their situation. How could she let Alejandro know where they were? In a flash, an idea occurred to her. She emptied her bladder, cleaned herself and then pulled out a lipstick she had in her jacket. Her abductors had patted her down, felt it, took it out, seen it and ignored it. Careful not to break the toilet paper, she wrote down that they had been kidnapped, scribbled the van's make, the license plate number, date and time. She rolled back the toilet paper, and came out.

"Don't lock it, let me take a look. Remember, you do anything I don't like and you can say *adios* to your son." Arturo held her by the arm and peeked inside.

There was a broken mirror above the washbasin and next to it an enclosed toilet closet.

Trembling with fear, she followed him, holding her breath.

"You afraid I'm going to fuck you here, *mamacita*? There will be plenty of time to do that later, don't worry." He smiled, showing a row of rotten teeth.

Arturo looked around the enclosed quarters, inspected the handwritten messages on the walls, went into the small toilet, closed the door half way and checked the writing behind it.

Satisfied, he pushed her out.

Exhaling quietly, the painful feeling at the pit of her stomach slowly went away.

On the way back, three truck-drivers walking back to their eighteen-wheelers whistled at her, one made an off-color joke, and another one made a lewd suggestion. Arturo ignored them and reached the van.

"How about we get some booze for the rest of the trip?" Rogelio said.

"Here." Arturo gave him a handful of pesos while pushing Virginia inside. "*Entra guerita.*"

Gabriel watched his mother come in.

"You okay, my love? I know Daddy is going to come back for us like he did for me before."

"Shut up, carajo." Arturo said in a harsh tone.

"Are you going to give us some water? Something to eat?" She asked. "If not for me, at least for my son, he's just a child. Don't you have any children?"

"Aah, mierda, guey, get some water for these two." Arturo yelled at his companion.

"I'm going to get food too." The man looked back and went in.

"Whatever, but hurry up. I don't think he heard me." Arturo shrugged his shoulders.

FIFTY

"What do you mean he's not there?" Raul asked, his cellphone glued to his ear.

"Who's not there?" Howard raised his eyebrows.

"Did he check out?" Raul raised his hand to keep Howard from interrupting him.

"Did that conniving Colombian leave?" Howard roared and banged on the hospital portable lunch table.

The doctor checking Domingo and Jacinto's vitals jumped. He stared at the angry man and ordered him to shush.

"Go to the train station, check the car rental agency, have one of the cars hit the road." Raul ordered his people. "He had a *Jeep,* look for it, he can't be too far." Raul looked at Howard. "Let's look for him too. We can come back later, you may be right, *ese cabron tiene algo con los narcos.*"

"I told you from the beginning. He is in deep. We put him in jail...no, actually, why don't we take him across the border? *Los Caballeros del Norte* have too many connections around here. Throw him in a cell here and those motherfuckers will come looking for him."

"I...you might be right." Raul wiped his face.

"He won't be able to get help in the States. *Hijo de la chingada.*" Howard scowled.

After checking on Jacinto, the doctor moved to Domingo. "Can you keep it down, please?"

"So? Are they getting any better? I thought you were a doctor." Howard said.

The doctor ignored the sarcasm. "Still critical…in a day or two, if their condition improves they can be airlifted to the regional hospital but at the moment they are in a coma and unresponsive."

****

Alejandro sat in the car near the other end of the street. Through his binoculars, he saw the two men exit the clinic and leave in a big *Ford Galaxy. I have to go in now, this may be my only chance to ask Jacinto.* He left the car and walked to the clinic holding his head down. *I hope I have enough time to talk to him before they come back.*

The soldier standing watch at the entrance saw him, smiled and let him in. No one had bothered to tell him they were looking for Alejandro.

He walked down the hall, turned the corner and headed for the injured men's room. Before going into the room he looked around and went in.

Coming down the hall, the doctor saw Alejandro. "Wait, stop right there!"

FIFTY-ONE

On the side of the road, Captain Karina Martinez stretched her arms and massaged her neck. She looked at her watch. "Two more hours?" And walked over to the passenger seat, letting Sebastian take over.

"I'm tired, why couldn't we fly? This is a long drive and some of those curves are...I mean, I like the landscape and the views are awesome but..." Sebastian came from behind some bushes, pulling up his zipper.

"No budget for it." She stared at the lone winding highway. Pines and other large leafy trees ran along the sides of the road. Ever since they had left the main road, there had hardly been any cars on the road. It was true; the seemingly endless panorama of hills and surrounding ranches, the bountiful coffee plantations, and cattle grazing on the verdant pastures on the skirts of the hillsides, gave them plenty of delightful eye-candy views. But they had been on the road close to five hours and were worn-out. "We'll spend the night in Santa Fe."

"Yes boss, I don't think I would want to drive back home on those roads in the middle of the night." Sebastian's stomach made a rumbling sound. "You think they'll give us lunch?"

The petite woman with the long eyelashes and black hair shrugged her shoulders. "Only one way to find out. Let's go. I'm tired of eating chips and *chicharrones.*"

****

Sitting under the stone arch with the wrought iron letters spelling LOS CIELOS, the cowboy heard the whine of a car stopping at the entrance. A heavy chain kept the gate closed.

"What do you want?" He stood at the edge of the arch, holding a carbine.

Karina and Sebastian bounced out of the car. "Good afternoon, we are police...from Medellin and need to speak to los Señores Calwel guests. Here's my detective badge." She moved closer, holding the black leather ID.

"They know you are coming?" He eyed them suspiciously.

"Yes, we called ahead." Sebastian said.

Snapping a two-way radio off his belt, he pressed the send button. Static noise broke the silence and seconds later a voice came on. After confirming that they were expected, the guard took out a big key and proceeded to unlock the gate. "Did you have a safe drive?" He asked.

"It's long." Karina looked at the uphill road that disappeared a few hundred feet ahead behind a curve. "How far up the road?" Her lips pointed to the road ahead.

"Half an hour, more or less." He said.

Sebastian sighed loudly. "Are you kidding?"

The man smiled and moved out of the way.

****

The more than a century old estate suddenly appeared in front of their eyes when they drove around a large promontory. The stately mansion took their breath away. The two-story house with tall white columns, faded bricks partially covered with climbing ivy, large French door windows, and towering chimneys at each end of the building, was a feast for the eye. A sizeable expanse of cropped green grass welcomed them.

"I told you, the guys that were here looking for his wife said it was like something out of a movie." Sebastian remained awestruck, his foot on the brake.

"Sebastian, move. I thought you were hungry and I need to go to a bathroom soon or I'll be making a spectacle of myself." Karina too, was enthralled, but her practical side, always won over her enjoyment of beautiful things.

Driving slowly, afraid the majestic villa was only a figment of his imagination, Sebastian stopped and turned off the car at the end of a long driveway. A wide porch and a broad polished wooden door invited the visitors to the quiet and majestic hacienda.

An attractive, well-dressed woman in her mid-fifties opened the door before they exited the car. "Good afternoon, come in please. I'm Teresa. I believe we spoke before, but you must be hungry and thirsty." She gestured with her arm, welcoming them in. "Are you Captain Martinez?"

"Yes, but please call me Karina, and this young man is my assistant, Sebastian." She shook hands with Teresa. The young detective followed on his boss' action and shook hands too.

They entered a large foyer, and Teresa led them through a highly polished mahogany hard wood floor. A magnificent black marble horseshoe stairway faced them, but Teresa made a right turn and they came upon a small dining room.

"We prepared some dishes and refreshments." She pointed to a sideboard with several pitchers and crystal water glasses. "Would you like to freshen up before we start?"

"Don't mind if I do." Karina said.

"If you follow that hall, it will be the first door to the left."

Karina hurried up through the path indicated by Teresa.

A young couple came into the room; accompanying them were two youngsters, one of them sat in a wheelchair.

"Detective...? I don't believe I know your last name." Teresa smiled at him.

"Sebastian Tomasseti at your service ma'am." He said.

"Let me introduce you. This lovely couple, Gianni and Zuri are long-time friends of el Señor y la Señora Calwel."

Gianni limped slightly when he walked forward to shake the detective's hand. Sebastian observed that he was slightly taller and it was obvious he worked in the field. His skin, bronze from being in the outdoors and his corpulence left no doubt. The young woman light chocolate skin color, well-defined curves and fine oval face with large almond eyes greeted him with a beautiful smile.

"That handsome young man is Andres, and Nicolas is my son." Teresa took her son's hand. "Gianni is el Señor Calwel's right hand man and is the caretaker. Zuri takes care of Gaby but as I mentioned over the phone, they are away on vacation. Andres works with Gianni. My son is a novice painter. El Señor Alejandro thinks he's very talented and is encouraging Nicolas to continue developing his artistic skills.

"What did I miss?" Karina asked the small group gathered at the entrance to the dining room.

"Teresa was just introducing me." Sebastian repeated everyone's name for her benefit.

When Karina finished acknowledging everyone, Sebastian excused himself and left down the hall.

When he returned, Teresa addressed them. "Shall we start? I'm sure you are both hungry." Teresa offered a chair to Karina and withdrew a second one for Sebastian.

"I'm starving." Sebastian waited until the women sat down.

"You're not supposed to say that. Where are your manners? Were you born in a stable?" But Karina's tone and wide smile implied that she was joking.

She had taken a liking to them immediately, noting that seldom she would feel that way about anyone she had just met.

The conviviality of these people was so evident, that she couldn't wait to find out how they had all come to be friends of the Calwel's. *I better restraint myself and go back to my usual guarded character.*

A short time after lunch was over, a maid came in and brought homemade flan and coffee. Karina decided it was time to broach the subject of their visit. "So, how did you all come to live here? I visited Mr. Draco's widow and in talking with some of her employees, found out that at one time or another you all worked for her husband?"

Before anyone could answer, Teresa took over as the spokesperson for the group. She went ahead and explained how she had ended up coming to work for el Señor Draco.

"And who can tell me about la Señora Calwel resuscitation?" Karina smirked.

Gianni explained that Alejandro had met with the people who had kidnapped her and had secured her freedom. But he didn't know the details.

"Excuse me...when is el Señor Calwel coming back?" Karina interrupted.

"...Ahh, I'm not sure, they are in Mexico visiting her parents." Gianni said.

"I guess we'll have to wait to meet el Señor Calwel. You will let him know we want to talk with him?"

"Of course." Teresa poured coffee around the table.

"Oh, Teresa? Who was the mystery man who helped you all escape?" Karina fixed her large black eyes on Teresa.

"Help us?" Teresa raised her eyebrows.

"Well, according to one of the people we spoke with, they saw you running from another house, I guess the guesthouse? And then, you are all getting out, or should I say escape, right? And to make this whole saga more interesting, you board a private plane with Mrs. Calwel on it? And shortly after Mr. Draco and his bodyguards are slayed right outside the airport building? My goodness, what a set of coincidences."

A smile appeared in Teresa's face. "Captain, I don't know what you're talking about. I can't tell you anything else. You'll have to wait for Alejandro to get back. I think those are fabrications from people with a very vivid imagination."

Sebastian snickered.

"Really?" Karina exhaled, an incredulous expression in her face. "Are you going to deny you were in that airplane?" She gave Teresa a skeptical look

"No, but it's not the way you are telling it. True, we boarded the flight but that was because I...we knew Virginia. She invited us to visit her here and stay with her. And we're very grateful for her courtesy. That's all." She smiled and busied herself with the flan.

"But you're not going back to work for la Señora Draco, are you?"

"Actually, Virginia and Alejandro offered us jobs. You know what happened here. So we decided to stay. Nothing wrong with that, is there?" She served Karina a piece of dessert.

"If you say so." Karina knew the gracious woman was lying but what else could they do. And besides, had she been in the woman's shoes she would have done the same thing. She didn't think too many people liked working for Mr. or Mrs. Draco. "Sebastian? Are you ready for the trip back?"

"Whenever you say boss." Sebastian finished his dessert and asked if he could have another piece.

FIFTY-TWO

At the shout to stop, Alejandro froze. The doctor hurried to him. "Where are you going?"

"I have to talk to Jacinto. Please, you must let me see him. My family is in danger." Alejandro pleaded.

"Come with me, hurry. The American wants you in jail. We must rush."

"I haven't done anything."

"I won't tell him I saw you." The doctor smiled.

The two men entered the room where the injured patients lay sleeping. Alejandro went to Jacinto's bedside and glanced at the doctor. "Can I wake him up?"

He nodded. "I'll stand watch by the door. I'll let you know if they're coming back."

"Jacinto, can you hear me?" With some hesitance, he took the injured man's hand.

Slowly, the eyelids of the bed-ridden man opened and his eyes gazed at Alejandro.

"My family was kidnapped about an hour ago. Howard is accusing me of being involved with the cartel. Can I trust him? I have the package."

"No." He replied in a weak hoarse voice. I'm not even sure about Raul," he continued, "Pancho mistrusted Howard. Do not share the files with them...your family, tell me..."

In an anxious tone, Alejandro told him, finishing with the call from his son.

"I wish I could go with you." Jacinto's voice was weak. "I don't trust anyone right now. You are going to have to find someone outside the police to help you."

"I heard them saying they were taking my wife and son to Chihuahua."

"Chihuahua?" Jacinto grimaced.

"I think so." Alejandro glanced back at the doctor, who was standing by the doorway. "I don't have much time. If Howard finds me, I'm going to jail and I won't be able to help my wife and son."

"There's a warehouse on the outskirts of town where they congregate. Write this down."

He watched Alejandro jot it down. "If they are not there," Jacinto paused and inhaled, "they may have taken them to Vicente's house in Culiacan...you'll never get in." He rested for a couple of seconds. The talk was taxing his meager energy.

"I'm not going to lose them again."

A faint smile passed through Jacinto's lips. "I don't doubt you're...the place is heavily guarded." He took several gulps of air and closed his eyes.

They were interrupted by the doctor's urgent plea. "Señor Calwel, you better hurry, they could be back any minute."

Jacinto grabbed Alejandro's hand. "Save your family...get those bastards." A renewed strength in his voice. "They killed my friend." His breath became more labored and he slipped away again.

****

"The man at the rental car agency lied to us. I bet you that Jeep being washed was the one Calwel was driving. He wouldn't tell us anything. Is everyone in the cartel's pocket here?" Howard sneered. "Let's go back to the clinic. Maybe Jacinto or Domingo are finally out of their coma and can talk to us."

With Raul at the wheel, they headed back.

"I can't wait until I get my hands on that lying, drug smuggling sonofabitch." The car picked up speed and turned on the street that led straight to the clinic. They passed a fairly new car parked about a block away from the clinic. Howard took a look at the car as they drove by. "A nice looking car...clean, most cars around here aren't that new...or clean."

Raul steered the car into the front of the clinic.

Howard jumped out of the car, wanting to run into the clinic. "Let's go, we can't waste any time. I want to get that double-dealer before he runs away."

"But we don't even know where he is." Raul hurried up and caught up with his partner.

Howard's cellphone buzzed again. He looked at it and flipped it open. "I'll call you." He shut the phone off.

Entering the foyer, they saw a soldier standing guard.

He was going to speak to them but Howard didn't let him, "not now," and continued at a fast clip with Raul trying to keep pace with him.

The curtains were closed, making the room dark and glum. The whirring of the machines and the labored breathing of the patients broke the dreary silence.

FIFTY-THREE

"**W**here is the goddam Doctor? The nuns? I need to talk to somebody. Shit." Howard's short temper was flaring up again.

"Quiet down Howe, there's no need to shout." Raul checked on Domingo and then slid the curtains a quarter of the way to let some sun light in. Both patients lay peacefully in their beds, fluids dripping into their veins in a slow monotonous cadence.

"I can't understand how you can take everything so calmly. We need to take action fast or we'll lose our only connection to the cartel." Howard pushed back his gray-black hair.

"We have no proof Howard. He maybe a suspect but to incarcerate him we need something."

"Oh? Fuck it man. How often have we dumped some asshole in jail on trumped up charges?" Howard was fuming. He could barely control his anger. What he really wanted to do was to trash the room. "When are these two malingerers going to wake up?

"Shhh." A nun came into the room and gave both men an irate stare. "What do you want? Neither of these men is in any shape to be disturbed. Please leave the room." She crossed her arms over her white tunic. Her pale face denoting an inflexible position.

Raul walked out first.

Howard followed behind. He muttered, "Sorry," which was almost unintelligible.

"So what do we do now? The only lead we have is that his wife and son left town in a gray Honda van...if we believe the words of a homeless drunkard."

Coming through the corner was the doctor. He seemed somewhat out of breath. "You're back?"

"Doc, when can we wake them up?" Howard signaled towards the room behind them with his thump.

"Maybe another twenty four hours? I'm counting on them being steady enough to be transported to Chihuahua."

A cellphone vibrated. "Raul here." He put his hand over the speaker. "It's the coroner. He says the bullets extracted from the dead gangsters do not match Pancho's."

"In other words, different guns were used to kill them?"

"He says his findings are preliminary." Raul paused and turned his attention back to the phone. "Yes, I understand...of course...you need a ballistics expert to confirm."

Howard interrupted. "How soon can I have the bullets?"

Raising his hand, Raul continued talking to the man on the phone. "Fine, thank you, because Pancho's wounds came from different caliber guns?" Raul nodded to Howard, acknowledging what the DEA man had already stated and then focused his interest on what the man on the phone was telling him. "Well, one of the doctors is here. I'm not sure but I think he may have been involved in assisting our men. Hold on." He eyed the doctor and handed over the cellphone.

"*Si? Entiendo. No, de acuerdo.*" The Doctor hung up. "The bullets extracted from Jacinto's wounds maybe a match with the ones that killed Pancho-"

"I don't need to be a freaking scientist to figure that out." Howard grumbled. "I want the fucking evidence."

"But the other men's fatal shots came from small caliber guns." The doctor handed Raul his phone back.

"There's just one slight problem. We don't have the guns to perform the tests. And until we talk to Jacinto we won't know what guns he and Pancho carried," Raul said, "assuming it was their guns."

"Except that we know Calwel was responsible for the killings. I bet you he did that to silence them." Howard grouched.

"But why would he let one of the assassins live?" The Doctor asked.

"Cuauhtémoc was the gang leader and Calwel killed him to cover his involvement. The wounded man? He probably didn't know Calwel." Howard scrunched his shoulders.

Jacinto heard the conversation. A faint smile crossed his lips. *I did the right thing.* He went back to sleep.

"If I were you? And I know I'm not, I would send an APB right now to find and apprehend Alejandro Calwel." Howard's cellphone dissonant tone jarred the relative quiet outside the room. "Wait." He lifted his palm to both Raul and the Doctor and walked away a few steps. "I told you I would call the moment I had something tangible." He scowled in silence listening to the other side of the conversation. "No, we don't have Calwel yet." He wanted to say something but was interrupted. "Yes, yes, I will call you the moment we capture him." One short pause. "Make sure alive? *Aja*, right." Howard hung up. "So? What are we waiting for? Let's find that mother..." A nun appeared out of an adjacent room.

Howard bit his lip to stop himself from saying a profanity in front of the religious woman. "Let's go Raul, *vamonos, vamonos!*"

"Doc, the moment Jacinto wakes up, call me." Raul handed the doctor a business card.

"Will do. This number?" He glimpsed at the card.

"Yes."

He watched both men leave and let out a sigh of relief.

On their way out, Raul remembered that the young soldier wanted to speak to them. "You wanted to talk to us?"

"Nah, I guess you saw him already."

"Who?" Howard stopped abruptly.

"You know...el Señor that stopped the killings."

"Where did you see him? When? Talk man." Howard, almost foaming at the mouth, towered over the soldier.

Nervous and stuttering from the unexpected and harsh questioning, the soldier told them that Calwel had been in the clinic a few minutes before they arrived.

"Sonfabitch." Howard looked like he was going to burst an artery. "And those cocksuckers didn't tell us." His face was angry red. "Did you see his car?" He yelled.

The head nun appeared, admonished him and asked him to quiet down. Howard ignored her. "Well? Did you see in what car he came in? Come on man, answer." Spittle left his lips.

"Noo, no, no. He...he walked in."

"Raul, that new Tahoe at the end of the block. Let's run over there."

When they gazed down the street, the car was gone.

"Send the APB, tell everyone; we're looking for a Tahoe. Let's go, maybe we can still catch up with him." He started running towards their car, Raul jogging along with him.

FIFTY-FOUR

"**Y**ou were right, I think I'll take the car you suggested before, more pep." Alejandro gave the keys back to the manager along with several thousand pesos. "Thank you for not telling them."

"I didn't like him anyway. I would have done it for nothing." He exchanged keys with Alejandro. *"Y vaya con Dios."*

"Thank you." Alejandro drove off, racing down the highway. He kept trying to think of ways to rescue his wife and son. But he understood that unless he knew where they were, any plan would be useless. The speed needle held at a steady one hundred and forty kilometers. He wanted to go faster, but was afraid of being stopped for speeding. The highway signs read one hundred and twenty and he felt that those few extra kilometers would not be worth the time of a highway patrol.

Traffic had dwindled on the undulating highway. The landscape had changed from scenic drive to a boring freeway. Occasionally, he would pass a road stand with Indians selling artifacts, or food. More than once, he drove by a lone individual on the side of the road hoping to catch a ride.

Glancing at his watch and then at the gas gauge, he estimated he'd been on the road close to two and half hours. A roadside sign advertised an upcoming gas station-restaurant coming up.

Alejandro wondered if this was the same place from where Gabriel had called. His heart started beating faster. He slowed down and pulled to the side to enter the adjacent road. A few eighteen-wheelers were parked on a dirt wide-open space with no clear signs.

A one story, no longer white but dirty gray building announcing a cafeteria waited in front of him. He slid into a gas pump, got out and waited for an attendant to come over.

A rather short man, with black hair plastered to his scalp and wearing dirty mechanic overalls that were two sizes larger, approached him. *"Cuanto jefe?"*

Alejandro told him to fill it up and on the spur of the moment asked the little man if by chance he had seen a *guera* and a *frezo* a while back.

"A lot of people like that stop here."

Laughing lightly, Alejandro agreed with the man and continued engaging the gas-station attendant in casual banter.

He then asked the man if he had been working all day and if there were others helping him.

"Yeah, I start in the morning and leave at seven."

"Long day. And you are here all by yourself? How do you do it?"

The diminutive man shrugged his shoulders. "But you know, now that I think about it. Yeah, there were some *cuates* with a *mamacita* y un *chaparrito.* To me they didn't belong together. Why you want to know?"

Taking out several extra hundred pesos, Alejandro casually asked him if he remembered what they looked like.

The man looked at the bills.

Alejandro added a few more one hundred-pesos.

"She was tall, *bien linda."* He made emphasis on the linda. The kid? I think he was kind of guero. It may have been a Honda, a van for sure."

"Do you see people like that all day long?"

"No, she looked like a *turista,* her clothes and the men's didn't match."

"What do you mean?"

"What she wore, it looked expensive. I can tell. I see a lot of people. And besides those that come in cars are mostly from around here, and they don't dress like her, not on weekdays anyway."

Peeling another several hundred pesos, Alejandro stuffed them in his pocket and smiled. "Oh, one more thing. When did you say they were here?"

"About lunch time, I remember, it was almost one o'clock."

The screams made them turn around. A frumpy middle age woman was running out of the ladies room. She held a long piece of toilet paper in her hands.

Rushing towards the woman, Alejandro asked her what was wrong, he glanced at the flimsy piece of tissue thinking it was smeared blood. "Are you hurt?"

The gas station attendant followed a few steps behind.

Several truckers glanced at the near hysterical woman.

A husky man walked out of the men's facilities and hurriedly approached them.

"Here, here, read this, *ay Virgencita de Guadalupe, Dios mio."* She made the sign of the cross.

"Let me see." Alejandro took the toilet paper from the woman's hand.

The woman's husband reached them. *"Que pasa Pilar?"*

Alejandro felt an ice-cold fear on his gut, a volt of current shaking him from head to toe. It was Virginia's handwriting.

Secuestrada con mi hijo de seis años

Honda van gris tres hombres Auxilio

The note ended with a license plate and the time. He checked his watch. *I'm never going to catch with them on time. They are more than forty minutes ahead of me, even if I go faster, I doubt I can...damn, I wish Jacinto could have given me someone else to confide with.*

"Should we call the police?" The woman asked. Her hair in disarray, half her blouse un-tucked.

"Nah, it's probably some teenager's prank." Her husband patted her back, trying to calm her down.

"But what if it's true?"

"Don't worry. I have friends in the police. I'll get going and make a call from my cell." Alejandro looked at the woman and her husband. "You are both okay?"

"*Si, si,* we need to get going, let's go Pilar." The man pushed his wife forward.

"*Pero,* Luis, what if it's true?"

"You heard him, he's going to take care of it. Let's go, woman." He grabbed her arm and stepped away.

"I'll call right now." Alejandro opened his cellphone and pretended to be making a call while walking to his car. Waving good-bye, he got back in the Yukon and drove away.

They are about an hour ahead of me. If I drive faster I may have a slight chance. Please God help me.

FIFTY-FIVE

God must have heard Alejandro because the van had a rear tire blowout. The driver was able to slow down and stop without getting involved in an accident.

"*Carajo*, why now?" Arturo opened his door and came out.

The driver came around. "We have to let them out to change the tire." He signaled to the woman and the boy.

Pointing at them, Arturo signaled. "Get out and sit there." He pointed to the side of the road. "*Guey*, you keep the *mocoso* right with you. She does anything and you know what to do."

Twenty minutes later, the flat tire was dumped on the back of the van. "We're going to have to stop at the next gas station. Another flat tire and we have to walk." Rogelio glanced to his side and sped out of the curb onto the highway.

"Yeah, if they don't sell tires, we'll have to get off the road and find a place that sells them. *Mierda.*" Arturo scratched his nose.

"I need to go to the bathroom." Virginia said.

"We'll see." Arturo said.

"There, Rogelio interrupted Arturo, "a sign for the next station." He checked the console. They had driven about one hundred or so kilometers. "Are we going to stop there?" He glanced at his companion but veered of the highway and took the exit road.

"Might as well, gas up and let's find out if they sell tires."

"Can I go to the bathroom, too?" Virginia asked.

"Shut up. What's with you? You already went once before." Arturo was annoyed, the unexpected delay had not been in his plans. He had wanted to reach Chihuahua sooner.

Rogelio slowed down and stopped by one of the pump islands.

"Find the mechanic," Arturo gestured at Ramon, "take the *frezo* to the bathroom and I'll take her." He glared at the woman. "This is the last stop, so you two better do it now because I'm not stopping anymore."

Ramon forced the child out of the van, holding on to his arm.

"Do you have to be so rough? He's only a child." Virginia protested, fury in her eyes.

"Shut up or I'll do worse with you." Arturo said. He grabbed her pulled her out of the car. "There's the women's room. Don't take long."

Virginia quickly stepped into the small room.

Waiting outside the ladies room, Arturo was becoming impatient. He wanted to get going, they had already lost too much time. His biggest worry was a police patrol.

He didn't want to arouse any suspicions. He knew that if things got out of hand, he would not hesitate at killing a policeman. The door opened and Virginia came out. "About time. What took you so fucking long?"

An older lady wanted to go in but he stood in her way. "Wait." Pulling Virginia inside, he inspected the small room like he had done before. Satisfied that she hadn't tried anything, he pushed her out.

Virginia tried to get the woman's attention by giving her an imploring look, but the woman avoided looking at her and went around them.

"Do you have to be so...?" She bit her lip and shut up. There was no point complaining.

She had left another message inside the toilet paper roll.

Arturo's companions were waiting by the van. "I'm going to call Vicente, tell him we are on our way." He took out his cellphone and punched in the numbers. He heard his boss's voice. "Vic, we are two thirds of the way there. What do you want us to do?"

"It's raining here. Take them to the usual place and wait for me."

"*Si jefe.*" Arturo hung up.

Inside the van, staring out the window Gabriel kept watching for his mother to come back. The loud racket caused by the engine of a large rig starting up, startled him, making him jump in his seat. He watched the truck pull out slowly.

FIFTY-SIX

The road sign indicated there was a gas stop down the road. Alejandro wondered if he should go in, he didn't need any gas and time was running. A stop would only make him waste more valuable minutes, minutes that he didn't have. *I'm not going to stop, there's no time.* He accelerated, the speedometer needle moved up, hovering around one hundred and seventy kilometers an hour.

Five minutes later he drove by the gas station. The driver of a long rig with a piggyback container attached was pumping diesel fuel on the truck's tanks. It hid the gray van from the highway. The urge to go back and stop at the gas station gnawed at him. He tried to reason with himself that going back was irrational and a waste of time. Inexorably, as if the car had a mind of its own, he slowed down, moved to the curb and waited for several cars and a large truck pass by. The car tires screeched and he was making a U-turn, going back.

The car picked up speed and within a few minutes he was crossing the traffic lanes and entering the station.

From a distance he saw Virginia come out of a women's rest room but almost immediately a man dragged her back into the room. He nearly drove to where they had disappeared, but a car was in his way and when it finally moved out of the way, she was out. A man held her arm.

He spotted a gray van by one of the pumping stations and two men stood outside. *Where is Gaby?* His heart was galloping. He imagined a thousand and one scenarios.

Was Gaby someplace else? That would make his mission much harder. Had they left him alone somewhere on the road? But wouldn't he have seen him? Could they have killed him, but what would that have accomplished? And besides, Virginia seemed fairly composed. He made a quick decision and took the spot a car vacated.

The rig impeded his view, which made him increasingly edgy. But at least now he knew where they were and he would be able to follow them. *Can I take them now?* He checked the floorboard and patted one of the guns.

"*Si Señor?*" The gas station attendant asked.

"*Llene el tanque, por favor.*"

The man nodded and asked him which type he wanted.

Alejandro indicated premium and remained partially hidden behind the pump.

The rig's driver jumped into the cab and the engine's roar immediately silenced any other noises. The cab shook and then the loud hissing sound of air brakes followed. In slow motion, the giant rig broke away from its mooring, giving him a clear view of the sitting van.

****

The van's rear door slid open and Virginia went in. Gabriel kept looking at the truck that had left the next island.

"Did you go to the bathroom?" She asked, but Gabriel didn't look back, just nodded. "Are you okay sweetheart?"

"Quiet." Arturo barked.

Standing behind the driver's seat, Gabriel ignored her or him.

Feeling Gabriel's tension, Virginia realized he wasn't paying any notice to her. Instead, his attention seemed to be focused somewhere else.

She put an arm around him and was startled when her hand fell on his chest. His heart was racing at full gallop. Gabriel was tense, stiff. Stupefied, Virginia sought what was holding her son's rapt attention. But Arturo's gruff voice startled her and made her turn around.

"This is the last stop. No more waste of time. If you need to pee again, you have to wait. There is a hole on the ground in the warehouse to take care of your needs when we get there." He laughed. "Ramon, Rog, if you need to go, do it now. I want to haul ass the rest of the way."

Both men nodded.

"Guey, I'm going to buy some beers, and cigarettes." Rogelio said

"Do it but move it. We got to get rid of these two soon." Arturo said.

Ignoring Arturo, Virginia went back to search for whatever it was that had her son enthralled. Across from the pump island the rig had just vacated, a SUV came into view. A tall man was watching the gray van while seemingly pumping gas.

She got a fleeting glance and almost gasped. A shiver ran over her body. Now her heart was beating fast too. She took Gabriel's hand and squeezed it gently.

Gabriel turned and looked at her. They both knew.

FIFTY-SEVEN

"There, there, stop there. I want to tell the highway patrolman what happened." The woman who had brought out the toilet paper note, begged her husband.

"I already told you Pilar, that was a teenager's prank. Do you think the police is going to pay any attention to you? *Estas loca.*"

"I'm not crazy, stop, Cuco, stop, please."

Slowing down, the husband brought the car to a full stop near the police vehicle sitting in the median. The police officer got out, his hand on the holster.

"Officer, I'm sorry to bother you but my wife is having a mental breakdown." Luis opened his door.

Pilar, came out in a rush. "I told him, I'm not cuckoo. Let me tell you what happened." She related the incident.

"When was this?"

"Not even twenty minutes...maybe less. He was driving a new car. I wrote down the license plate." She handed him over a piece of paper with the letters and numbers from a State of Chihuahua plate.

"What did he look like?" The officer took the piece of paper and peered at it.

"He was tall, almost looked like a gringo but he spoke in Spanish, but not from around here."

"You mean an American accent?"

"No, no, like he...is not Mexican, more like from another country. He said he was going to call the police and tell them. Did he?" Pilar was getting agitated.

"I'm calling headquarters. Wait." The broad-shouldered policeman entered his car, picked up the mike and called. He related the story and asked if anyone had called reporting the situation.

"No but there's an APB regarding someone...let me patch you through. Stay on the line." The dispatcher looked for a phone number and made the connection. "Ahhh, I have the highway patrol on the line. Go ahead Morales."

The officer introduced himself and told Raul what had occurred.

"Go after that SUV and put the driver in a holding cell until we get there."

"If I catch up with him..."

"Why do you say that? Do you think we won't be able to apprehend him? We'll alert all the patrols."

"It depends on the speed. If he gets to Chihuahua, it will be a problem."

"Go. I'll inform the Chihuahua City police."

"Will do." He hung up the mike. *"Señora gracias por avisarnos."*

The highway patrol officer turned on the police lights and the car sped out of the median, leaving the husband and wife in a cloud of dust. In less than thirty seconds, all one could see was a speck on the horizon.

Choking and moving her arms to dispel the dirt cloud the woman watched. "See? I was right. The police thanked me and they are looking for that man. We should have kept the note. I shouldn't listen to you."

"Yes, Pilar, you're right, as usual." He exhaled in defeat. "Let's go." He strode towards their car. His wife kept chastising him for not standing his ground and believing in her.

FIFTY-EIGHT

S eeing two men leave the van, Alejandro grabbed one of the guns from underneath the car seat and crossed the pumps island, sidestepping two cars and a pick-up and ended about five feet from the front of the van. Trying not to look too conspicuous, he gazed to his right.

A man seemed to be standing by the passenger door, waiting and playing with his cell phone. Alejandro tried to look inside but he could barely discern Virginia. He thought Gaby was next to her in the rear seat. He slowed down his walk and watched one of the two men head straight for the concession area and disappear inside. His companion turned right, going to the men's room and entered it when a man opened the door and stepped out.

Virginia muffled a cry of joy. She held Gabriel tightly. *What should I do, how can I help him? He knows we're here. Oh my God, please help us.* She knocked on the side window, making Arturo look at her.

"What now?" He said. "I told you, no more *favores.*"

Satisfied, Alejandro switched his focus on the felon standing guard. The man seemed to be focusing his attention on the inside of the Honda. Without missing a step, he quickly covered the distance.

From the corner of his eye Arturo saw a man approaching. He started turning but then noticed the gun in the tall estranger's hand.

"Open the door. Now." The voice sounded menacing.

Arturo did as told.

"Get in and move to the driver's side." Alejandro roughly pushed the man inside, making him stumble. He nearly hit his head with the steering wheel.

Smiling at Virginia he handed over the keys to the big SUV. "Here's the key to my car. Take Gaby with you and follow me," he winked at them, "hurry, his companions may be here any minute now."

Arturo couldn't understand what they were saying. He didn't speak much English and the man spoke very fast, but the meaning was clear. The man had a relationship with the *gringa* and the *freso*. He tried to think of a way out but the man holding the gun to his side was much taller and muscular. He didn't think he had too much of a choice at the moment but to follow the man's instructions. "My friends are coming, you can't shoot me here."

"You want to try me?" Alejandro smiled.

Arturo tried to think of something else to say. *"El Chapo-"*

"El Chapo? He is my friend. Start the car, get going. And fast. " He pushed the gun's barrel into the man's right ear, making him wince in pain.

The engine started and the van left with a jolt.

Rogelio, leaving the small store with a six-pack of *Dos Equis* and a pack of cigarettes, watched the van leaving. He stood outside confused.

Ramon stepped out of the men's room and went to meet Rogelio. "What did you buy? Did you get any tequila?" His head moved seeking the van but instead saw the rear of the van entering the highway. A SUV followed closed behind.

They started yelling but it was too late. The Honda was gone and they were stranded in the hot sun.

"What the hell happened?" Ramon said.

"I...I think Arturo took off."

They both looked at each other in total confusion.

"What do we do now?" Rogelio, the younger of the two, held the bag with the beers in his hands.

"Call Arturo?" Ramon pulled out his cellphone and punched the numbers.

Jumping at the sound of his cell phone, Arturo gazed in fear at the big stranger sitting next to him.

"Take it out, I'm going to put it on speaker mode. You say anything I don't like, I'll whip you with the gun. Take off the seatbelt in case I want to throw you out of the van. Move it *pendejo*."

With his eyes as big as saucers, Arturo fumbled with the seat belt.

"If it's your friends, tell them you received an urgent call from the boss. Do it." Alejandro put the gun barrel against the side of Arturo's head for more emphasis. Squirming, Arturo took out the cellphone but Alejandro snatched it from his hand.

"I'll hold it." He flipped it open and held it close to the man's ear.

"What's going on man?" Rogelio shouted on his cellphone. "What the hell did you do? How are we going to get back to the city?" He was in the middle of a large dirt field at the edge of the gas station, nervous and sweating.

"Remember what I said." Alejandro whispered.

"Vicente called...told me to head for the warehouse right away. The police are looking for the woman and the *frezo*."

The gun's barrel stroke the side of Arturo's scraggly beard. Reminding the man that any false movement would have dire consequences for him. *So Vicente is their boss. But I still can't fathom why he's after us.* Alejandro continued pressing the gun to the man's jaw bone.

"What about us?" Rogelio demanded.

His comrade, in the meantime came back, looking miserable. He had been trying to get a ride with one of the truckers but his looks made even the swarthy men avoid him.

"Tell him to get the bus." Alejandro prodded the man. His voice barely audible. "Where are you supposed to hide the woman and the child?"

"Ahhh, get a bus or whatever. I asked Vicente and he told me that was your problem. I'll be at the warehouse."

Mouthing his words, Alejandro told him to hang up.

"I got to go."

The cellphone was snapped shut by Alejandro. He took a quick glance behind him. Virginia was keeping a steady pace, maintaining a distance of about four cars. *Hmm, I think we are far enough now. I'll have him take the first country road off the highway.*

****

The drab, dusty landscape did not offer much in way of sightseeing. It was mostly deserted with only a few cars coming and going every now and then. A few scrawny low hanging trees and cactuses dotted the bleak surroundings.

Staying close to the fast moving van, Virginia had no problem keeping up with it. The Yukon was purring along, the older Honda being no match for the truck's powerful engine.

Her mind was swirling with the emotions of the moment, and for the second time in a short period it was her husband who had come to her rescue, and succeeded. She couldn't think she could love him anymore than she already did. Even though they were not physically together she felt protected and, safe. And though she knew they were not out of harm's way, the man ahead of her was her knight in shining armor. He was always there for her. Could she love him anymore? Probably not. Her thoughts were interrupted by Gabriel's voice. She glanced at him and thought of how blessed she was.

"Mami, I knew daddy would come for us. When you were lost, he found you."

"Yes sweetheart. You're right."

"He promised he would find you and he did. Even Zuri thought you were dead, but I knew you were alive, and I told her."

"Yes, Gaby, you're right. Dad is very good to us. He's-"

"Daddy is awesome!" He smiled broadly and rested his head on the seat's back.

"Yes he is." She glanced at Gabriel's happy face, smiled too and sighed with relief.

A road sign announcing a turn off came up. She saw the van's break lights go bright red. It slowed down and headed for a small dirt road that seemed to disappear in the undulating background.

Arturo added pressure on the brake pedal. The Honda entered the road. He glanced at the rear view mirror and saw the woman doing the same.

"Keep going, I'll tell you when to stop."

There was a slight curve and the road dipped, temporarily hiding the highway from view. There were no signs of any ranches or any other human presence nearby. The dirt trail disappeared behind a small promontory.

"Stop there." Alejandro signaled at a large cactus with long vertical limbs. He looked back. He could not see the highway. "Keep going...a little more, there. I think we are good."

Virginia wondered why Alejandro had turned off the main highway but knowing that she would be able to hug and kiss him in a few seconds filled her with ecstasy. She briefly gazed at Gabriel, who had fallen sleep. The Honda stopped.

The small boy stirred up and opened his eyes. "What are we doing, mami?"

"Don't know sweetheart, daddy is in front of us."

He pushed himself up and peered through the windshield. His dad was coming out the van backwards, holding a gun pointed inside.

Seconds later, the man who had kidnapped them struggled out through the passenger door.

Virginia waited and watched Alejandro march the hoodlum to the back of the van. The thug opened the rear door.

"Bring out the tape and some rope. No sudden or jerky moves. You try anything and I won't hesitate to put a bullet through the back of your neck."

Arturo numbly nodded. He bent over and forayed through the back of the van.

Alejandro watched him several feet back.

A thick roll of black tape and a long piece of rope were tossed out of the van.

"Lay on the ground, put your arms behind your back."

"Are you going to leave me here?" He looked around in despair. "I'll die."

"Shut up and do as I say or you'll have to deal with a lot more than being tied up."

Resigned, he went down on his knees and then lay flat on the dirt. He turned his head to the side and put his arms behind his back.

"Virg, please come over," Alejandro called.

Virginia approached her husband.

Handing the gun to her, he admonished the prone man. "She's a sharp shooter, so don't fool yourself by getting any fancy ideas." He straddled the man, taped his wrists and then did the same with his ankles. Soon Arturo looked like a trussed pig.

Handing back the gun to Alejandro, Virginia hugged and kissed him profusely.

Gabriel opened the car door, came out and ran to his parents. Alejandro caught him and lifted him up.

FIFTY-NINE

"Y ou will be here later then?" Vicente, the butcher, asked Fabian over the phone. "I'll be at the airport. When we take off, I'll let my men know so they can pick us there."

"Have you spoken with them? Fabian stared out the back window of his limousine. Traffic was moving at a snail's pace. "Do you know where they are?"

"Yeah, about five minutes ago. They had a flat and stopped. Should be in the city in about an hour."

"I want to see who these people are. They have pissed me off and I don't like it."

"If you want, I can have them find out for you." Vicente said.

"No, I want to hear her scream when I start burning her son's fingers and toes, maybe put a rat on his stomach after that. I want to inflict as much pain on the kid and her without killing him. You think they'll last a day? I want him alive when the men rape his mother. Before I forget, set up the video. We'll send it to her husband."

"The equipment is in the warehouse." Vicente made a mental note to remember to bring new cassettes just in case. "Anything else?" Vicente watched his men load a small truck with fifty-five gallon oil-drums full of packed powered cocaine in plastic bags. Each bag held about two kilos with a street value of close to forty thousand dollars. And each barrel had a street value of approximately four million dollars. About a third from the top, a flat top was added and sealed with plumbers' gunk to prevent leaks dripping into the hidden bags. Once this last step was completed, gasoline was added to fill the barrel to the top and then a metal seal with a spigot was screwed on. If anyone opened the lid and looked in, all they'd see and smell would be the oil. If a stick was inserted it would come back out with the oily sheen of fuel.

"The late afternoon traffic is a bitch. I'll call you the moment we get clearance to take off. There are some showers around, so I don't know. Call me if there is any news. I got too hung up, I'm getting another call."

Fabian checked the caller ID. "Any news?"

"As a matter of fact, we got a tip. Our man is on highway sixteen. A woman took the car's license plate. I already gave instructions to stop him and keep him in a holding cell until I arrive and the police have issued an APB. And I requested a helicopter. We'll get him, don't you worry."

"Find him before he reaches Chihuahua. Don't lose him. Damn it."

"We have a fix on the car he's driving. It shouldn't be too long before he's ours."

"I'll see you there. But first I have to pick Vicente in Culiacan," he looked at his watch, "say by eight or nine."

"I'll have him by then. I'll let you know the moment we grab him."

Fabian relaxed in the plush back seat of his limo. His chauffeur was left to worry about the driving snafu caused by the thousands of cars congesting the smug filled streets.

SIXTY

"What are we going to do now, love?" Virginia said. They were standing a short distance from the two cars. Arturo was sitting on the ground, his back resting against the Honda's side and out of earshot.

"There's only one way to end this." Alejandro didn't elaborate. His mind was working out different scenarios. "Jacinto warned me not to trust either of the men who came down to see him. The documents from the safety deposit box incriminate someone high up in the DEA."

The ringing of Arturo's cellphone interrupted his monologue. He retrieved it from his pocket and looked at the caller ID. He looked at Arturo. "Your boss is calling. We're going to play the same game as before. Got it?"

The man nodded with his head and mumbled yes.

Alejandro went to him and flipped open the cell phone.

"Where are you?" Vicente asked with no preamble.

Looking at Alejandro, Arturo coughed, his mouth, dry. He was parched. "One moment."

"Are you there? What the fuck is going on, Arturo?"

"Sorry...I...we are very close. There's some traffic, we are having a little bit of a delay." He gazed at Alejandro, as if asking for approval.

"Get to the warehouse without delay. Fabian is picking me up and then we are flying there. He'll be here any minute. If you are not there when we arrive, you'll be in deep shit. Don't waste any more time."

"I won't, I won't."

Alejandro shut off the phone, picked Arturo off the ground without much struggle and sat him in the passenger seat.

In a way, Arturo was relieved; he had thought he was going to become fodder for the desert animals. On the other hand, not knowing where he was going and not sure of what the rugged man might do to him gave him little peace of mind.

Walking back to the black Yukon with Virginia and Gabriel, Alejandro opened the driver's door. "Okay, my sweet, here's where we go our separate ways. I'm taking him to the warehouse in Chihuahua. Once there I'll call the police and tell them about the hideout."

She sat on the driver's seat. "Please, be careful."

"Dad?"

"Don't worry, the moment I notify the police, I'll leave for the airport. You head straight there now and take the first flight to Mexico City. We'll meet at your father's house."

"I...I don't want to go without you..."

"We'll stay in touch via the cell phones. Here, take mine. I'll use his." He pointed at the van. "Gaby, you still have yours?"

The boy nodded. He was already seated in the passenger's seat. "Dad, can we go with you?" He seemed unhappy.

"I know son, I don't want us to be apart either but where I'm going, it could be dangerous and I don't need to put you or mami at more risk."

He gave Alejandro a pleading, desperate look.

"Daddy is right." She smiled but Gabriel remained forlorn. His face was pasty. "Are you getting sick, sweetheart?" Virginia put her hand on his forehead. "You don't have a fever." She gave Alejandro a worried look.

"Go, it's getting dark and I want you in Mexico City tonight." He advanced to the window and gently kissed Virginia on the lips. He extended his arm and ruffled his son's hair.

"You take care of mami, okay?" Alejandro winked at his son and moved away from the Yukon as Virginia started the SUV and began to back out.

A minute later, the car had disappeared and Alejandro went back to his quarry.

"Here is what you are going to do if you want to live another day. It will be your choice. I can tie you up to that tree," he pointed at the thick trunk of a nearby dead tree, "and you can take your chances that someone will drive by and see you before the wild beasts decide to get a taste," Alejandro paused, "or you can work with me and tell me what I want to know and we'll be in Chihuahua together...tonight." He gave Arturo a hard look. "Well?"

"I'll work with you, I will, I will."

"One lie, just one, and I'll dump you off some dirt road with bullets on your legs. I'm sure the smell of blood will attract a coyote, or a jaguar."

"I will do whatever you want." What unnerved him the most was Alejandro's quiet demeanor. There was no menace in his tone, no shouting, only the calm voice. It made him quiver in fear.

"We'll have a nice drive to Chihuahua. Now tell me where is this warehouse, and how do we get there."

He gave him directions and Alejandro drove off.

"How well guarded is it?" Alejandro entered the highway.

"At least half a dozen men. The depot is used for transporting the coca."

"If I find different..." he let the thought hang in the air. "Tell me about Vicente. Who's his boss?"

Scared and totally defeated, Arturo rambled on and told him what he knew.

"See? We will have a nice and pleasant drive the rest of the way." He patted the man's leg. Arturo jumped in his seat.

SIXTY-ONE

Flying low towards Chihuahua, the Bell 206B helicopter followed the two-lane highway. Anytime Howard or Raul saw a black SUV they would command the pilot to dive in closer to obtain a better view of the car and check drivers. Both men sat in the back with the rear doors open. The huge draft caused significant wind noise but it made it easier for them to peer through their Steiner 7x50mm M50RC binoculars. Their helmets minimized wind noise, and allowed them to give instructions to the pilot via the imbedded mikes at the front of their headgear.

So far, they had only seen three SUV's that somewhat matched the description given. Each time, they would ask the pilot to drop down so they could get a fix on the license plates.

In one case, an old man received the scare of his life and almost rode off the roadway. The farmer was driving along listening to a popular *ranchera*. He looked at his rearview mirror and saw a helicopter hovering almost at road level behind him. He swerved off the road, the helicopter lifted up and the oldster opened his window, cursed and gave the helicopter the middle finger.

****

"Dad, we're making a quick stop at a gas station." Gabriel spoke on the cell phone.

"Good son, how is mami's driving? Are you feeling better?" He smiled and looked at his watch. They had been on the road for more than an hour. From what

Arturo had said, he had enough gas to get him to the warehouse.

"We are okay."

Alejandro could tell Gabriel was unhappy but it was better this way.

"Tell mami I'll call you when I'm near the city."

"Take care daddy."

"Bye son." The connection went off.

Ten minutes later, he drove by a gas station on the side of the road. He took a quick look but couldn't tell for sure if that was a Yukon parked by one of the gas pumps. He thought it was. He called. "Are you still at the gas pump?"

"Hi love," Virginia exclaimed with delight, "we got some sodas and chips and are headed for the car now. Maybe we'll catch up with you before we take the turn for the airport."

"Just don't drive too fast," He smiled to himself, "I'm going to hang up, love you."

"Love you too, bye." She waited for Gabriel to enter the car and then she checked the pump's meter and paid the gas attendant. "Thank you." She went around and entered the Yukon.

A few seconds later, she was near the entrance to the highway. She let several cars pass by and then entered the two-lane road. Traffic had picked up. They were getting closer to the city of Chihuahua. She thought she noticed a low flying helicopter in the distance.

****

"There's the gas station," Raul pointed excitedly, it's the only one we have seen and there's a black SUV entering the highway." He knew that Howard could not see it from his seat and asked the pilot to turn the helicopter so his partner could check it from his side.

The helicopter lifted up higher and made a slight turn to the right, but kept going straight. The DEA agent brought the binoculars to his eyes, fiddled with the center wheel, adjusting the power and focused the powerful eyeglasses on the black truck entering the highway. "Yep, it has to be him." Howard asked the pilot to head straight for the car.

SIXTY-TWO

"How's my Mexican partner? She didn't bother to hear his response. "I'm planning to meet with Eric in Miami. But you and I need to get together. I could stop in Mexico on my way back." Claudia played with a five-karat solitaire in her weeding finger.

"I'm headed for Chihuahua. Seems, that our mutual acquaintance, Alejandro? You remember him, right?" Fabian paused and smoothed his mustache, "he is here."

"He what?" She almost yelled.

"Yes, here in Mexico. I'm arranging a meeting with him and…his family. The wife and the son."

"What is he doing there?" She couldn't believe what she was hearing. *I may need to change my plans and go to Mexico first.*

"It…I don't really know, but from all appearances, it was a vacation…that went awry."

"Oh? Go ahead tell me more."

Fabian went on and related all that he knew, being careful to keeping his comments neutral. One never knew if a phone was being tapped.

"It would be wonderful if we could all get together. I haven't seen him in a long time. There are so many things I need to catch up with him and his wife." *I should find out about her. I wonder what she looks like…him too. I have been so busy with all this other shit.* "Please tell him that I'm planning to fly there. You wouldn't mind, would you?"

"I thought you were going to Miami."

"Oh, I can, after we meet, don't you think?"

"Sure, but I don't know how long he's going to be around."

"Please try to convince him. Can you do that?"

"I'll do my best, but no promises. Okay?"

"I'll start making plans right away." She hung up but dialed another number. "I need pictures and information about a man named Alejandro Calwel and his wife. How soon?"

The detective glanced around his desk and looked at the office a few feet away from him. His boss was gone for the day. His partner, whose desk was across from him, had stepped away to get coffee. "Let me check what we have on him."

"Call me the moment you got it. I'll send one of my men to pick it up." She said.

SIXTY-THREE

The helicopter hovered overhead, its white, green and red colors of the Mexican flag shone brightly under the last rays of a disappearing sun. A small red light twitched intermittently underneath the carriage. Gabriel instinctively took the cell-phone out and dialed his father. Virginia slowed down unsure of what to do. She looked at her rear view mirror and saw the red and blue lights of a police car telegraphing its imminent arrival.

"Daddy, there's a helicopter in front of us and a police car is coming."

"Gaby, let me talk to dad." She grabbed the phone. "Sweetheart?"

"Be calm, it's the police. Call me when you know what they want. Don't tell them about my plan. Do you have the other cellphone I gave you?"

"Yes, yes," she looked at her jeans pocket in an involuntary reaction, making sure the cellphone was still there. Be careful, my love." She handed over the cellphone back to Gabriel. "If they ask you; you don't know anything, and you don't where daddy went."

"Okay mami."

"All you know it's that the men that kidnapped us were very dangerous."

"I will mami." He stashed the BB in his back pocket. He looked back and saw the highway patrolman come out of his car and walk over towards them.

The black Yukon waited on the road's shoulder. The police officer kept one hand in his holster, ready to take his sidearm out if the need arose. He wasn't too concerned though, with the helicopter touching down a few feet from him on a patch of hardscrabble ground, he knew he had sufficient back up. But he had been told the driver could be dangerous, so he was being careful just in case.

"What is the problem officer?"

He was taken aback, he expected a man, not the beautiful woman with the gorgeous large dark-almond eyes and the easy smile. He almost gasped at seeing her mesmerizing face framed by cascading black shimmering hair. He pulled back his hat somewhat. *"Buenas tardes señorita."* He peered into the back of the large SUV but nothing seemed suspicious. "I think there may be a mistake." He switched on his shoulder mike. "Aah, I think we stopped the wrong car."

Before Raul, could respond, Howard was already talking, "what do you mean?"

Raul stepped down from the helicopter.

"Well, the driver is a young woman and there is a child with her."

"What?" Howard hollered. The big burly man trotted past Raul towards the large truck. He reached the officer and stared inside too.

"Who are you?" He asked, although he was fairly certain he knew the answer.

The officer tendered Virginia's driver's license but Howard ignored him.

"Virginia Calwel, and you are...?" She held his gaze.

Brusquely snapping the ID from the policeman, Howard switched his attention to the document and then looked back inside.

"That's your son?"

"Yes-"

"Where is your husband? He told us you were kidnapped this morning. We have been looking for you all over the place. How come you didn't call us?" He barked in a resentful tone.

"We barely escaped an hour ago. I thought my husband had called. Anyway, we are free now. You should go after the men who took us. The last I know, they were at a gas station."

"This is your husband's car, isn't it? So, where is he?"

"He didn't tell me, he commandeered the thugs van and gave me his car. We're going to the airport and flying to the D.F. where my parents live. Can we leave now?"

"Not yet." Howard stepped away and signaled Raul to come over. "I want to hold them as material witnesses or some other bullshit like that."

"Under what grounds, Howe?"

"Don't know. Offer to take them to Chihuahua's airport in the helicopter."

"...I don't know, they are not Mexicans, I don't want to get into some jurisdictional scuffle." Raul said.

"I don't care, make something up. I want to hold them as hostages until we find that sonofabitch. He's a sleazy bastard. I won't let him escape."

"Are you sure? We can get in real trouble if this-"

"Come on man! We went through this already. I'll take the responsibility, don't worry. Let me clear it with my higher ups."

Howard stepped away to make the call but there was no response. "Fuck," he muttered, and put his BB away, then went back to Raul.

"What is it?"

"He's not answering. Give them to me anyway. I'll take them and it will be out of your hands. It's easier that way."

"Are you sure?"

"Alejandro will have to come to me. He doesn't have any other choice but to enter the U.S. if he wants his wife and son back." He grabbed Raul's arm, and they both walked back to the SUV.

"Are you done with me?" The patrolman asked.

"Yes, we don't need you anymore. Go get back on the road. We'll take it from here." Howard said.

The officer glanced at Raul who shrugged his shoulders. The highway patrolman took another look at the beautiful woman. "Goodbye, ma'am." He touched the tip of his hat and walked back to his car.

"I want you to come with us." Howard addressed Virginia and smiled. "We'll fly you to the airport."

"But, what about the car?"

"Don't worry about it. The officer is already calling a tow truck."

"It's a rental car..."

"I'll have it towed to the rental car office at the airport." A smile lingered in his lips.

"Can I call Alejandro?" She said.

"Sure, as a matter of fact, after you talk to him, let me..."

"Why do you smile when you don't mean it?" Gabriel asked.

A coughing fit erupted in Howard's throat. "I...never mind." For once, he was out of words.

Virginia looked at Gabriel and gave him a quiet smile. She brought out the cell phone and called her husband.

"Sweetheart, the DEA officer and his Mexican partner are taking us to the airport in their helicopter. A truck will take your rental to the agency."

"That's good, my love. I don't have to worry about your safety."

"I sure hope so." She said but her voice sounded skeptical.

"Yeah me too." *Jacinto doesn't trust him but he's with other policemen. He wouldn't do anything to her. Would he?* The question lingered in his mind.

"Mrs. Calwel, we have to get going. Hurry up." Howard gave Gabriel a sour look.

"The DEA officer wants to speak with you. I'll call you from the airport."

"Okay, my sweet, let me talk to him."

Virginia handed over the cellphone to Howard.

Taking the phone, he stepped away and when he felt he was out of earshot, spoke. "Calwel, you are in deep shit. You know?"

"I have done nothing wrong, agent Howard."

"Well, if you are really innocent, why don't you give yourself up?"

"Why? What have I done?"

"All I know is that you're getting into a hell of a mess."

"What are you accusing me of?"

"I'm not accusing you of anything...yet. I just want to have a word with you."

"I'll meet you at the airport. Once I know my family is safe, I'll address all your questions and concerns. Did you have your Colombia counterparts check my background?"

"Where are you going now? Why don't you give yourself up? Why are you running away from me?"

"I'm not running away from anyone but I can't meet with you now."

"You're in hot fucking water, man." Howard's face was getting red. "Raul has asked all the police agencies to look for you and detain you. If you give yourself up now, there will be lesser chances that we charge you for obstruction of justice, aiding and abetting a criminal enterprise and whatever else I can think of."

"I think you're stretching yourself a little, don't you think?"

Barely able to hold his anger, Howard struggled to speak calmly. "Don't push me boy. I can put all the resources of the U.S. at my disposal. You continue defying me and I'll throw the book at you. Could be looking at a long stint in a federal prison."

Raul watched from a few feet away. He thought Howard was really pissed off. He walked closer, in case he needed to intervene.

"Howard, you can threaten me all you want but the truth is that when my wife and son were kidnapped you didn't move a finger to help me. So I can argue that I had no choice but to take matters in my own hands. Which I did and now my wife and son are out danger."

"Oh? You are lawyer now? You'll need a good one to represent you." He growled.

"Fine, I'll give myself up when I get to Chihuahua and know that my wife and son are on the airplane to Mexico City. Do we have a deal?"

"It's your skin man. I can't vouch for your safety from here on."

Bastard, he's up to something. He turned off the cellphone. "Ready? We should get going." Howard walked over to the pilot while Raul went to pick up Virginia and Gabriel.

She approached Howard, who was still talking with the pilot giving him the coordinates to a location.

"May I have my cellphone back, please?"

"No, I think I'm going to keep it for now."

"Why?"

"I have my reasons. Let's move. We don't have much time." Howard glanced at Raul. Both men let Virginia and Gabriel walk ahead of them.

"Why don't you want her to have the phone?" Raul said in a low voice.

"I'll tell you later."

The helicopter lifted up. Virginia and her son sat across from the two lawmen. This time Gaby did not look outside but kept his eyes fixed on the men. He had an uneasy feeling.

SIXTY-FOUR

Forcing himself to relax, Alejandro thought about what had just transpired. Although, he didn't trust Howard, the man was in Mexico and with Mexican officers. He was almost sure the DEA agent didn't have the leverage he would otherwise enjoy if his wife and son were in the U.S. Besides, Alejandro reasoned, I can't give myself up. If I go back, my plans will be thwarted. The Mexican authorities will protect my wife and son.

He exhaled and glanced at his prisoner. He had kept Arturo's arms tied behind his back, with another piece of rope going from the wrists and under his backside to his ankles, which were also tied up with rope and tape. Given sufficient time, he didn't discard the possibility that the man could eventually untie himself but for the time being, he knew that was not going to happen. His years of roping cattle gave him the kind of dexterity and knowhow that few of these men probably had.

The cellphone rang again, Alejandro looked at the caller ID. It said Fabian Negreto. Alejandro raised his eyebrows. "Looks like Vicente's boss want to talk to you. Interesting. You're getting high up in the world. You know the drill; be careful with what you say. Lying on the side of a highway at nighttime cannot be very nice, especially here in the desert. Gets to be cold." A short while back he had turned the air conditioner knobs to fresh air. Alejandro flipped open the cellphone, put the volume up and pressed the green answer bottom.

"Si? Diga?"

"Where are you?"

"Outside Chihuahua, near the warehouse, Don Fabian." Arturo said.

"Good, I'll see you in a while. Everything all right?"

"Si, si."

"How are my guests?" Fabian smirked.

"No problem. They are fine."

"Ask him when he's coming to the warehouse." Alejandro whispered.

Arturo did as told.

"I'm picking up your boss first. We should be there by nine, ten. Why, are you going somewhere?" Fabian let out a loud laugh and hung up. The plane took off and all land communications were cut-off.

A brooding looking Arturo glimpsed at Alejandro.

"Very good. I see we're getting close." The Chihuahua city lights seemed inviting in the distance. Dusk had overtaken the highway and traffic had increased. Alejandro followed the thug's instructions. During the journey to the warehouse, Arturo had opened up and spilled his guts about Vicente and Fabian.

He hoped that his captor would show him some mercy and let him live. His survival instincts told him to cooperate with the man driving the van. He prayed in silence, although he had never shown any compassion or experienced feelings of remorse to those he had dispatched.

He told Alejandro that he was only a minion in the cog and that he had never tortured or killed anyone. But he now remembered the fathers and mothers who had begged him to spare their lives or at least the lives of their children.

His innermost desire was that when his cohorts arrived they would disarm the bastard. He would then enjoy torturing him slowly, and roast him like a pig on a poke. He imagined driving small nails in his eyes and puncturing his eardrums with a screwdriver. Arturo moaned and shook in fear. He didn't want to think bad thoughts in case God was paying attention.

"What is it?" Alejandro asked.

"Nothing, nothing, really. Take that side street...there." They came upon a dimly lit road with more potholes than asphalt.

Alejandro noticed that it was a dead end street. He turned his lights off and stayed on the corner. Most of the poorly constructed houses in the area seemed to have been built with discarded materials. There were no two-story buildings, with the exception of the warehouse at the end. "Is there any other way to get in and out? Who's in there now?" The building's façade had seen better days. Part of it showed the cement blocks, the paint having peeled off long ago.

"There...there is a small dirt road in the back that comes out on another street. But it's hardly used." He told him how to find it.

"And who is there now? How many?"

"Don't know for sure. Maybe one or two men, I don't come here often." He lied.

"You really have a death wish, don't you? Do you seriously believe I will swallow this crock of shit?" Alejandro stopped, took out the gun, and pressed the barrel against Arturo's knee.

The man recoiled in fear. He tried to put distance between his bound legs and the gun, but Alejandro pressed it against the knee. "No, please, no. Please, please."

"Should I believe you?"

Arturo whined. "Sometimes, there may be four, maybe even five or six. I'm telling you the truth. There are never too many in there."

Taking the weapon by the barrel, the gun's butt was slammed against Arturo's knee.

He screamed, "Shit, oh, shit, you broke my knee." He whimpered. "What did you do that for? Oooh, shit, it hurts." Snot covered his upper lip but he couldn't wipe it off with his hands tied behind his back.

"You are lucky I didn't blow your kneecap with a bullet. I told you, don't lie. I have very little patience." Alejandro opened his door and went in the back. He grabbed the tape and a piece of oily cloth and came back in. He took the dirty rag and forced it into Arturo's mouth, and then ran tape around his face, preventing Arturo from making any loud, distracting sounds.

Putting the Honda in gear, Alejandro followed the man's directions. Several minutes later he came upon precariously built shanties, which seemed to defy gravity and only remained partially upright by tilting against each other. He found a dirt trail. About a fourth of a mile from his vantage point, he saw the warehouse's second floor. The building appeared to have a large backyard enclosed by a six-foot brick fence. He turned off the headlights and drove down further until he found what looked like a group of abandoned huts, and parked behind them.

The van could not be seen from the building. He assumed he was far enough that no one inside would have heard the engine's noise. He pressed the hood's lever and popped it open.

Alejandro got out and made some faint noises, scraping and twisting and bending things. He then walked to the back and returned with a set of pliers and screwdrivers.

Seconds later, he opened the driver's door and snared around the handle what looked like a thin wire that disappeared under the steering wheel. Alejandro went around the front and reappeared by his side. Taking another piece of thin wire, he secured it against the passenger's door handle and ran it underneath the dashboard.

Arturo watched in fear.

"If I come out alive, you will too. If not, when your pals come to free you, the van will blow up," he smiled, "you'll try to warn them but they won't be able to hear you, will they?" *I hope he believes me. It may buy me some precious time.*

Arturo's eyes went wide, he made muffled sounds, kicked the floor with his feet, tried to jump and down to little avail. "Uuugh, uugh, uugh."

"What is it? You have more to tell me?"

With eyes that wanted to pop out of its sockets, Arturo nodded furiously.

Using the pointed end of one screwdriver, Alejandro broke the tape, nicking the man's cheek, and then pulled enough tape off to allow Arturo to spit out the rag. "Aargh, that hurt."

"Speak up." The gun barrel was pressed against his kneecap.

"Don't hit me again, I beg you."

"I'm all ears."

"The...place, it is where they mix the coca with baking soda and water, to make crack."

"Go on."

"They put it in small zip lock bags. If there has been a recent shipment and people are working, there could be more than thirty or forty workers, and a dozen men watching. You see, the building looks like it is almost ready to crumble, but inside it's all new."

"So, this is a factory."

Arturo nodded. "They were talking about installing infrared cameras, front and back. Please, don't hurt me again." The hound-dog face implored. For the first time in a while, he felt he could hang up his sneakers at any moment.

"Well, that could complicate things. Open your mouth." The wet rag went back into Arturo's mouth. He stuck the tape around the man's face and added another strand around his head for good measure. "I guess you are going to have to pray a little, right?" He patted the man's knee.

Arturo jerked at the touch but at least he wasn't hammered with the gun. Alejandro grabbed the hoodlum's legs, making the man's body twist. The legs hung outside the door. He grabbed Arturo by his shoulders and pulled him up. In a quick move, he bent down, pushed the man over his right shoulder, and stood up. He slid open the side door, threw him on the floor and closed it. Alejandro heard a faint muff.

Walking to the brick wall, Alejandro peered inside the yard. His height allowed him to peer above the wall. He fixed his eyes on the closest far corner of the yard, then on the other, but there was nothing resembling any type of surveillance gear. Picking up a stone, he flung it close to the back of the building.

The rock bounced a few times and stopped about a foot from the building's back wall. Alejandro waited a minute, squatted, picked two more nice size rocks and proceeded to toss them near the corners where the brick fence met the tall walls.

Again he waited, but nothing seemed amiss.

A faint moon, obscured by dark clouds, hardly offered any light. A single yellow bulb lit a rear door. One window on each side of the wall and two more on the second floor looked nailed shot.

Alejandro jumped to the top of the fence and immediately went down the other side, ducking and waiting; one gun ready to shoot in his right hand. He carried another gun under his belt, and held a long Phillips screwdriver on his other hand.

The silence was unnerving. He inspected the yard littered with oil drums and pallets. An old, banged-up lift truck with hardly any of its original yellow paint visible was plunked down near the back entrance.

Alejandro ran closer to the building and hid behind five open drums stinking of fuel. He looked around, trying to find how the lift truck was driven to the backyard.

Near the rear of the building was an area cleared of debris. If he were going to get closer, he would have to run across the empty space. Only a pile of discarded pallets would give him any cover. He looked to his right, then to his left. If there were cameras he would be exposed. The right side was worse. Nowhere to hide.

He heard a faint rumble and stayed hidden behind the empty drums. The reverberation got louder. Alejandro recognized the sound. It was the flap-flap of helicopter blades.

A minute later he looked up and saw landing lights shining on the flat ground below. About the same time, powerful floodlights came on. Now he could see the garage door. It was painted a dull, almost black-gray and in the darkness had been invisible. Alejandro shifted his attention to the landing aircraft. He recognized the Mexican national colors and shield.

Cigarette in his mouth, a man opened the back door and held it open. Fluorescent lighting outlined his short solid body.

A second man came out. He was taller and held an Uzi submachine gun. Alejandro noticed that both wore what looked like surgical masks around their necks.

Alejandro wondered who was arriving at the warehouse and why?

****

"Where are we going?" Virginia asked.

The helicopter was dropping altitude.

She could see shacks and poorly built small houses below. This was not the airport.

"Making a small detour. Some people who want to talk with you." Howard said.

"Where the hell are we landing?" Raul looked suspiciously at the ground below.

"Don't worry, I'm taking care of this."

"You said you wanted to take them across the border." Raul looked perplexed.

"I told you. I'm handling it." Howard gave him a hard look, and taking his gun out, pointed it at the Mexican drug official. "Hand over your gun. Now." He shouted.

"What are you doing man?"

Howard discharged his gun. The bullet passed though Raul's upper arm and lodged in his chest, piercing his heart. He was gone in a second.

Virginia screamed, and snapped off the restraining belts of her seat to shield Gabriel.

"What is going on back there?" The pilot yelled from up front.

"Raul got shot. The woman was hiding a gun. She was trying to escape. He's badly hurt but we have medical facilities available where we're landing. I'm sure they'll be able to help him. Hurry up and land. We don't have much time." Howard moved the gun from Raul and pointed it towards the woman. He put an index finger on his lips and said, "shhhh, be quiet."

Virginia and Gabriel stared at him in shock.

Within seconds, the whirling blades raised a cloud of dust. The helicopter landed gently in the area highlighted by the spotlights.

"Don't try anything. I don't give a rat's ass about you or your boy."

Making a small ark with the gun from her to Gabriel, Howard began to back out of the compartment.

SIXTY-FIVE

fter finishing telling the maid how to pack the last valise, Claudia-Lucia heard a knock on the door. The old manservant held a large sealed manila envelope in his hands. "Bring it." She said.

Entering her bedroom, he handed over the packet and waited. Claudia-Lucia stared at the thin envelope and turned it over but there was nothing written either front or back. She ripped it off the top and looked inside. Then stared at the woman-servant. "Close the damn thing and put it with the others." Three large Gucci suitcases stood on the floor. The butler remained standing by the door. "What are you waiting for? Help her, take the luggage downstairs and close the door." Once the servants were gone she took out several pictures and three pages of printed computer pages. "She is the bitch? Fucking whore. So she was the one living here under my nose, fucking my husband?" Her voice rose in anger. "*Puta de mierda.* Oh, baby, I'm going to make you pay, oh yes, yes. And this is your *huevon, malparido* husband eh?"

The old man and the servant heard her angry tirade and rushed down the long corridor carrying the heavy suitcases.

"You are the one who killed that good for nothing husband of mine." She went on. "Well, maybe I'll keep you alive, you'll be my slave, have you serve me. You look like a nice hunk of meat." Her fit simmered down. "I'm going to have sex with you until you bore me. Then I'll cut your balls and send you to the jungle to be those maricas girlfriend."

The maid was about to knock on the door but she heard Claudia's continuing shouting and cursing. It scared her, she thought the woman was going crazy. She waited and when the screaming simmered down she knocked on the door. "Señora Claudia, your bags are in the car."

"Fine, fine, oh this is going to be such a good trip. Tell them, I will be right down." She wore an embroidered diamante snake cording pantsuit created by a famous designer. *I look stunning, if I do say so myself.* She smoothed her hair, slid her hands down the black tight fitting pants, picked a leather jacket, and a large matching black handbag, and then walked out of the room, envelope in hand. "Who has my other hand bag?" She yelled from upstairs.

The maid, waiting at the bottom of the stairs said, "I have it Señora."

****

The pilot, copilot and a handsome thirty-some steward stood in line in order of status to welcome their curvaceous new client.

Slowly swiping her hand through the lustrous, light brown leather seat, Claudia-Lucia inspected the Lear Jet 60 that was about to fly her to Mexico. The aircraft was expensively appointed. Fine wood grain polished to a brilliant shine covered the inside walls. The plane, custom made, and holding only six wide armchairs, was immaculate.

The tall steward with black curly hair and thick eyebrows escorted her inside.

Claudia inspected the other men.

The pilot and copilot moved inside the cockpit and sat down to begin the departure process.

The steward offered her one of the plush wide leather lounge seats.

Seemingly satisfied, she sat down and sighed. "What do you have to drink?"

"Whatever you desire. I'm Alberto, and I am at your service for the duration of this flight." His deep but pleasant voice had no specific accent.

"Oh, my, aren't you sweet?" She gave him a languorous look from head to toe. "Hmmm, is there a mile high club here?" She let a hand slide down the attractive looking man's cheek, stopping at his chest. "Is there a bed here?"

Alberto smiled. "Yes, a partition behind the lounges can be closed to offer privacy and that sofa becomes a bed." He pointed to a sofa placed sideways against the plane's wall.

"I have always been curious as to what one has to do to become a member. Would you happen to know?" She gave him lustful glance.

With a suggestive smile he responded. "Ma'am, I'm here to make sure all your desires are satisfied during your voyage." Moving forward and slightly brushing Claudia's arm with his groin, Alberto bent over and pulled out a small collapsible wood table hidden on the wall. He laid on it a white linen tablecloth. "Would you like some champagne with strawberries?" An allusive grin, showing a row of perfect white teeth, unveiled from behind his pulpous lips.

Her eyes became smoky, and she looked at him with abandon.

He turned and walked to the galley in the back. Inside a wood cabinet was an array of various size fine crystal glasses, securely held in wood shelves. A silver container filled with ice, sitting on the top of a small credenza, held a Louis Roederer 2006 Cristal champagne bottle.

Taking a flute from one of the shelves, he examined it against the light. Using a cloth napkin, he wiped it and poured in it the faint yellow liquid. Next, he crouched and opened a small refrigerator, and took out a white plate with thin silver edges.

It was filled with carefully laid out chocolate covered strawberries.

He placed it on a silver tray next to the glass. He walked back to Claudia and placed the display on the side table. "Is it cold enough?"

"Will you have something hot and hard for me later?" She smiled and brought the cup to her lips while fixing her eyes on him. The moment was interrupted by unexpected commotion at the door entrance. Irritated, she took her eyes off him.

The pilot came out of the cockpit and approached her. "We have been asked to wait a few minutes. A police officer wants to see you Señora Draco."

"Who? What for?" Claudia's eyes glinted with anger.

"They didn't tell me. "I'm sorry for the delay. Hopefully we can take off right away, but the tower will hold the flight until they have clearance from the authorities...she's waiting at the bottom of the steps."

Furious, Claudia got up and went across the aisle to peek through one of the portholes. "What the fuck does that bitch want now?"

Captain Karina, one foot on the first step of the retractable ladder, spoke with a customs officer. A few feet back, standing by the side of a police car was Sebastian her young assistant,

The customs and immigration officer started climbing up the ladder, with the policewoman following close behind.

The pilot retreated to the entryway and greeted the new arrivals. "Good evening, I'm Fernando Bellazuela, the officer in charge of the airplane." He extended his hand.

The officer turned sideways and introduced Karina. "Good evening Fernando. This is Captain Karina from the Medellin homicide division. May we come in?"

Fernando stepped back, allowing the visitors to enter the cabin.

An indignant Claudia-Lucia, legs crossed, a high heel shoe dangling from one foot, waited impatiently. A frigid smile was cemented in her face. She held the champagne glass in her manicured hand, long fingernails painted a bright, blood red, matching her toenails. Her cold stare could have frozen the devil's caldrons.

Captain Karina walked over to her. "I heard you were living the country, and wondered if you were being threatened, what with the latest spat of prominent citizens being killed. I wanted to offer our services in case you need police protection." Karina's mocking comment only served to further infuriate the already fuming woman.

"Stop the bullshit. What do you want?" The insipid smile disappeared from Claudia's face.

"A couple of questions, that's all." Karina noticed the manila envelope on the tabletop. The color and size were similar to the ones used by the police force. The edge of the packet had a distinctive, red edge. "Is that from us?" She wondered who in the force was being paid off but was not surprised.

"None of your business." Claudia-Lucia hurriedly retrieved the envelope from the tabletop and squashed next to her in the seat.

"Where are you flying to and how long do you plan to be out of the country?" Karina already knew she had seen the submitted flight plan. It had raised her eyebrows. What a coincidence, she had thought. The two people that held the most interest for her at the moment were going to be in the same country. Long experience in the police force told her otherwise. Nothing happened by chance.

"I'm flying to Mexico. I'm visiting some old friends, why? Is that a crime?"

"Not at all. Where in Mexico?"

"Right now, Mexico City, then maybe I'll go into the countryside."

"I see...but the pilot's flight plan didn't say Mexico City. It only specified Chihuahua. Am I mistaken?" An indulgent smile appeared in Karina's face.

"If you know so much, why the fuck are you asking me?" Claudia's foot moved at a fast pace, the loose shoe dangling and close to falling on the carpeted floor.

"Only wanted to have my facts straight, Señora Draco...in case there was a mistake."

"No, there's no mistake. Friends invited me, and I may go to Mexico City afterwards."

"And do you know how long you plan to stay?"

"My visa is for thirty days but I can't stay that long. Have your moron and incompetent assistants found any leads as to who did him in?" She waited for a response but none came. "I have too many responsibilities taking care of all his businesses. Anything else?"

"And you are not being threatened and that's not why you are leaving so suddenly?"

"Of course not." The high heel Manolo shoe fell off. "Who would want to hurt me?" She scoffed.

"Very well, sorry for delaying your vacation. Would you mind letting us know when you return, in case we have any news about your husband's killing?"

"Sure..." Claudia stared at the tarmac dismissing the stupid idiot standing in front of her.

Glancing at the airport officer, Karina shrugged her shoulders, thanked him and ignoring Claudia, turned and walked to the exit. The airport policeman fell in step behind her.

SIXTY-SIX

Hiding behind some oil barrels, Alejandro was taken aback when he saw Howard getting out with a gun in his hand.

The pilot emerged from the cockpit at about the same time and rushed to the rear compartment to look in.

Howard pointed his sidearm at the back of the pilot's head and shot him dead. Repulsion and anger at the cowardly act, Alejandro did all he could to contain himself from shooting at the turncoat agent. *He is the one that Pancho and Jacinto feared was involved with the drug cartel. No wonder he's been after me all this time.*

Half the man's body fell on the cabin's floor. Slowly the body slid and slumped on the ground. Seconds later, Virginia came out. She carried Gabriel and tried to block his eyes from the gory scene.

A desperate impulse to rise and fire at will almost overcame Alejandro. But the men at the back entrance had their weapons ready to shoot. He wanted to rescue his loved ones, but restrained himself, gritted his teeth, and waited, trying to listen to what was being said, but he was too far to hear.

Howard was pointing with his gun towards the small stone steps that led to the entrance.

The man with the cigarette flipped it out to the ground below, scattering the ashes on the dirt floor. "Who the fuck is going to fly that shit out of here?" He yelled from the top of the steps. "Can't have the *federales* come in here."

"I called Fabian. He's taking care of it." Howard shouted.

Virginia holding Gabriel in her arms, and bowing slightly under the still gyrating blades, walked ahead of the traitorous DEA officer.

The spot lights had been turned off and except for the dim glow of the bare bulb above the back door and the light stemming from inside, the backyard was mournfully black.

Virginia, an arm over Gabriel's shoulder in a protective gesture, went up the up the set of cement steps, keeping her son close to her. Howard followed them close behind. The man holding the submachine gun went inside too, while the smoker took out another cigarette and lit up.

Watching from behind the oil drums, Alejandro tried to determine if there was any way he could get in without being caught.

He needed to find out how many men were inside and whether it would be safe to rescue his wife and son without exposing them to more danger. *Can I take him without making any noise? I don't think so. I have to wait. Come on, move.*

After taking a couple of deep puffs the guard threw the cigarette away, walked behind Howard and closed the door.

Taking careful aim to avoid hitting the helicopter, Alejandro threw another stone near where the spotlights had shined before. The backyard remained dark and quiet.

If there are sensors, they are not on? He stood up slowly and quietly walked around the barrels.

Nothing.

In a gradual, paced motion, his weapon at his side, Alejandro approached the lift truck and waited. He kept his eyes set on the door. *Still, no noise.* No spotlights were activated to expose him. Alejandro looked in the machine. It ran on natural gas not diesel fuel. *Probably to avoid fumes inside the building or the possibility of an accidental fire.* He thought.

The forklifts were about a half-foot off the ground. Turning around, he walked to the mound of discarded pallets a short distance away. With hardly any light from a morose moon, he inspected the wood planks, chose one, and taking it, brought it back, rapidly sliding it into the truck forks.

He walked to the small garage door and checked it. He couldn't tell whether it was locked or not. Skimming close to the dank wall, Alejandro reached the cement steps. He estimated that the top landing was about five feet from the ground.

The door opened with a creaking sound, the obscure surroundings conquered by a burst of fluorescent radiation. Alejandro crouched and glued himself to the side of the cement steps.

It was the guy who smoked. Closing the door behind him, he began taking out a cigarette.

Alejandro waited.

The man lit a match and put it close to the cigarette.

Taking advantage of the man's momentary loss of depth perception caused by the flame, Alejandro stood up, grabbed the man's ankles and yanked him off the platform.

Caught by surprise, the hoodlum didn't have a chance to shout. His head cracked loudly against the top of the steps; his body stumbled to the ground.

Alejandro checked for a pulse, pressing on the carotid artery. There was none. The thug's neck had snapped. Pulling the dead man's body by its ankles, Alejandro hid it on the opposite side of the steps.

Rummaging through the pockets he found a cellphone and a spare cartridge. Next, he picked a Beretta 921A1 9mm lying on the dirt floor. *Now I have three guns, I guess the odds of my survival have improved somewhat. All I care about is for Virg and Gaby to be safe.*

Going back to the lift truck, and working as quietly as he could, he put four barrels in the pallet while keeping a wary eye on the door. If anyone came out looking for the thug, he would be toast. Trotting back to the steps, he mounted them two at a time. After reaching the landing, he unscrewed the light bulb and then checked to see if the door was unlocked. With great care, he turned the knob. It moved, and after turning it, pulled the door slightly ajar. It creaked faintly. Alejandro peered. Bright lights illuminated an array of aluminum or steel benches in the center of the building. Stools underneath completed the ensemble.

Where are they? He waited for his eyesight to adjust to the darkness surrounding him. He opened the door further and pacing his steps, slowly entered the building. He thought he could distinguish two semi parked near the far entrance.

Drums, similar in shape to the ones outside were piled two and three high on a corner.

Cardboard boxes of various sizes and identifying different types of zip-lock bags were stacked near him.

A metal staircase led to a second floor wing of offices that looked down on the center of the large hall below.

Light from a large pane glass window above told him where the men might be.

Creeping along the far wall, and partially hid by the assembled boxes, Alejandro reached the roll up garage door. He felt around the edges, then crouched and found a dead bolt at the bottom.

He was able to slide it out without much effort. He tried raising the door but it would only budge a little. *There must be another bolt at the other end.* Sticking to the metal contraption he moved to the other side, and squatted looking for the other cylindrical iron bar. His eyes remained vigilant, looking up at the door at the top of the staircase. He felt it and pulled it out. He tried raising the door again. It moved, so he pushed it back down softly.

SIXTY-SEVEN

irginia and Gabriel sat on the floor their backs resting against the wall. They were almost smack center of the long office. A few feet from them and near the window, Howard was gulping a tequila shot. The man with the Uzi and another cohort sat on a nearby sofa watching TV. The man who had poured the drinks looked at Virginia and shouted. *"Quieres un poco de tequila, mamasita?"* He laughed in a lewd manner.

Virginia recoiled and ignored the thug.

"When can we have her?" He looked at Howard.

"Don't even think about it. That's the boss prerogative." Howard said.

"The what?"

"Fabian decides what to do with her. Come to think about it, he hasn't returned my call. Well, it doesn't really matter. Pour me one more and that's it for me. Is there anything to eat here? I'm starving." Howard's stomach made a loud rumbling.

"Mr. Silverband, can we have some water?" Virginia said.

Howard didn't seem to hear her or didn't care.

She spoke louder this time. "Mr. Silverband, can we have water, please?"

"Do you have anything to drink other than that?" Howard asked.

The man holding the bottle of booze looked at the bottle. "There are probably some cokes in the cooler. You want me to give her one?" The skinny, bony, bronze-color man ran his tongue over his lips.

"No, bring me two, one for her and one for the boy. Where did your other companion go?"

"Vampiro? He went out for a smoke. Vicente don't want no one to smoke here, too many fumes. He is always afraid this shithole is going to go bhruum." He raised his hands up and out.

"Why do they call him Vampiro?"

"He likes to torture people by biting off chunks of their flesh. Women give up right away. I have seen men faint. No one holds for more than three bites. We had one policeman who would not accept bribes...bit his ear off in one bite, then while the man was howling, Vampiro held his head and chomped off his nose. Man, it was bad, really, really bad."

Howard gave him an incredulous look.

"Blood all over the place. He's fucking scary, man." He squirmed.

"Are you shitting me?" Howard said. A disgusted look on his face.

"You should see him do it one day. Even the men pee on their pants when they see him come close to them. But then, they talk real fast, oh, yeah. He had these teeth sharpened," he opened his mouth, his teeth looked rotten, and rolled his index finger through the front row, "said it made for a better bite. Maybe Vicente will ask him to demonstrate with the *gringa*."

"Just bring me the goddam cokes." Howard shuddered. "I'll give to them. I'm on my way down to look for...Vampiro." Howard winced, and glanced at Virginia and the boy.

Walking away with an unsteady gait Flaco stopped by a large cooler sitting next to the threadbare sofa, opened it and came back, handing two bottles to Howard.

"Did you have a little bit too much of that stuff?" He asked and took the sodas and approached Virginia and Gabriel.

The skinny man remained standing but swayed unsteadily. He saw the DEA man give the sodas to the prisoners. A snarl came up in his mouth as he watched Howard walk away to the door and step out of the room. "How about if we put the *mocoso* in a closet and we play with the *mamasita*?"

"Have you lost your mind?" The man with the Uzi said. His head was shaved clean. It showed two long scars on one side.

"*No seas pendejo,* Fredy," Flaco said, "I only want to play with her a little. Feel her boobs. She how wet is down there."

Fredy turned and saw the woman handing a bottle to her son, he kneaded his companion in the ribs. "What do you think?"

"Uh? What?" Bleary eyed and slurring his words, Carlos held up his shot glass. "Give me ano...ther ooone, Flaco."

"You want to play with the *gringa*?" Fredy asked.

"What...ever...I don't..." He held his arm up waiting for the tequila.

Flaco poured with a shaky hand, which resulted in half the tequila to splash on the man's hand and the gritty floor.

Carlos trembling hand reached his mouth, he gulped the drink and licked his fingers.

"I'm gonna get the *freso.* You watch he don't get out of the closet, okay?" Flaco turned but almost fell. He stopped, cursed and stared at the woman sitting on the floor.

Gabriel, drinking the soda, watched the wobbly man start walking slowly towards them. "Mami, that man is coming." He whispered.

Deep in thought, trying to figure out a way out of their dangerous predicament, Virginia looked up with alarm.

In woozy legs, Flaco stood in front of Virginia and her son. "Get up." He pointed at Gabriel. "Come with me."

"No, he stays with me." Virginia said and started to get up. Flaco pushed her down.

"Leave mami alone." Gabriel shouted and stood up, only to be slapped on the head by Flaco and making him fall. He tried to get up again. Flaco raised his fist.

"Don't hit him! Please. Where are you taking him?"

He stopped in midair and stared at Virginia. "You stay here." Flaco snarled. "I'm going to put him in there." He pointed at several doors facing the far end of the room.

"He hasn't done anything." She whimpered. "Please, let him stay with me."

"If you're nice to me, nothing will happen to him." Grabbing Gabriel by the scuff of the neck, Flaco stood him up and half dragged him across the room.

"Please, please, don't hurt him." She started getting up.

Flaco turned and threatened her. "If you move, I will hurt him bad, real bad." He slurred.

"Gaby, do as he says, baby." She gave Flaco an imploring look.

Holding Gabriel by his polo shirt collar, the pockmarked Flaco pushed him past the sofa.

His cohorts watching a soap opera paid no attention as he pushed Gabriel ahead of him.

"You two watch him." He growled at the two men. "Don't let him out."

Virginia watched in fear.

Flaco opened a door and flung Gabriel in a dark room. He closed it and leered at her.

Gabriel looked around. He was in a closet. Darkness didn't frighten him anymore. The cave experience had taken care of that. He had counted how many steps the man had taken on the way to the door. Once Flaco closed him in, he listened to the man's boot strides. When he could no longer hear him over the muffled sound of the TV, he stopped counting.

He inspected his surroundings. Other than a bucket and a mop, there didn't seem to be anything else in the small space.

Taking the BB out of his back pocket, he called his father.

SIXTY-EIGHT

T he plane sat on the tarmac of Culiacan's private airport section. Its engines on idle. Inside, Fabian waited for Vicente. His cellphone buzzed. "Alo?"

"Hallo, my darling. I have a surprise for you."

"Claudia-Lucia? What a...tell me, please." Through the porthole he watched Vicente approaching the ramp.

"I'm on my way to visit you. I rented a private jet. I can see why you own one."

"Oh? Splendid. And to what will I owe the pleasure of your visit?" Vicente was at the cabin entrance and Fabian beckoned him to come forward while gesturing that he was on the phone.

"After learning that my friends and neighbors are visiting you, I got the urge. Why should you have all the fun? And I thought, I have never been to Mexico, so why not go now?"

"You will be most welcome, that is certainly absolute my dear."

"And now that I'm a widow, maybe I can find me a nice Mexican *torero* and marry him." She laughed.

Fabian chuckled.

"And after seeing how nice this plane is, not like that small shit, Victor used to fly, I may buy one too. Do you think they would let me paint the outside pink?"

"Are you pulling my leg?" He laughed. "Are you really coming to Chihuahua?"

"Yes, I am. The pilot told me it might be about five hours. I wanted to see my friends tonight but I think I will be too tired by the time we land. You won't spoil the surprise, right? Don't tell them. I want to see their faces when they see me. It will be the surprise of a life time."

"Don't worry, we'll hold all the festivities until you arrive."

"Who's picking me up at the airport? I haven't made any hotel reservations. I'll leave those details to you, right?"

"In the morning, Vicente and I will pick you up at the hotel. You'll be able to spend as much time with el *Señor y la Señora* as you want." Fabian laughed at his own joke. "Give me the plane's ID number. My men will be waiting for you in the private terminal."

"You're a darling."

"You should be arriving around three in the morning...I think." Fabian took a cursory look at his Hublot.

"Write this down." She gave him the plane's flight plan and other information. "I have to hang up. We're about to take off. Bye, cheerios, as you like to say."

"Cheer..." She had hung up. *Cheerios is a cereal, stupid bitch.* "Vicente, anything to drink?" Fabian asked. He held a glass partially filled with whisky and ice.

An attractive brunette had welcome Vicente when he had stepped into the plane. Now, she approached him from the galley. "What would you like?" She smiled graciously.

"Bring me a tequila." Vicente took off his jacket and handed it over to the stewardess.

"Have you talked to the men?" Fabian motioned with his hand for Vicente to sit across from him.

"No, I'm sure I would have heard from them if something had gone wrong."

"I spoke with Arturo before I left *el Distrito Federal*." Fabian took a gulp as Vicente sat.

"How was the weather in the Capital?" Vicente asked.

"Smoggy, the usual. I'm glad I live far from downtown." Fabian emptied his glass and jiggled his glass for the stewardess to take notice.

"They should be at the warehouse by now. I'm going to call them." Vicente said.

"I missed a call from my inside-man." Fabian stared at the number in his cellphone.

The plane started moving slowly towards the runway but then stopped. The pilot's voice came on the loudspeaker. "We have one commercial flight taking off and then we are next. I don't expect any weather delays. We should be landing in about forty five minutes."

"I think I have time to call him real quick." Fabian called Howard. "Hey, you called me before. I hadn't had time to call you back. I'm about to fly there. I hope you have good news."

"You finally called." Howard stepped down gingerly. The stairway wasn't lit and he paused in one landing.

"Are you with my Colombian friend?" Fabian asked.

"Negative, but his wife and son are here with me. That's the good news."

"What are you saying?"

"Your men fucked up.

Fabian looked at Vicente confused. "Wait. What do you mean?"

"The woman and the son got lost. It's a good thing I found them. Your friend would have been very upset."

Fabian jiggled the empty glass with fury.

"Our friend thought to bring his wife and son in your van. I think he didn't get your message." Howard waited. When Fabian didn't respond, he continued, "the car broke down and they were stranded. I found them and brought them home. But he was gone looking for help. We left him a note in the car..." He hoped Fabian was reading between the lines. They were never comfortable speaking on the cellphones. "And by the way, you need to get a fucking government helicopter out of here. Both the pilot and my counterpart got real sick."

"Blimey. Balls up, mate." Without thinking, an upset Fabian, had switched to his Oxford English. "But, but I spoke with Arturo a while back. He told me everything was fine."

"Arturo isn't here, I don't know where the fuck he is." Howard went down one step and stopped.

"We're fucking buggered. I'm browned off with that fucker. Any ideas where Alejandro is?"

"No, but his wife loaned me her cellphone and I spoke with him already. He thanked me for bringing them here and he's stopping by to pick them up. You owe me big time. Your boy Vicente is not too reliable is he?"

"Bollocks. Fucking right mate. What a load of cack."

"Does that mean a load of shit?" Howard said. "But, you understand, right?"

"That fucking cheeky monkey. Listen mate, the pilot announced we're about to take off. I'll call you when we land in Chihuahua." He turned to his attention to Vicente. "Your men lost the woman and her son, and you didn't even know it."

Fabian, visibly angry, told Vicente the jest of the conversation. "Is that the best you can do? Do you normally send arses to do a job? Beastly, simply beastly, how did three men manage to botch it? Blimey. Howard saved the day."

"I...I." Vicente stammered. He was at a loss for words and worse he didn't have the slightest idea of what had happened. "I'm going to-"

"You can't talk to them now. If that's what you're planning..."

Vicente gulped the tequila in one quick move.

"We're taking off but you better find out how they could screw-up something as simple as holding a woman and a child. They even lost their van. How is that possible? One man in the middle of nowhere finds his wife and son and gets rid of..." Fabian pushed his seat back and closed his eyes but quickly opened them and handed Vicente a piece of paper.

The younger man stared at the paper, afraid to look at Fabian.

"You better not cack up this assignment. Have your men pick up my Colombian partner in the private section of the airport. That's her plane ID number. And make sure they are there at least an hour before she lands."

"Will do." It was all Vicente managed to say. He would have to wait until they landed and he had a chance to find out what had happened. He knew he'd have to make up for the blowout.

The stewardess handed him a tall, slim glass with a double shot of tequila.

SIXTY-NINE

L urking behind a slew of boxes, Alejandro heard the whirring of the front garage door and watched a SUV enter. *Well, this certainly complicates things. The odds were stacked against me before, but now?* His vision had adjusted to the darkness and he surveyed the rest of the large storage space. It was a shadowy amalgam of pillars, boxes, oil barrels, discarded and crumpled cardboard containers and large sacks of white powder.

Sandwiched between two semi-trucks were a Dodge Dart that had seen better days and a Nissan Xterra.

He watched Howard pocket his cellphone. He was half way down the stairway. He too, was staring at the wide front garage door opening up. Both men's attention was momentarily distracted towards the entranceway above. Freddy came out, his outline, illuminated by the inside light. He stood at the top of the stairway.

"We got company." Howard shouted.

A black Suburban entered the cavernous building. It stopped inside and one man got out from the passenger door. Once the SUV was inside, the garage door began to roll down automatically. The driver parked the Chevy Suburban between the cars. A small group came out of the car and walked towards Howard. They passed him by, barely acknowledging him and went up the stairs single file.

"Damn, he's taking a long cigarette break. What else can he be doing? It's so damned dark. I can't even see where the exit door is." Howard took his time going down the steps.

With the upstairs door closed, the penumbra invaded his environs. What glimmer reached him from the whitish lighting in the middle of the warehouse was of little help.

With great care he treaded down, holding on to the one rail, afraid he might miss a rung and tumble down. He looked around but it was hard distinguishing anything. Something bothered him but he couldn't pinpoint it. "Where is that fucking door?" He barked and squinted towards where he thought the door was, stopping again as if trying to get his bearings. He was near the bottom landing.

Alejandro wondered if the DEA man had heard him and was getting suspicious.

Howard kept holding on to the balustrade and muttered to himself. "This place gives me the creeps." Creaking noises from the roof caused by the outside cooling temperature made the metal rafters compress and groan.

"Vampiro." Howard half yelled. He called again, this time a little louder and at last landed on the floor. He took a cautionary step forward making sure he was on firm ground.

Then everything went black. His falling down was stopped and noiselessly his body was laid on the floor.

Pulling Howard's arms behind his back, Alejandro tied him up and wrapped tape around his mouth.

Howard started coming around and realized his mouth couldn't open.

"Your friend is taking a long nap. Vampiro? Is that his name? Maybe he is not dead and is going to suck your blood." He scuffed.

How the hell did he get in here? How did he find us? Fuck, I hope Fabian and Vicente arrive soon and get this son of a bitch. Howard tried to see where he was.

Alejandro looked up at the window. Shadows would intersect and encroach on the light that filtered out of the room. Everything seemed normal. One of the cellphones he carried buzzed. He took it out. "Si?"

"Dad, we're in a building. A helicopter brought us-"

"I know where you are son. Quickly, how many men are holding you? Is mami with you?"

"You do?" He asked confused. "But dad? How-"

"Listen Gaby, I need to know how many men are with you and if mami is there too."

"There were five men but two went downstairs. They shoved me in a closet. I hear more voices. There are other people here. Mami was outside in the big room but I don't know if they moved her too. The men are drinking."

"Very good, son. Don't do anything. Wait for me, okay?"

"Yes, yes, daddy." He was giddy with happiness. His dad was nearby.

SEVENTY

The men slapped Fredy in the back as they entered the large suite. Each one made some snarky remark about each other.

The driver, a short, crew cut man with hardly any facial hair asked Fredy who the tall man in the middle of the stairs was. His companions, in the meantime went on to greet Carlos and Flaco.

"He's Fabian's friend." Fredy said noncommittally.

"Oye puto. Quieres un tequila?" Flaco yelled from the middle of the room. When said in jest, puto was not considered an insult. They sat around a cheap aluminum table, its chairs covered in an ugly plastic flower pattern.

"Are we partying already?" Asked an albino thug, who had arrived with the others.

The man who had exited last from the SUV walked into the wide room with Fredy at his side. "Who are they?" He pointed at the woman. She had an arm wrapped around the shoulders of a forlorn looking child. They were sitting on the floor with their backs resting against the wall, their legs stretched out on the grimy surface.

"Fabian's guests." Fredy smirked. They walked towards the group but not before Damian made a bawdy comment to Virginia.

"Damian, do you want a tequilaso or not?" Flaco yelled again. He was taking out beers out of a corroded old fridge.

"Go ahead, pour me one." Damian said.

Smoothing his handle bar mustache, his face a wide grin, Flaco left the group and stood in front of Virginia. "How about you and I have a little fucky-fucky?"

"Stay away from me. Howard will be very angry if you try to touch me." Virginia pulled her knees back and wrapped her arms around her legs. Her feet were flat on the floor.

Towering over her, Flaco snickered. "Fuck Howard. He'll be gone for a while. And even if he sees me, what is he going to do?" He bent down towards Virginia, his mouth, an ugly snarl. One hand got hold of her hair, and he pulled her head back, grabbing her chin with his other hand. "I'm going to taste your delicious lips *mamacita*."

The coke bottle shattered on his head and his groin felt an unbelievable, excruciating pain that took the air out of his lungs, cutting short his scream. Unable to stay up he crashed to the floor whimpering in anguish. "Aaaauch." He groaned in agony.

At the same time Virginia snatched the gun he held in his waist and hid it.

"What are you doing Flaco?" Carlos snickered and then roared with laughter.

The rowdy group watched Flaco on the floor writhing in pain. They started laughing, made lewd remarks and jokes and then made a toast to Flaco for letting the woman kick his balls.

The loud yell, the raucous laughs and shouts from the upstairs room made the hairs rise in the back of Alejandro's neck.

Taking the pistol by the barrel, he hit Howard on the back of the head, knocking him unconscious again and raced upstairs. Ramming the door he crashed through. He tripped and fell but began shooting at the startled men gaping at him.

Carlos jumped when he heard the door bang against the wall.

Fredy flew out of the sofa and twisted around. A third man, choking and coughing when his tequila went down the wrong pipe, tried to fire. Instead, he collapsed when several bullets hit him in the mid-section.

Taking his pistol out, Damian began firing.

A lanky thug with frizzy hair did the same and fired his revolver at the shadow that had burst through the door.

Holding both guns in his hands, Alejandro fired indiscriminately at the men around the table and sofa.

The albino, whose back had been against the door, turned around, but at that moment his head shattered.

The room had exploded in gunfire.

Half way down the room, Virginia instinctively fired at the door, realizing at the last second it was Alejandro. She barely missed shooting him in the head. She threw herself on the floor and fired one shot after the other at the men standing around the sofa and the table.

The TV set detonated in a million bits of glass, and so did the large pane window.

Alejandro heard a bullet whiz by and rolled on the floor, but a slug nicked the back of his leg. Another skirted the side of his previously injured arm, but he kept shooting.

The walls were getting splattered with blood.

Wedged in the middle of the gun barrage, the gang members were exposed to the maddening firefight that had erupted in the room.

Fredy and one of the new comers went down with bullet holes in their chests.

A man fell backwards, his machine gun clattered on the floor shooting a volley of fire and hitting both of Carlos' ankles. He fell down, his knees hit the floor, and he went down, face first.

Virginia felt the sting of a bullet on her right shoulder. Another bullet hit her in the lower leg. She went on firing, despite the pain.

A bullet punched Damian in the stomach. He tottered, fell backwards, and disappeared behind the window. A loud thud was heard despite all the noise.

In the meantime, Flaco had started getting his breathing back. He clutched his head with one hand, while holding his battered balls with the other.

The smell of cord infused with a gray cloud of dust and residue from the guns enveloped the room.

"Gaby, where are you?" Alejandro shouted. He looked at Virginia, who was disheveled but held a gun at the man near her.

"Are you hurt?" Trying to stand up, he kept a wary eye on the group of men lying on the floor a short distance away. He could hear moaning behind the sofa and two hands rising in the air. It was Carlos, who had half raised his arms, unable to get up.

Virginia wobbled but managed to get up. She felt the blood trickling down from her lower leg. The top of her shoulder hurt too. Her blouse was tainted red.

"Where did you get hit?" Where's Gaby?" Alejandro's words rushed out of his mouth. A bullet had nicked his temple; his face was covered with blood.

"He's back there." She pointed towards a door. "I'm coming baby." Virginia sobbed.

Helping her along, but glancing back every other second at the injured thug, Alejandro reached the door and opened it.

Their son lay unconscious on the floor. "Gaby, baby you're hurt!" She said.

The right side of Gabriel's white shirt was slowly turning darker in color.

She held him close to her chest, sobbing.

"How bad?" Alejandro's voice sounded full of concern and misery. He wanted to crouch next to his son but had to keep a wary eye on the other man.

"I don't know yet." She blubbered while opening the blotched shirt.

There was a large flesh wound on his side, below his thorax.

Virginia bundled the shirt and packed it against the wound.

"Are you okay mami?" Gabriel's big gray eyes, stared at his mother.

Her blouse was speckled with both of their blood.

"Is daddy here?"

"He's here, baby."

"Hi son, you were very brave." He ruffled his hair. "I have to secure the bad guys. I'll be back in a minute, okay?"

Gabriel nodded and gave him a light smile.

Flaco looked aghast at the scene around him. Surprisingly, he had escaped the shooting unscathed. All his friends were dead or badly wounded, and he could barely stand up while holding his groin.

"Move to the sofa." Alejandro commanded.

"It hurts, man," he whined.

"That's what happens when you try to mess around with my wife, asshole."

Flaco sulked. With his legs wide open, he staggered towards the sofa.

Examining the room, Alejandro reassured himself that the danger for the time being had ebbed. Pointing his weapon at Flaco, he ordered the man to sit the middle of the room, where the rest of his companions lay dead or injured.

After picking all the guns, Alejandro took hold of a belt and grabbed Flaco's wrists, tying them behind his back. He heard Virginia talking, but she hadn't called him. He desperately wanted to be with them. He walked around checking on who was still alive. All the men were dead but for Carlos who was incapacitated with wounds on his ankles.

He didn't like killing, even though he'd been forced to do so in the last several months. He walked over to the window and looked down. A body lay splashed on the floor. He went back to check on Virginia and Gabriel, whose head now rested on Virginia's thigh.

Alejandro felt an immeasurable amount of love and admiration for his wife. Her first inconceivable act of valor was to risk escaping from Victor Draco's estate not knowing who to go to, who she was or where she was. And only a moment ago, daringly confronting the thugs, took an incredible amount of courage. He shook his head.

"What is it love?" She asked him.

"Nothing. Let me secure this one."

She went back to render help to her son.

Alejandro knew they had to move fast. Fabian and his cohorts could arrive at any moment.

Taking the belts off two of the dead, Alejandro used them to fix tourniquets around each of Carlos' legs. "This will stop the bleeding for a while." He seriously doubted they could survive another skirmish if they were caught in the warehouse.

He walked over to his wife and son. "I hadn't thanked you for telling me how many men were up here. You were terrific." He kneeled and kissed Gabriel on the forehead. "How is your wound?"

The boy gave him a feeble smile. "It doesn't hurt too much."

The two surviving thugs sat on the floor looking dejected and miserable. But Flaco's attention was on the man and his wife. While they were talking to their son he pushed himself closer to Carlos, who cringed when he though Flaco's feet would bruise his injured legs.

"Pendejo," Flaco whispered, "take the gun out of my boot and kill them."

Carlos turned his head and looked back, but the couple was talking to the *frezo*. Not wasting another second, he slipped his hand into one of Flaco's boots and felt the revolver. He took out the small caliber pistol, turned around and pointed.

The loud crack of a gun cut through the eerie silence.

Smoke spilled from the gun barrel of the Smith & Wesson Virginia held.

A second earlier Carlos saw the flash, heard the sharp boom, and felt the pain in his chest. His arm went down, and looking at himself, he tumbled forward, dead.

"Don't kill me, don't kill me. I didn't do anything. I swear." Flaco, pushing with his legs, frantically moved as far as he could from the dead man. "Who the hell are you people?" He cried, unable to understand how all his accomplices could be dead.

"Shut up." Alejandro felt the quiet buzz of one of the cellphones in his possession.

Flaco stopped his pitiful and insincere diatribe.

SEVENTY-ONE

The plane landed and ran down the runway towards its parking location.

"When are you going to call your men?" Fabian said. The inefficiency of the man he had entrusted with the transit of drugs through Mexico really pissed him off.

"I was about to do that. I was waiting for us to get out of the airport." Vicente took out his cellphone and called *Vampiro*. No answer. He smiled at Fabian and then tried Arturo. Same result. Now he began to feel a dampening sweat under his armpits.

He tried one of the men supposed to be waiting for them at the airport. The man answered and told him that Arturo had left his companions stranded at a gas station and any attempts to find him since had been fruitless.

"Puta madre." The expletive escaped from his mouth louder than he wanted.

"Bad news, mate?"

"You were right. My man has disappeared. No one knows what happened to him."

"Check with the men at the warehouse." Fabian said.

After dialing three different numbers without success, Vicente grew more furious. But deep inside, he was very worried. He feared Fabian's wrath.

Before the plane had stopped, he unbuckled his seat belt and stepped towards the exit door.

"Who did you call?" Fabian asked him calmly; he too unfastened the safety belt but didn't seem in a hurry to get off the plane.

"I...I, Fredy, Vampiro. Where the fuck are they? They know we are arriving-"

"Well...?" Fabian asked.

"I don't know. No one is answering. I'm going to try Carlos." He pressed the buttons.

"Don't waste your time. I'll call Howard and I'll find out what's going on, but you have some serious issues." The sarcastic tone in Fabian's voice left little to be desired. He stood up and left for the gangway. Together the two men went through the terminal towards the late model black Cadillac Escalade waiting for them on the curb at the private business section of Chihuahua's airport.

Six men created a protective ring around them as they walked out.

The man in front opened the SUV's passenger door. Vicente moved aside and let Fabian go first. Once both men entered and sat down, the man jumped in the front, sitting next to the driver. The other five men quickly scampered to a Ford Expedition in front of the Escalade.

Not wasting another second, Vicente pulled out his cell and called Carlos.

One of the cell phones buzzed and Alejandro searched his pockets until he found the right phone and took it out. "I can't stall any longer. Answer and don't try to play any games." Alejandro's stern voice ran chills through Flaco's body.

"Jef-"

"Who the fuck is this?" What the hell is going on?" Vicente wiped his upper lip and then his forehead with the shirtsleeve.

"It's Flaco, *jefe,* there's no problems. *Todo tranquilo.*"

"Why are you answering for Carlos, and where are Arturo and Vampiro? Those motherfuckers haven't answered. We're already heading for the warehouse."

"They are...are down in the...yard. I'll tell them you called."

"Never mind, I'll be there soon enough." Vicente hung up. His face was red.

"Tsk, tsk, not very good, not very good at all, mate."

A brooding looking Vicente stared out the window. He wanted to call again but if no one answered, what would Fabian think? He thought about it and decided not to. "We'll be there soon."

"I know that, I see your men called back." Fabian's sarcastic tone irked Vicente. He wanted to blast the arrogant *hijo de puta*.

"I'm wondering if I'm going to have to spend more time around here. Looks like things are run very loosely under your leadership." The last word came out at a lower decibel.

"This has never happ-"

Fabian raised his hand. "Do not waste my time, mate." The lead SUV turned at a corner. They were within a few miles from the warehouse.

SEVENTY-TWO

"We can't waste any time. They'll be here any minute. Let's go downstairs." He pushed Flaco towards the exit door. "How are you feeling Gaby?" Alejandro picked up Gabriel with great care.

"I'm okay, daddy." Gabriel laced his skinny arms around his father's neck.

"He stopped bleeding, I think the bullet just scraped the skin. Thank God." Virginia said.

"Dad, are we leaving now?"

"Where can we go, love?" Virginia asked.

"What about your friend in Creel, dad?"

"That's an excellent idea and I may have his number in Howard's phone." Alejandro took out the cellphone and checked the index. Jacinto's number came up. "I hope he's not under sedation and can talk."

"What about my father?" Virginia said.

"Only as a last resort, I'm afraid for his health and his contacts are in Mexico City, not here. We could be in a hell of a mess by the time they respond."

"Can we run away in one of their cars?" Virginia asked.

"Maybe...I'm concerned that with all the shooting, their accomplices may already be on the alert. We could end up being easy prey." Alejandro called Jacinto's number.

"Señor Howard?"

"Jacinto, this is Alejandro. Can you talk?"

"*Si.*" Jacinto's face expressed surprise. He wondered why Alejandro had the other man's phone. *Has Howard apprehended him?*

"I don't have much time. I'm in one of Fabian's dens with my wife and son. Howard is the one involved with the cartel. It's a long story." Alejandro gave him a succinct version of the events. "Can you help us? It won't be long before they get here."

"I'll make some calls right away. Don't wait and get out of there fast. Call me when you are safe."

"Okay." Alejandro closed the cellphone and opened the upstairs door, washing the top landing with light.

Howard had awakened from the wallop on his head. He had heard the shooting, then everything had gone quiet and then he had heard one or two more shots, he wasn't sure.

Pushing his prisoner forward, Alejandro glanced at Howard below who was still resting on his belly.

Making muffled noises to get the men's attention, Howard tried to roll over. *I hope they killed the bastard, but if not, I'm going to. Fabian will be upset. I know he wanted him alive but what the hell, you can't have everything.* He wanted the men to find him right away and untie him so he could unleash his wrath on Alejandro. He finally managed to roll his body and looked up. His elation was short lived. To his chagrin, it was not Alejandro but the man nicknamed Flaco coming out with hands tied behind his back.

Alejandro was prodding him forward with an Uzi machine gun and carried his son in his other arm. The woman followed behind. All three looked bloodied but were walking unaided. *How the fuck? What happened to all the men?*

Flaco was pushed next to a column and Alejandro tied him around it. Howard heard the familiar buzz of his cellphone.

Alejandro took it out from his pocket and looked at the screen. "It's Fabian. You're going to tell him that everything is okay and you have all three of us and you are waiting for him. You change anything and here's a bullet with your name headed for your balls."

"Hmm, hmm." Howard nodded.

The tape came out of his mouth in one swift pull, which made Howard howl. Alejandro put the cellphone to Howard's ear. "Talk." He had the loudspeaker on.

"Howie, are you there?" Fabian, settled in the comfortable leather seat of the car, smiled at Vicente. He was delighted watching his man squirm.

"Yes, yes, waiting for you."

"Is everything okay? My man here hasn't been able to get a hold of any of his people." Fabian's lips curled in a cruel smile.

"Everything is okay."

"Ask him when will you see him." Alejandro mouthed the words.

Howard did as he was told.

"I don't know, about fifteen, twenty minutes? Maybe less? Have you had dinner?" Fabian asked.

Alejandro shook his head.

"No, no, I'm waiting for you." Sweat bids were pouring from his forehead.

"Wonderful. You came through, as I knew you would. I'm going to ask my Colombian partner, Claudia-Lucia, to personally deliver to you a special gift, but you'll have to pick her up at the airport." Fabian gave him the itinerary and the plane's identifying numbers. "I gave her your phone number. Wait." Fabian asked Vicente if he wanted to speak to any of his men. "Put one of Vicente's men on the phone. He hasn't been able to get a hold of anyone." He chuckled.

"Tell him you are alone with Flaco upstairs." Alejandro whispered.

Fabian offered his cellphone to Vicente.

Alejandro approached Flaco, his hand over the cellphone microphone part. "Talk. If you warn him, it will be the last thing you'll have done on this earth." His voice had a menacing tone.

"Diga?" Flaco's eyed Alejandro nervously. He didn't doubt the man could kill him.

"What the fuck is going on?" Vicente said, visibly upset. "I can't get a hold of anyone. Are you all getting drunk? *Donde esta Vampiro*?"

"Ahh...*Vampiro* is...outside smoking, yes."

"I don't give a shit." He hollered. "Find him. I want to talk to him now. You hear me?"

Flaco looked at Alejandro with a questioning look in his face. *"Si, si*, I'll go find him and have him call you."

Alejandro pressed the end call button on the cellphone.

"I told that asshole to have Vampiro call me and I'm still waiting. Somebody is going to die tonight." The galling disrespect of his men enraged him.

SEVENTY-THREE

Alejandro ran to the large garage door and pushed the open door mechanism. He waited until it was half way up and stopped it. He bent down and came out halfway, peeking at the dark street. It looked deserted. He took a couple of steps and canvased the sides of the building. The lugubrious surroundings didn't give him any clues. Going back inside, he pushed the close door button.

After tying Howard to another column, Alejandro ran to the rear garage door and opened it. "Sweetheart, follow me in one the cars." He sprinted to the lift truck, turned on the engine and drove it to the back patio wall.

Virginia took Gabriel and chose the less conspicuous Dodge. When she started it, a strong roaring sound came out of its engine. She had been deceived by the looks of the car. A powerful motor purred with a smooth sleekness. She drove it outside and waited. "What is he doing?" Alejandro had stopped at the end of the backyard facing the brick wall.

"I think I know." Gabriel giggled.

"Why are you smiling?" *Considering you got hurt, and have seen horrible things...all of a sudden you're very cheery.*

"Something daddy and I did before."

"Like what?"

"Wait, let daddy show you."

Raising the fork lifts half way up, he pressed the accelerator to the max and attacked the brick wall. The upper portion of the wall came tumbling down. He backed up, dropped the long steel shafts to ground level and rammed the wall again. A gaping hole appeared in front of him. Backing one more time, he stood up, checked and pushed the truck through. He backed out again, turned the machine around and drove to the edge of the back garage door. He looked at his watch. "Damn, it took me almost ten minutes."

"I told you." Gabriel laughed. "We were playing with Legos and he built a castle. I put together a forklift and pushed down the castle wall. He remembered." He snickered.

Before Virginia could say anything, Alejandro called her over. "Can you drive this? Let me show you."

He explained the driving mechanism and the lever that moved up and down the blades. "...and that's what I want you to do."

He started trotting towards the warehouse and asked Gabriel and Virginia to follow him. "Let's hurry, I don't know how much time we have left."

They moved fast despite the lingering pain from their various injuries. Alejandro reached one of the semis. "Love, check the other one, see if it has the keys in it." He clambered up the huge truck and started looking inside. "Gaby, you stay by the big garage door. If you hear a car, kill the automatic switch. It's the red one next to the button that opens and closes the door. And run back to us."

Rummaging inside the semi, Virginia couldn't find any keys on the starter. She opened the glove box. It was full of papers, maps, a partially consumed packet of cigarettes and a truck registration. "Nothing so far." She cried in anguish.

Alejandro was experiencing similar results. There were no keys anywhere to start the big truck. *I may have to change plans, shit.*

"Bingo." She yelled. She had dropped the sun visor and a set of keys dropped but she was able to catch them.

"See if it starts, hurry." Four minutes.

With a loud rumble the big semi shook and trembled, spewing diesel smoke in the room. "Gaby, push the button to open the door." Alejandro jumped down, opened the hood of the second truck, climbed on the front fender, took out the distributor cap and darted to Virginia's truck. "Go to the car." He said and then drove the big semi to the front. "Okay Gaby," he shouted, "close the door and go with mami."

SEVENTY-FOUR

Virginia finished the tasks Alejandro had given her and now mounted the forklift.

Gabriel stood at the bottom of the steps.

She switched on the engine of the forklift, left it in park, walked to the roll-on door and pulled it down with some effort. Her shoulder wound opened up again. She winced, walked back to the yellowish truck and pulled herself in by grabbing the steering wheel. "Go ahead Gaby."

The boy ran up the set of steps and kept going until he reached the back garage door. He pushed in the two metal bars that secured the door and kicked the metal panel twice. He ran back out. His side hurt a little bit but he didn't mind too much. "Done, mami." He yelled.

She put the forklift in gear and picked up a pallet that Alejandro had set up with four full oil drums.

"Okay mami, stop." He watched a few inches away from the truck forks facing the cement steps.

Slowly, Virginia raised the forks holding the skid with the drums.

"Okay mami, you are now higher than the platform."

"Move away in case that thing tips over." She gently drove forward until the mast touched the wall of the steps. The lifts raised over five feet high were inches above the platform were the steps ended.

"How does it look?" She stood up.

"Good." He said.

The forklifts came down, dropping the pallet on the base at the top of the steps. She backed away softly. The forks came out from under the skid. She stood up on the truck.

"Are the blades even with the wood?" She put the truck in gear and advanced, the metal made a scratchy noise on the cement when it slid forward.

"Good, mami, good, stop."

"The fork is even with the wood base?"

"*Si, si.*"

"Okay, move away, just in case." She pushed the accelerator softly and the blades made contact with the wood base. Virginia felt the resistance and put a slight amount of pressure on the accelerator.

The grating noise of wood against cement told her that the heavy loaded platform was moving forward. "Gaby, tell me when it's pressed against the door."

He went up the set of steps. "There, there," he said excitedly, "it's hitting the door now."

Putting the forklift in reverse, Virginia turned the wheel and had the forklift face the roll-up garage door. She pushed the lever and the steel blades went down to about a foot of the ground. The small truck jumped forward when she pressed the gas pedal all the way. The blades cut through the metal door. She kept going, although slowly, until the thick steel swords were imbedded in the door to the hilt. She turned off the engine and ran to the Dodge.

Gabriel waited by the side of the car. He called Alejandro. "We are ready, dad."

"I'll be there soon." Alejandro flipped off the cellphone. He looked at his watch. Time had expired. They should be arriving at any moment. He kept the large semi engine on idle, halfway down the side of the warehouse. To Alejandro it sounded too loud. He hoped they wouldn't hear its rumble or if they did, it would not make them suspicious. He shouldn't have worried.

The radio in the Chevy Suburban was blasting away with a regional ballad, and the heavy bulletproof windows on both vehicles didn't allow too much noise to filter through.

He saw two cars turning into the street, heading for the warehouse. He ran to the truck and put in gear. With the headlights off, he drove at a snail's pace to the corner.

SEVENTY-FIVE

"How soon do you think you'll get there?" Jacinto asked the Mexican marines commander over the phone.

"We are ready. The coordinates you gave me are correct and the cartel members are there?"

"That's what my source told me."

"We'll let you know in about fifteen minutes." The burly, barrel chested officer gave the pilot the go ahead sign.

"I'll call my friend. Thanks." Jacinto punched the cellphone numbers from where Alejandro had called. "Alex, it's me, the cavalry is on its way."

"I hope we get out on time." Alejandro curled his lips in a grimace. "Don't know what's going to happen in the next few minutes."

"Just get the hell out of there!"

"I'm getting another call." Alejandro looked at the name, but didn't recognize it. *Shit, what if he's one of those guys?* His next thought was that his plans had gone to waste. He decided to pick it up. *"Si?"*

"Quien es?"

Muffling his voice, Alejandro coughed and mumbled. "...los."

"Okay *guey*, get everyone ready. We're going in." The thug sitting next to the driver pushed the wireless garage door opener.

The driver sped through and the Cadillac followed close behind.

Alejandro turned the corner when the rear end of the limo disappeared through the door. He pressed the button on the contraption attached to the visor. The entryway began to close while the men were still getting out of the SUV. Behind them the Cadillac's driver and his companion rushed to open their respective back doors for Fabian and Vicente. The driver thought he heard the rumble of an engine, but was distracted opening the door for Vicente.

The automatic door went down and shut with a sharp clank.

"What happened here?" One of the men in the first group asked his companions. They were grouped in front of their SUV. "Is the window-?"

"I smell gun powder and..." Another man said.

A loud crashing metal sound came from behind them.

Fabian, Vicente and their two henchmen spun, startled. The garage entryway had been banged up and pushed in after it closed. The other men ran to the door.

One of the bodyguards pressed the open button. The electric motor whined but the large metal gate didn't budge.

Alejandro had driven the semi into it, making the corrugated metal buckle and inoperative. The front of the truck was stuck to the door. He jumped out of the truck.

A dark, oil sleek pool covered a corner by the edge of the banged up door. He lit a match and dropped it. A whoosh, and the flame quickly gathered speed, and slid through the blocked entrance. Alejandro called Virginia, "Now!" And dashed around the building, running towards the back corner.

The rear entrance was splashed with a similar gasoline puddle. Virginia lit a match too. The ignited fuel went under the door and followed a path towards a group of oil barrels. She ran to the Dodge, and began counting the seconds. It seemed like an eternity. She saw Alejandro turn the corner. At the same time she heard a loud roar.

"Move over, quick." He yelled.

She went over the console, leaving the driver's seat available for Alejandro, who put the car in gear and took off. A few seconds later they passed the abandoned van. Another louder explosion seemed to rock the car as it swerved over a deep hole. Before long, a few fearful faces were staring out of their darkened hobbles. Others, more curious, began to emerge from their huts and pointed behind them. From his rearview mirror, Alejandro could see flames licking the roof.

SEVENTY-SIX

Fabian, Vicente and their men ran frantically looking for a way out. The man that had been trying to open the roll-up door was rolling on the floor shrieking in pain, his clothes and body on fire.

"Run to the back." Fabian shouted but then stopped dead on his tracks. He stared in disbelief. A fast running snake of fire was moving unimpeded towards a bunch of oil drums.

A tremendous explosion shook the place. Pieces of burning metal and material flew everywhere and ignited the closest car. The men were thrown around like matchsticks, some of them mortally wounded. A second car became another fire torch. In a matter of seconds the entrance and exit to the warehouse were impassable. Fabian fell on the floor. The roaring blast of the first car blasted his ears. Large pieces of shrapnel spread around hitting, cutting and killing those still standing.

The fuel tanks of the semi parked inside, blew up with a tremendous thunder.

Those not mortally wounded or on fire, perished with the last blast.

Eyes wide with panic, Flaco stared at the furnace surrounding him. He'd seen a man running to the back door get his head snapped off by a piece of scorching tire hurled by the explosions.

Vicente, badly burnt but still conscious, tried to escape to the back, only to be smashed to the ground by a piece of hood from a third car.

Struggling to get up, Fabian wobbled away from the increasing heat and the cars that were now catching fire. He had burns on his scalp and blood was seeping through different wounds and blisters he'd suffered. He saw Howard tied and unable to speak. Not too far, he caught Flaco in the same situation. Both men gave him desperate, pleading looks but he needed to get out of the increasing inferno. He yelled for his men but they were already dead or dying.

The flames were now spreading around the whole structure. The electricity went off.

An acrid black smoke, the result of burning fuel and tires, started to mix with the white smoke and sweet, chemical smell of burning sacks of cocaine. Light bulbs exploded from the intense heat. The flames rose and began to engulf the walls of the sealed building.

Fabian staggered through the floor gasping, coughing and chocking.

He desperately wanted air to breathe, but the pungent fumes would not relent. His eyes were tearing with the burning chemicals. He watched in horror Flaco being consumed by the flames.

Howard's ropes and clothes had caught fire. He was badly burned but had been able to free himself. He staggered towards Fabian, but collapsed before he could reach him.

A large piece of the aluminum roof caved in and fell on Fabian. It began to fry him alive.

His desperate screams and wailing was silenced by more blasts from exploding fuel drums.

****

The marines' leader and his twenty-two heavily armed men, wearing bullet proof vests stared at the sight of a furious conflagration a few kilometers ahead of them. Flames were leaping in the air and brightened the sky only to be dampened by dark clouds sprouting from the bowels of a hellish chaotic scene.

"Commander, that looks like the location we're supposed to hit." The pilot announced on his mike. He checked his coordinates one more time.

"See if there's any space where we can land. Ask the other helicopter to go down on the other side." *I think we're arriving too late.* In the distance he saw the bright red lights of several fire trucks making their way to the imposing fire. "They're not going to get there on time, and besides what can their equipment do to fight that?" He realized he was still talking to the pilot and switched channels. He communicated with the men in the aircrafts. "Ah...men...it seems like this is going to be a search and recovery mission." He kept his eyes fixed on the intense blaze.

SEVENTY-SEVEN

"Where are we going?" Virginia asked.

"Away from here. Someplace where we can have peace and quiet." He sighted. "We have to stop somewhere where a doctor can take care of us. I'll call Jacinto."

"Daddy, the fire is really big." Gabriel, wide-eyed, stared out the back window.

A fire truck whizzed by, siren blaring.

"Love, please take this number and also write down this address." He repeated the information Jacinto was giving him over the phone. "No, I would prefer to keep this under wraps." He said on the phone. "I think it would be best."

"You're probably right." Jacinto said.

The car reached a main street.

"I doubt if they knew your wife and son had been kidnapped and were being held."

"Let sleeping dogs lie, as my friends in the U.S. like to say." Alejandro checked the street.

"Thank you for all your help and get well soon. You know you have a friend in me."

"Same here. If I can ever be of help, call me. Thank you Alejandro. Bye."

****

Sometime around three in the morning a private jet arrived in Chihuahua. A good-looking woman exited the plane. She was sleepy, but satisfied. If anyone ever asked her about the mile-high-club she could tell them that probably she had earned more points than anyone else in one flight. How many could compete with her? She had done it not with one, but with three different men, all in one evening. She grinned, the captain had had more vigor than she had thought. He had come twice for more. She stepped into the tarmac, and the tired smile left her mouth. No one was there.

A drowsy Alejandro heard the cellphone in the nightstand and picked it up. "Who's this?" He yawned.

"What the fuck is going on Howard? Fabian told me you would be here to pick me up. The goddamned airport is deserted."

"And...?"

"And? What the fuck is wrong with you? Where am I going to sleep tonight, asshole?"

Suddenly he was wide-awake.

"Were you guys screwing Calwel's wife? That bitch is mine; I can't wait to get my hand on her. That whore beat me up."

Alejandro looked at his sleeping beautiful wife. He switched off the phone and smiled.

"Hallo? Hallo?" Claudia-Lucia looked at her cellphone with an incredulous look.

He laid back, put his hands behind his head and let out a profound sigh.

"Who was it?" A sleepy Virginia snuggled closer to him.

"No one. Wrong number." He kissed his wife's lips in a tender gesture. He draped his arm around Virginia and gently cupped one of her breasts in his hand. She moaned softly and went back to sleep.

THE END

About the Author

Jorge G. Reyes Serrano was born in Cuba. His parents fearing the Communist dictatorship sent him to the United States. He began high school in Philadelphia and completed it in Newark, N.J.

Continuing his studies while working, he received a bachelor's degree in Business Administration from Rutgers University and later obtained his Master Degree in Finance from Seton Hall University in Orange N.J.

Most of his professional life he has dwelt in the international finance field, working for Fortune 500 corporations and traveling extensively throughout Latin America, including living for extended periods of time in Mexico and Venezuela.

After a successful career he decided to leave his field of expertise and embark on a new career, writing fiction. The first two books of a three part; "The Retribution Series" have been published and he is working on the third installment. The first book "Justified Retribution" depicts the travails of a family turn apart by a drug lord and his accomplices.
Road to Redemption is the second book and in it the pursuers continue their bloody attempts to kill the Calwel family.

The third book of this series "The End Of The Road" is a work in process. Be sure to subscribe under my author page (http://amazon.com/author/jorge.g.reyes.s.) for information on all NEW Releases and future work.

Stop by on any of these locations or contact me:
Email: jorgegreyes.author@gmail.com
Twitter: @jorgegreyes
Facebook: https://facebook.com/Jorge-G-Reyes-S-831524603633871
Website: http://jorgegreyes.com

41606159R00193

Made in the USA
Middletown, DE
17 March 2017